Save the Date

∞∞

A Romantic Anthology

BELLA BOOKS

2021

Copyright © 2021 by Bella Books. Contributors retain the rights to their individual pieces of work.

Bella Books, Inc.
P.O. Box 10543
Tallahassee, FL 32302

All rights reserved. No part of this book may be reproduced or transmitted in any form or by any means, electronic or mechanical, including photocopying, without permission in writing from the publisher.

This is a work of fiction. Names, characters, businesses, places, events and incidents are either the products of the author's imagination or used in a fictitious manner. Any resemblance to actual persons, living or dead, or actual events is purely coincidental. The publisher does not have any control over and does not assume any responsibility for author or third-party websites or their content.

Printed in the United States of America on acid-free paper.

First Bella Books Edition 2021

Editor: Ann Roberts
Cover Designer: LJ Hill

ISBN: 978-1-64247-232-5

PUBLISHER'S NOTE

The scanning, uploading, and distribution of this book via the Internet or via any other means without the permission of the publisher is illegal and punishable by law. Please purchase only authorized electronic editions, and do not participate in or encourage electronic piracy of copyrighted materials. Your support of the author's rights is appreciated.

Table of Contents

Jaime Clevenger, *New at Love* 1

Kay Acker, *The Wedding Party* 23

Louise McBain, *Trouble in Mind* 47

Tagan Shepard, *Out with the Old* 71

Celeste Castro, *Queen for a Day* 93

Dillon Watson, *The Magic of the Coin* 123

Cade Haddock Strong, *Inn Trouble* 149

Kate Gavin, *Liberty* 177

M.B. Guel, *Grounds for Panic* 199

Jessie Chandler, *Send Out the Clowns* 227

E.J. Noyes, *Something (Really) Old* 243

About the Authors i

Introduction

Back in May 2020, an avid wlw fiction reader I follow on Twitter sent out a tweet:

"Question for you married folks:
How long did you date your spouse before getting married?"
(@notsoteenwitch Twitter, May 21, 2020)

The answers queer folks gave to that question were so telling.

"About 15 years before we were legally married. Considered ourselves married long before that."
(@CHaddockStrong, Twitter, May 22, 2020)

"Jamie and I were together for 8 years, but if it was legal, we would've gotten married much sooner."
(@HeatherBotteon, Twitter, May 23, 2020)

"31 years.
(The government made us wait from 1977-2008.)"
(@Kallmaker, Twitter, May 22, 2020)

My own answer was five years, and that was based on a Civil Union in Vermont. Because we weren't residents, it had no legal effect. We had to marry again when it was legalized nationally.

When my wife and I met, our relationship was a felony in the Commonwealth of Virginia. The law wasn't overturned until March 2014. It was called the Crimes Against Nature Law. There is a special kind of cruelty in one's government calling them a crime against nature.

Our right to marry—to have our love acknowledged and legitimized by our governments—has been a long-standing fight for the queer community across the world. Generations of queer folks lived and died without ever having that right. Generations put their blood, sweat, and tears into giving us the opportunity to love legally. In much of the world, that fight is ongoing. In America, that right is so fresh, and so fragile.

Because of that fight, however, we in the queer community sometimes overlook one important aspect of weddings:

They're awesome!

They're big parties with free food and booze and CAKE! People get drunk and do stupid things! There is terrible dancing and, if you're very lucky, terrible karaoke-style sing-alongs!

More than dancing and singing and, yes, even more than cake, what makes weddings awesome is what's at the center of all of them.

Love.

Love between the couple and the celebration of that love with family and friends.

Save the Date is a chance to celebrate all the best and worst of weddings. This anthology will have it all: action, disaster, meet-cutes, and romance galore. There'll even be an appearance from Death herself. Mostly, there will be a celebration of our wonderful community and the passionate women at the center of it.

So join us as we gather something old, something, new, something borrowed, something blue, and a sixpence for our shoe!

Tagan Shepard

NEW AT LOVE

Jaime Clevenger

"Wait, she's gonna be packing? In a strapless dress?"

Macy Evans bit her lip and focused on the hem she was busy pinning. Blushing wasn't an option. Neither was jumping into the conversation to volunteer that packing in a dress sounded red-hot.

Most of the customers at Pin-Up Girl Alterations came from the bridal shops in town, so she fitted more than her fair share of brides and bridesmaids. Pre-wedding gossip and jitters were par for the course. But the topic of strap-ons had positively, one-hundred percent, never come up.

"She hasn't decided yet on the dress." The bride-to-be, Sarah Fitzsimmons, pursed her lips and shifted her weight from her right to her left foot. "Honestly I think a dildo would be subtler under a dress but she looks damn good in a tux too."

"Everyone looks good in a tux," the maid of honor said. "Knowing Izzy, I bet she waits til the last minute to decide."

"I know," Sarah huffed. "I love her but sometimes spontaneity is annoying."

Sarah tapped her foot and Macy resisted the urge to grab ahold of the dress. All she needed was five minutes of no moving. *Just five bleeping minutes.*

"If she's wearing pants, there's gonna be a bulge," Sarah mused.

The maid of honor nodded at her in the mirror. "Would that be a problem for you?"

As essential as the big mirror was, sometimes Macy hated feeling like she was in a fishbowl while she worked. Everyone stared at her from all different angles and the number of not-helpful comments on how she should do her job were annoying to say the least. But there were no critiques this time, and even better, she was making the mirror work to her advantage—stealing glances at the maid of honor while pretending to be checking out how the dress hung on the bride.

As soon as she'd walked into the shop, Macy had been certain the maid of honor was a dyke. And the way the woman looked back at her had sent her pulse through the roof.

"I think I might be distracted during the ceremony if I can see it," Sarah continued.

"The bulge?" The maid of honor laughed. "I figured you were worried because the in-laws would talk."

Macy wondered if there was any not-awkward way to ask the maid of honor's name. She had all of the bride's info, but no reason to ask about the maid of honor since she hadn't mentioned needing any dress alterations.

"Oh, I don't care what the in-laws say. I'm in love." Sarah lifted her shoulders and then swished her hips back and forth, sending the hemline on a rollercoaster ride.

Macy barely held back a frustrated growl as one of her grandmother's oft repeated adages came to mind: "Love is sweet but overrated compared to a perfect hemline." She was one pin away from being done.

"I think you need to stop wiggling," the maid of honor said.

"I'm not wiggling." Sarah glanced down at Macy almost as if she was surprised Macy was still working on the dress. Sarah held perfectly still for about two seconds, but before Macy could set the last pin, she spun around and narrowed her eyes at her friend. "When was the last time you had to stand still in a pair of heels while someone stuck pins in you?"

"Um, never. But I'd think you'd be used to holding still with all the times Izzy's tied you up."

"You can keep your trap shut back there, Devin." Sarah wagged her finger in the mirror, chastising her friend, but a smile stretched from ear to ear. She looked down at Macy again. "Sorry about all the wiggling. I'm a little nervous. Never thought I'd be doing something like this. Getting married, I mean."

"I get it," Macy said, reaching again for the hem. Her thoughts were entirely distracted now, however, by the silent back and forth that was going on in the mirror between Sarah and Devin.

Sarah made a finger gesture in the mirror but Macy missed whatever Devin had done or mouthed to earn it. A moment later Sarah spun around and said, "Remind me why I brought you along?"

"Because I'm the only friend you have who will watch you get pins stuck in you for an hour?" Devin grinned. "Remember that time you tried to get a tattoo?"

"Only you would bring that up now. Only you."

Suddenly the two of them were laughing. Macy didn't stop herself from looking at Devin. She loved the way her laugh warmed the room. However, that wasn't the only thing she liked.

Devin stopped laughing and looked right at Macy. The smile didn't leave her face but she added an, "I'm not sorry" half-shrug either meant for Sarah or for her.

Macy smiled back and Devin chuckled again. Her gorgeous dark brown eyes were quick to crease with her smile and Macy felt an overwhelming urge to hold her gaze longer. She'd thought the other times she'd caught Devin looking her direction had been accidental or careless, but this time when Devin didn't glance away, she knew it was intentional. And it turned on every nerve in her body.

Aside from her distractingly pretty eyes, Macy guessed that Devin was otherwise someone most people wouldn't notice. She'd probably pass through a room and no one would be able to recall exactly what she looked like. That wasn't exactly a bad thing. She had no features anyone would complain about—smallish nose, roundish face, medium-length, light brown hair that was mostly hidden under a faded blue Cubs baseball hat, and average height. Her blue jeans and loose T-shirt concealed a good bit of her body, but her forearms were well muscled and her bulk had an athleticism to it that made Macy guess she'd find more muscle if she went looking.

But there was something about how she carried herself, and even the relaxed way she took up space on the sofa, that seemed to broadcast how much she didn't care about other people's opinions of her. Or maybe it was that she was so accustomed to no one looking her way, she'd forgotten to be nervous like most people were. Being completely at ease and comfortable drew Macy to her all the more.

"So am I done?"

Macy looked up at Sarah. She'd paused too long and now fumbled for an excuse. "I have to see how it moves with you. Mind taking a little walk around the room? You can tell me how the length feels."

Sarah clearly was no expert at walking in heels and teetered more than once, then tugged at the waist of the dress. "I think the length's fine but maybe it's too much lace?"

"That part's hard to change." Aside from the lining and layers of chiffon, the whole dress was lace, including the entire back side.

Sarah scratched at the neckline and then at her arms. "I know, but I want to be able to move in this thing and not feel like a weird mannequin." She held her arms out at her side and took a few steps looking more like a robot than a mannequin but getting a good laugh from Devin.

"Maybe all the lace was a mistake…"

Devin shook her head. "You liked the dress when you picked it out. You sent me about a hundred pictures of it. And you look gorgeous."

"She's right," Macy said. "You really do look beautiful."

Sarah bit her lip. "You think so?"

"I do. The dress is a perfect fit."

Behind her, Devin held up her hands in with an, "I told you so" look. "I might be the one who's single, but I know a few things. Izzy's gonna love you in that dress."

"Well, yeah, but she thinks I'm hot in a bathrobe." Sarah sighed. She put her arms down and eyed her reflection again. "I'm just not sure this is me. It's an awful lot of lace."

"Sometimes it's hard seeing yourself in a wedding dress," Macy suggested. "It's a lot to take in."

"It's a little late for second guessing the dress anyway I suppose…Have you ever fitted someone who wanted to hide a dildo under a dress?"

Macy was caught off guard by the question but didn't want to let it show. "No. But I could. I have friends who are into cosplay and I've worked with about every kind of material you can imagine."

"I guess I'm wondering if you think it'd be better to wear it under a wedding dress or a tux," Sarah continued.

"It'd be easier to hide it under a dress, for sure, and maybe more comfortable. But why hide something like that?"

Devin chuckled and Sarah grinned. "Good answer," they said in unison.

Sarah looked back at Devin. "Jinx. Double blackout."

"We're not in grade school anymore. You can't call double blackout."

"I totally can. And I did." Sarah turned back to the mirror. "You guys, this is happening. I'm wearing a wedding dress—and I'm actually getting married." She took a deep breath and exhaled. "Lace and all."

The dress moved with her seamlessly. At least Macy could say she'd done her part of the job. "You look amazing. Your wedding's going to beautiful." A little hiccup of fear was normal. All brides felt it at one point or another. Lifelong commitment was no joke. "The dress is perfect. And your fiancé sounds perfect too. I mean, anyone who can rock a ball gown, as well as a tux, and is ballsy enough to wear a strap-on, has my vote."

Sarah laughed. "Thank you for the pep talk. Izzy is perfect."

Macy eyed the dress one last time and gave a nod of approval. "Let's schedule one last fitting two weeks before the wedding to make sure I don't need to make any other adjustments, okay?"

Sarah nodded and took off her heels as Devin got up from the sofa and gathered their things. Macy followed Devin with her eyes, wondering how inappropriate it would be to ask for her number. It wasn't that she hadn't asked a woman out before, but lately she'd been spoiled by women asking her. And being at work was completely different than walking up to someone at a club.

Her cheeks burned with a blush as she considered some question that might get Devin's attention. "So what's the maid of honor wearing?"

Devin straightened up. "Fluorescent pink. No joke."

"Fuchsia," Sarah corrected.

Macy laughed at Devin's pained expression. "Fuchsia can be nice."

"Yeah, and don't let her fool you. She looks sexy as can be in fuchsia."

"Well, if you need any adjustments on that fuchsia dress, let me know." Macy handed Devin one of her cards.

Devin took the card but seemed to hesitate. "I'm not actually wearing a dress. Sarah's letting me get by with a bright pink vest with a matching bow tie. I really shouldn't complain."

"Fuchsia," Sarah said. "And you shouldn't. Because you're going to look damn good."

Devin started to hand the card back but Macy held up her hand. "You can keep the card. I do alterations on everything."

"Okay thanks." Devin eyed the card. "This artwork is amazing."

"One of my cosplay friends drew it," Macy volunteered. "And she is amazing." She'd wanted to keep the name of the business from when her grandmother was running the place but "Pin-up Girl Alterations" had needed a new image for a while. She'd been thrilled with the artwork her friend Nina had sketched and was especially glad now that she'd thought to add her cell to the back of a few of the cards.

"My cell's on the back in case you ever need an emergency seamstress. No one thinks it'll happen to them but you'd be surprised the calls I get." Chances were, she'd never see or hear from Devin again, but she could hope. "And good luck with your fuchsia vest."

"It's all about the cute bow tie," Sarah said.

Devin groaned. "I'm going to look like a teddy bear."

"I say own it." Macy doubted that Devin would look anything like a teddy bear, but the smile she got in response made her wish she could see the outfit herself.

* * *

Maybe all weddings had mishaps. But this one was bordering on the side of catastrophe. The caterer was running late—three hours late and counting. A bee had stung Izzy's aunt, who was also acting as the wedding officiant, and since she was highly allergic, she'd gone to the ER after someone managed to jab her with an EPI pen. Then the photographer had insisted on taking pictures outside. In the mud. The storm the night before had effectively overwatered the grass and Sarah had managed to find one unfortunate low spot. Two group shots in, she'd rolled over on one of her heels, caught the wedding train in the process, and tumbled onto her side.

"Do I want to know how bad it is?" Sarah peeked between her fingers that were plastered over her face as Devin inspected her heels.

Izzy had helped Sarah up from where she'd landed and then hurried off in search of a wet washcloth and some soap. Devin had instantly known that wouldn't be enough but didn't want to stop her from trying to help. She was as stressed as Sarah.

"These heels are kind of ridiculous. They really had no business traipsing around on wet grass." Devin's brow furrowed. The right one was broken and the left one had a quarter inch of mud.

"How bad?" Sarah pressed.

"Pretty sure they're toast."

Sarah's chest heaved. "Okay. I'm getting married barefoot. No big deal."

"That's the spirit." Devin smiled encouragingly. Sarah wasn't much of a crier but she could hear the shakiness in her voice and knew it wasn't only about the shoes. The pressure was high having her whole family around, let alone all the dozens of Izzy's relations, and everything else that had gone wrong didn't help.

"Can you see the backside of my dress? I think I might have heard something rip." Sarah craned her neck, clearly hoping to see the damage she'd done to the dress.

Devin lifted the torn train. "Well, this is a casualty for sure but do dresses really need trains anyway?"

Tears welled up in Sarah's eyes. "I'm such a klutz. Just one time I wanted everything to be perfect."

"I think the bigger problem is the grass stains." Devin held up a section of the gown that was decidedly more green than white. "Oh." Above where the train should attach a huge section of lace had torn. From her angle, Sarah couldn't see it, but Devin was certain there was no repairing it.

"What do you mean, 'Oh.' I don't like it when you say things like that."

"Well…there's another tear. It's kind of big. And without the train part…"

"Maybe we should cancel the whole thing." Sarah didn't hold back the tears now. "We have nothing to feed all these people. Aunt Esme is still stuck in the ER and even if she gets out on time, I'm sure she's going to be on a bucket of drugs. Who's going to marry us?" She wiped her running mascara. "And I'm a total mess."

"Didn't your cousin Joey get ordained online? You told me he married his friends in the Cheesecake Factory. He's coming anyway, right?"

Sarah's tears slowed. "You're brilliant, Devin. Can you text him?"

Devin reached for her phone and then remembered she didn't have it. She'd left all of her things upstairs in the changing room. She also didn't have Joey's phone number. "Does your mom know his number?"

Sarah nodded. She took a shaky breath and pulled back her shoulders. "Maybe there's still hope."

"There is. Totally. I'm gonna go find your mom and get her to text him. Then we're gonna get help for your dress."

Sarah tugged at the torn train. "How exactly are we going to do that?"

"I may have saved the number for that cute seamstress," Devin admitted. In fact she'd put the number from the woman's card in her phone on the off-chance she found the guts to text her and ask her out. So far that hadn't happened. "She said she did emergency alterations."

"That's right!" Sarah's face lit up. "And you should have called that girl weeks ago—what was her name again?"

"Macy." Devin was only a little embarrassed that she had no trouble remembering.

"You know she was into you."

"I don't know for sure," Devin argued.

Sarah rolled her eyes, then made a little gasp. "After she fixes my dress—if it's even possible—you should invite her to stay for the wedding. You need a date anyway."

"I can't ask her to come fix your dress and then say, 'Hey, I haven't stopped thinking about you but I'm too shy to call you up, but maybe you wanna go out with me anyway?' It'd be too weird."

"It wouldn't be too weird. It'd be sweet." Sarah reached out and caught Devin's hand. "As much as I love having you as a best friend all to myself, you know I wouldn't mind sharing you. A date wouldn't kill you."

Devin rolled her eyes. "I don't want to date only to say that I'm dating."

"But you also know you liked that seamstress. You can't pretend you didn't. And if you never take a chance and go out with someone, you're going to pass someone good up. You are the most loveable person I know. You deserve to be loved back."

"Second most loveable—remember you're getting married to Izzy. Today in fact." Devin added a wry grin.

"Right. That. I was wondering why I was in all this lace." Sarah made a face.

"You okay waiting here?"

"Izzy will be back any minute. Hopefully with wine. Go call that hot seamstress."

Dating wasn't Devin's forte, but Sarah already knew that. She'd witnessed all of her attempts. It wasn't only the awkward, "getting-to-know you while I try and impress you" part. She simply never seemed to connect with anyone that she dated. Macy probably wouldn't be any different, so what was the point in taking the risk of asking in the first place? Even as she tried to talk herself out of it, she pictured the way Macy's eyes had met hers in the mirror's reflection. Her heart tap danced in her chest all over again. Maybe this time would be different.

After she found Sarah's mom and asked her to call Joey, she went back to the dressing room where she'd left her things. She'd listed the seamstress's number in her phone under the heading "Macy Pin-up Girl" because it had made her smile. Pin-up Girl Alterations was an awesome name for an alteration shop and in other clothes, Macy could certainly have fit the classic pin-up girl image. In fact, she was so pretty that Devin hadn't believed her flirty looks could be for someone like her until Sarah had pulled her aside and whispered an earful.

And now she was going to call her and ask her out? *No way would she go out with someone like you.* Or would she? Unfortunately, the only way to find out would be to ask. Devin rolled her shoulders and neck. *First the dress.*

"Hello?"

"Hi. I'm looking for Macy from the Pin-up Girl shop?" The line had been answered on one ring and Devin hadn't had time to gather her thoughts.

"That's me. How can I help you?"

"You did some alterations on my friend Sarah Fitzsimmons's wedding dress and there was a little accident." Her palms were sweating but she squeezed her eyes closed and reminded herself that the call was only about the dress.

"That doesn't sound good. What happened?"

Devin launched into a description of the stains and the ripped section and then waited hopefully for Macy to proclaim it was no big deal to fix. Maybe it could even be done within the hour. But the longer she waited for Macy to say something, the more reality kicked in.

"The dress is screwed isn't it?"

"Without a picture, I can't say for sure. But probably, yes. Grass stains are one thing but torn lace is…well…"

"The wedding's at four."

"Today?"

Devin dropped her head in her hand. Why had she even given Sarah any hope that she could fix this situation? "Yeah, today. But there might be a delay because the person who was supposed to officiate went to the ER for a bee sting. And the caterer's MIA." Could she convince Izzy and Sarah to push the wedding back to six? That would give the caterer time… And hopefully Joey would fill in for Aunt Esme. Which only left the dress. "I know you said you did emergency alterations so I thought maybe you could take a look. We'd pay anything."

"This is Devin, right? Sarah's maid of honor?"

"Yeah. Sorry. Should have said who was calling at the beginning." Except she'd been too nervous then. The more she talked with Macy, however, the more her nerves had quieted. Telling Macy that her voice was soothing was out of the question but true anyway.

"It's fine. I can tell you're stressed. Where's the wedding?"

"Do you know the Oakley Farmstead? It's a little ways out of town…" Devin searched the room until she found a guest sign in book with the address.

"I know the place. I'm about an hour away. Should I text this number?"

"You can come? Really? That's awesome. Amazing. Great. Thank you." Devin's hopes soared. For more than one reason.

Macy laughed. "I wish I always had people that excited to see me. Tell Sarah I'm not making any big promises but I'll see what I can do."

* * *

"If I had a little more time, I could open the seams and release some extra fabric." Macy shook her head. She knew that wouldn't be enough. No matter how she tugged on the remaining fabric, she couldn't close the gap that the shredded lace had left. "I can make a repair but there's no way to hide it completely. And this tear is only part of our problem. These stains are going to be tricky." She let out a long sigh. "We do have an alternative option."

"What do you mean?"

"Devin gave me a heads-up on the damage, so I swung by the shop and grabbed another dress." Macy knew Sarah wasn't going to be thrilled with her plan but it was the most likely to succeed given the time frame. "My grandma used to make wedding dresses instead of only doing the alterations. She left a closet full at the shop—dresses she never sold or never wanted to part with. The one I grabbed is an older style but it's brand new. I checked your measurements and I think it would fit."

Sarah's eyes watered. She twisted around to peek at the tear and the stains. With a big sigh, her shoulders dropped.

"I really wish I could fix this," Macy said. Really, she did. Not only because she liked to make a customer happy but because she'd love to impress the maid of honor. Also, she didn't want to have gotten up their hopes for nothing.

"It's okay. I knew it was a long shot." Sarah squeezed the bridge of her nose. Another big sigh followed. "If you really don't mind loaning me the other dress, that'd be amazing."

"It's in my car. Give me a minute to run out and grab it and you can try it on and decide."

"Not to throw another wrench in things, Sarah, but apparently your mom is freaking out about the flowers," Devin said. "The corsages are missing. Sounds like Izzy's managing things but…" She loosened another button on her shirt, exposing the white tank top under her white tuxedo shirt. Macy did her best not to stare.

Devin had mostly kept quiet since Macy had arrived, clearly stressed, trying to manage texts and calls coming through on

Sarah's phone as well as her own. The fuchsia bow tie hung loose at the collar and all the buttons were undone on the vest. Macy was tempted to put all the pieces together so she could see the complete picture but Devin looked damn good half undressed. When she stood up to hand over Sarah's phone, Macy's breath caught. *Damn good* was an understatement. This woman needed to always wear tuxedo pants.

Sarah read the screen. "I don't know how Izzy puts up with my mom. Corsages are the least of our problems."

"I'm thinking Izzy would appreciate being rescued," Devin said.

"Do you mind?"

"Not at all."

"Maybe we can head down together," Macy suggested. "It'll only take me a minute to grab the dress and then you can get me back in. That security guard takes his job seriously." No one but the wedding party was allowed into the building, but she hadn't expected a full-on search. Of course that was only part of the reason she wanted Devin's company.

"Oh, that's thanks to my mom too," Sarah said. "She tipped him extra to make sure he checked IDs."

"Who let your mom watch that wedding crasher movie?"

Sarah grinned. "Not me. Oh, Macy, there's one other thing." She held up a white satin shoe with a jack-knifed heel and mud splatters. "Any chance you know how to do shoe repairs? I know it's silly but I love these shoes way more than this dress. I picked them out first."

"I could do a temporary fix but it'll be tight time wise to get the glue to set…" Macy took the shoe from Sarah and surveyed the damage. "Even with that, probably you won't be able to dance on them—"

"I'd fall right on my face if I tried to dance in heels. I only need to walk down the aisle."

"If you want, you can start on that project and I can grab the dress from your car," Devin offered.

Macy hesitated. As much as she wanted an excuse for a few minutes alone with Devin, the hopeful look on Sarah's face was hard to ignore. "That'd be great." She handed Devin her keys.

"My car's the old-school VW Beetle—cherry red—you can't miss it. The dress is in the backseat. You won't miss that either."

As soon as Devin had gone, Sarah sank down on the seat in front of the mirror. "This day really couldn't get much worse. I shouldn't say that. Who knows what will happen next. I can't remember if I said thank you for coming all the way out here. But thank you."

"No problem. I'm happy to help." Macy went back to her sewing bag and pulled out a tube of superglue. Not knowing what repairs she'd be in for, she'd brought the same bag of supplies she used for all the cosplay repairs her friends needed.

Sarah stared out the window, looking as forlorn as a bride in a torn dress could be. The dressing room was a converted bedroom in the old farmhouse that now served as a bed-and-breakfast—and apparently sometimes as a wedding location. From the bedroom window, there was a perfect view of the back lawn where chairs were lined up in front of a gazebo.

The old farmstead really was a perfect location. Close enough to the city to not be a hassle for guests but far enough away to feel like a different world. And with the sun shining and the temperature in the mid-seventies, nothing about the day could have been more perfect. Except for everything that had happened to Sarah, Macy thought with a pang of commiseration.

"I'm sorry today's been so awful. Your wedding day isn't supposed to be like this." Macy scraped off some of the crusted mud and then set to work repositioning the heel.

"It's fine. Really. No one died. Yet. Aunt Esme did look awful after that bee sting but...they say she's better now." Sarah forced a smile. "I'll get out of my funk, don't worry. Just having a moment. And I probably shouldn't tell you this, but a little part of me is happy I tore the dress."

"Why?"

"Devin has a crush on you, but her calling someone she actually liked would take an act of Congress. Or a torn wedding dress. This was the push she needed. And she will absolutely kill me if you ever tell her any of that."

Macy couldn't hold back her smile. She wanted to bounce up and down but that would be over the top. Not to mention unprofessional. "My lips are sealed. You getting killed would make your wedding day a real bummer."

Sarah laughed.

"But thanks for telling me. I may have let out a little shriek after I got off the phone with her this afternoon. I mean, I was sad about your dress, but after a week passed and she didn't call, I figured there was no chance I'd see her again."

"I knew it!" Sarah clapped her hands together. "I knew you were into her. I kept telling her to call you but she's never really had a girlfriend and she's terrible at asking women out."

"Seriously? She's so hot." Macy sucked in a breath. "I probably shouldn't have said that out loud."

Sarah smiled. "Relax. You're fine. She's good-looking and she's a complete sweetheart. I keep telling her she's a catch, but she doesn't see it."

"Why doesn't she date?"

"She says she doesn't have time. Which isn't completely a lie. She's in grad school, and between her dissertation and teaching, she's somehow always too busy to date. But she's also shy around women. Sometimes I forget until I see her around someone like you. She's so confident the rest of the time."

Before Macy could ask more, the door opened. Devin walked in with the garment bag carefully held high in the air.

"You found it," Macy said. She felt shaky with excitement now, knowing Devin was into her, but if one of them needed to be brave, she was up for the challenge. "Hope my car wasn't a total mess." In fact she hadn't thought to be worried about that until this very moment.

"Not at all."

Devin held out the garment bag and Macy's hand brushed hers as she went to take it. A blush sent heat barreling up her neck. Being brave hadn't lasted long.

"Izzy's on her way up," Devin said to Sarah. "I may have told your mom that you were bawling and needed Izzy."

"It's not far from the truth," Sarah said. She wiggled out of the torn wedding dress and tossed it on the bed. "Let's see this exclusive vintage wedding gown. Should I ask first how Grandma feels about lesbian weddings? She won't get mad at you or anything for letting me wear it, right?"

"If she's mad, there's not much she'll be able to do at this point. She's dead." Macy unzipped the garment bag and slipped the dress out. She hadn't had time to air it or check for any wrinkles but was pleased to see it looked great. When she glanced up, she noticed both Sarah and Devin looking at her with concern. "Oh, don't worry. Grandma died ten years ago. But I was mostly joking about her being mad. I think she'll be up in Heaven cheering if this dress makes it to a wedding."

"That makes me feel better." Sarah stepped forward to examine the dress. "I like this…It's simple but sexy. Good job, Grandma."

"Turns out Grandma was très chic for the fifties," Macy said. "She was doing this same sweetheart neckline for years after it was out of vogue. but I think it's a look that's universally flattering. And this is one of my favorites of hers."

Sarah took a deep breath. "Let's hope it fits."

"If not I have time to make little adjustments. I'm a whiz with my sewing machine."

Grandma could have made the dress specifically for Sarah. The fit was perfect and Macy silently congratulated herself on knowing it would be. Once Sarah had a look in the mirror, she got quiet and only then did Macy worry.

"Do you not like it?" Macy glanced at the bed and the rumpled torn wedding gown from earlier. "We can go back to the original plan and I can do my best fix your dress. The lace isn't going to be perfect but maybe no one will—"

Sarah caught Macy's arm. "No. This is perfect. I don't know why I went for that other dress. It wasn't me at all. But this…is exactly right."

Someone knocked, and a moment later the door cracked opened. A Latina woman in a white suit peeked in. "Did I miss all the tears?"

"Izzy!" Sarah opened the door the rest of the way and then threw her arms around her fiancé. "Do you know how much I want to marry you?"

"Hopefully a lot." Izzy brushed Sarah's lips with her finger and then leaned close and kissed her.

Macy averted her eyes, thinking it wasn't polite to stare no matter how good the kiss seemed, but then suddenly she was looking right at Devin. Her heart slammed to a stop. One second and then another. She managed to swallow, knew she should busy herself with something—tidy up the mess she'd made fixing the broken heel or at least start gathering her things—but Devin's dark eyes held onto her and she didn't want to move.

"You look amazing. Where'd this dress come from?" Izzy asked.

Still Macy didn't break eye contact with Devin. Had the room gotten a hell of lot hotter all of a sudden?

"Macy brought it," Sarah said. "She saved the day and fixed my broken heel too. Thank God Devin had her number and thought to call her. I owe them both."

Devin cleared her throat and looked over at Sarah and Izzy. "I only made a phone call."

"To someone who could save the day."

"It was no problem at all. I'm happy Devin called," Macy said.

Devin looked her direction again but didn't say a word. Sarah glanced between them. Maybe she sensed that something had changed?

Macy wanted to tell her it had. She might not have been the one who'd been kissed, but her lips buzzed and her heart had yet to come out of orbit. But she also knew that for better or worse, she was going to have to take the lead if she wanted a date with Devin. And she definitely wanted a date. Coaxing Devin out of her shell might take a little time, but if the look she'd given Macy earlier was any indication, the fire in her would make it worth all the work.

Macy turned back to Sarah. "If you're happy with that dress and don't need any other adjustments, I probably should get out of your hair. You've got a wedding to go to."

"Oh, right. That." Sarah squeezed Izzy's hand. "But I need to pay you before you leave."

"It's okay. You can pay me for the house call and shoe surgery when you drop my grandma's dress back at the shop. Unless you'd like to keep it. Then I can just bill you."

"I'm keeping this one forever," Sarah promised, running her hands over the dress's full skirt. "Don't tell me how much it costs yet."

"You got it." Macy went to gather up her things, pretending not to notice when Sarah made a "go talk to her" sort of gesture at Devin. She wanted to tell Sarah not to worry. She had a plan. No way was she waiting for another dress emergency to get Devin to reach out.

"Oh, Devin, I think you still have my keys," Macy said. "And maybe you wouldn't mind helping me carry the sewing machine out? I clearly brought a few more things than I needed."

"Sure." Devin stopped, patted her pants pocket and then opened her mouth. "Oh, shit."

"You don't have my keys?"

"I think I might have locked them in your car."

* * *

Before they even got to the car, Devin knew the keys wouldn't be in the door handle. She'd replayed everything in her head and was certain she'd set them down when she'd carefully lifted the dress out of the car. Then she'd locked the door with her free hand, making certain the bottom of the garment bag didn't brush the rain puddle next to the car. And she'd been so focused on making sure she got the dress up to the room without a wrinkle that she'd entirely spaced on the keys. Macy probably thought she was a complete idiot.

Macy tried the handle and then shook her head. She peered through the window. "I see them."

"On the backseat, right?" Devin resisted the urge to swear out loud. "I'm so sorry."

"It's fine." Macy pursed her lips. "To tell you the truth, this isn't the first time I've been locked out of this car."

"Don't worry. I got this," Devin said. "Roadside Assistance to the rescue." She'd brought her wallet and her phone, guessing they'd find the keys locked inside, and set the sewing machine down to reach into her pocket.

"You've got to get back to the wedding. It'll be starting soon. I really can figure it out."

"No way. I'm not leaving you. This is my fault. Besides, I've got a little time still." Devin made the call and then breathed a sigh of relief when the agent promised someone would be there within a half hour. If all went according to plan—not that the day had followed any plan so far—she'd make it to the altar with ten minutes to spare. "They're on their way."

"You don't have to wait with me. Really. Your best friend is about to get married."

"With the way this day is going, I'm not betting on it happening on time."

Macy laughed. "I won't ask what more can go wrong."

"Please don't." The truth was there'd definitely been good parts to the day. Well, one good part.

"Sarah told me you're in grad school. What are you studying?"

Devin cocked her head, wondering how that topic had come up. She'd only left Sarah and Macy alone for twenty minutes but Sarah could tell a stranger a lot in that time. "Sociology. I want to teach someday."

"What's your dissertation on?"

"You really want to know? It's kind of wonky academic stuff…"

Macy folded her arms. "Are you suggesting that a seamstress wouldn't care? Or wouldn't understand? I happen to have a bachelor's degree in chemical engineering. I'm not dumb."

Devin's mouth dropped open. She promptly clamped it shut and gave herself a virtual kick in the ass. "No. Not at all. I'm sorry you thought I might be suggesting that. Shit, I'm a total idiot today."

"Not totally. You finally called me." Macy arched her eyebrow.

Devin forgot it was her turn to say something. Macy's reprimanding tone turned to a playful smile that scorched through her brain. She'd been charming and definitely sexy at the shop in leggings and a scoop-neck knit shirt with her little wristband pincushion and her wavy, dark brown hair pulled back in a ponytail. But now with her hair down and in a sundress? And looking like she knew exactly what Devin was thinking? Showstopping. Also brain zapping.

"Sorry it took a dress emergency for me to call. I wanted to before but—"

"You don't have to apologize. If I tell you I like you, will you tell me what your dissertation is on?"

Macy's playful smile made Devin unsteady. She swallowed. "The impacts of natural disasters in areas with high economic and gender disparities. But you know, I don't really want to talk about it. It's not that I don't think you'd understand or be interested. I'd just rather talk about other things. Can I ask you something?"

Macy laughed. "Okay. Go ahead."

"Chemical engineering?"

"Yeah. I know. Why would a seamstress study that?" Macy shrugged. "I found it interesting. And I guess I never thought I'd take over my grandma's shop. She passed away my senior year of college. Left me the little shop and everything in it. I live in the apartment above the shop."

Before Devin could ask more, a yellow tow truck pulled into the parking lot. "They're fast," Devin said, eyeing the time. Too fast. She raised her hand to flag the tow truck driver, wishing they'd taken the full half hour as promised.

"Keys locked in the car?" The driver hopped out still talking. "Usually I get calls for these old bugs not starting. You know you can jimmy them real easy. I'll show you the trick."

Devin started to say it wasn't her car but then thought better of it. She tried to pay attention to the rundown on all the ways to unlock the door but the whole time she was too focused on Macy watching her. And then the door was open and she was waving off the driver. Once Macy's sewing machine was loaded up, Devin knew she had to ask the question on her lips. She couldn't simply let Macy leave.

"So did you get all that?" Macy asked.

"All of what?"

"The three ways to break into my car."

Devin smiled. "Sure. Seemed easy. Hopefully you won't have a reason to test out—"

Macy tossed her keys on the seat and pushed down the lock. She swung the door closed with her hip. Devin lunged forward but missed. Macy only laughed.

"I wasn't…I don't think I can…" Devin stopped stammering and shook her head. "I can't believe you locked the door."

Macy went around to the back of the car and popped the trunk. She pulled out a metal clothes hanger and walked back to the door. In about three seconds, she had the door unlocked.

"You knew how to do that all along?"

"I might have majored in chemical engineering but it was a toss-up between that and mechanical. Did I mention I'm a whiz with my sewing machine? Pretty much any machine." Macy's eyes sparkled mischievously. "I know, not what you expected, right?"

"Why didn't you say something earlier?"

"Maybe I wanted an excuse to spend more time with you. I almost told you not to call Roadside Assistance but you wanted to help."

Devin couldn't help laughing. She'd never enjoyed being duped so much. Macy leaned against the car. "You're not mad?"

"No. Impressed but definitely not mad." Devin hesitated. "I've never met someone like you."

Macy spread her hands. "I like to surprise people."

"Do you think I could ask you out on a date some time?"

Macy tilted her head. "You could. I might even say yes."

Devin's heart raced. It wasn't a yes but she loved the way Macy pushed her.

"Honestly I thought I might be the one doing the asking."

"'Cause I'm shy?" Devin guessed. "I'm not always shy."

"So I've heard." Macy narrowed her eyes. "But I appreciate subtlety."

"What are you doing tonight?"

"Eager, huh?"

Macy practically batted her eyes and Devin's breath caught in her chest. She could hardly believe she'd been brave enough to ask, but now that her question was out there she desperately wanted Macy to say yes.

Macy continued, "I think you have a wedding to go to tonight."

"Well, yeah, but…maybe you'd like to join me? I mean, you're already here. And you're already wearing a really nice dress." Devin gathered her courage. "Plus I feel like you're a really useful person to keep at this disaster of a wedding. Would you be my date?"

Macy laughed. "That might be the most honest offer I've ever received. I'd love to be your date."

The look in Macy's eyes was something Devin had only dreamed of seeing before. Tonight was the start of something big. She knew it.

When Macy held out her hand, Devin didn't hesitate. The soft warmth of her skin sent a rush through Devin's body. Her chest felt full, and she was glad she'd said all she needed to say. For now.

THE WEDDING PARTY

Kay Acker

Melody's blood sugar was dangerously low the first time she asked Nikki to marry her.

"If I say yes, will you drink your juice?" Nikki asked, and Mel downed the whole glass in two gulps. Nikki didn't think she'd remember.

They were sprawled naked and panting in bed together the second time Mel proposed. Nikki shifted from the mattress to her wheelchair and unlocked the brakes with a snap.

"We could never afford it," she said over her shoulder. "You know that."

The third time, Mel got down on one knee and presented her favorite hematite ring on a discreet silver chain.

"Just a commitment ceremony, it'll be fun!"

"That's 'holding out as married.' It still counts against us with Social Security," Nikki said, her head in her hands. "They could reduce both our benefits, and if your computer business made a dollar too much, I'd lose my health insurance. It took years to convince those people that Ehlers-Danlos is even a real condition, let alone that they should give me help. I can't do it all again."

Mel's shoulders slumped and she put the ring away. "I know, baby."

"Then why do you keep asking me to do this?"

"You've never quite said no." Mel played carefully with the tips of Nikki's fingers.

Nikki wrapped Mel's hand in hers, part comfort and part apology as she said, "I didn't think I'd have to. You know the rules and you know the risks of trying to get around them."

After all, they weren't the first lovestruck pair to think they could keep a secret. They'd attended a commitment ceremony for friends two years ago, and one photo on social media plus one spiteful neighbor filing a complaint with the Social Security Administration had been that couple's undoing. They weren't even together anymore, and they were both still fighting, alone, to get their benefits back.

Mel and Nikki both did their level best not to sulk, but the atmosphere was cloudy. Even after Mel left to do some work in her own apartment, the dourness lingered. Nikki cooked stir-fry in the massive skillet Mel had bought her for her birthday, ate alone at her neat table for two, and loaded the leftovers into every Tupperware she owned. There was still food in the skillet because she'd cooked as if Mel would be eating with her.

She texted Mel, *can you eat about this much stir-fry?* and sent a picture.

Anything for you, babe, Mel replied, pretending it would be a hardship.

Nikki filled a plate and balanced it on her lap as she wheeled out of her apartment and over to Mel's door, right next to hers. She rang the doorbell Mel had installed so she wouldn't hurt her hands knocking; her knuckles would pop out of joint under that much force, the connective tissue too rubbery to hold them in place. Mel answered the door and took the plate of stir-fry with a smile.

"Are you coming in or dropping off?"

"I can come in," Nikki said, grateful to be invited.

Computer hardware spilled from the tables lining three walls of the living room onto the floor. Mel settled a half-built tower on the carpet to make room for the plate and followed the taped-off pathway toward the kitchen to get a fork. Mess was Mel's natural habitat, but she always kept it within the tape so Nikki could move through the apartment easily.

Nikki hadn't asked Mel to do that. She hadn't had to. Mel made space for her as easily as she calculated the amount of insulin she needed to inject after she ate, like she'd been doing it all her life. Nikki wanted to take up space in Mel's life for the rest of her own.

She put a hand on Mel's hip when Mel moved to sit at the table.

"Can you stand for a minute? I can't kneel, but I'm about the right height from here."

Mel set her fork aside and looked down into Nikki's eyes.

"I love you," Nikki said, "and I'm right that we can't afford to get married, but you're right that I don't want to say no. So how about this? Will you, Melody Michaela Sanders, perpetrate a zany scheme that's technically fraud with me?"

Mel's frown of confusion melted into delight. She bent down to kiss Nikki, then asked, "What do you have in mind, honey?"

* * *

The building supervisor, Ruth, was thrilled that Mel and Nikki wanted to use the community room in the apartment complex at all, let alone six times. She'd been desperate to get tenants to "engage with their community" for the entire year she'd been working there.

"Just one party every two months? You sure you don't want a full dozen? There's plenty of space on the reservation calendar!"

"The budget's a bit tight for twelve parties," Nikki explained, "but if other people have ideas, they can fill up the alternate months."

Ruth finished writing their names on each date they'd reserved, then hung the calendar back up on her wall.

"You can go through the closet for any supplies you need, if that helps. I've never had tenants come up with ideas as clever as these before, but this might be the perfect way to spark even more creativity. I'll ask around and see what folks come up with. It's just cute little twists on classic parties, that's all?"

Mel and Nikki nodded.

Ruth shimmied in her chair. "Fun! Here's the list of rules for using the common areas. Do you both know how to operate a fire extinguisher? I'd be happy to show you if you don't. Oh, and I'll make sure we haven't accidentally scheduled this 'un-birthday' party on anyone's actual birthday. That'd be a shame, wouldn't it? Is there anything else you need?"

"We'll let you know," Nikki said.

"I'll set an appointment with you and that fire extinguisher," Mel added.

And that was step one of the Fake Married Plan, done with no difficult questions or strange looks. So far, so easy to get away with.

They explained the whole plan, including the theme of each silly party, to Mel's mother over speakerphone that night.

"We can try to keep people from sharing pictures or mentioning the wedding in public or online, but everyone makes mistakes, so being careful is no guarantee. Social Security isn't a detective agency, though. If we get reported, they won't pick apart every detail. All we need is an excuse, an answer for any questions we might get asked," Nikki said.

"And the answer is that the wedding is clearly a joke!" Mel said. "It's part of a series of six parties that are all jokes! An un-birthday party, a book signing where we sign random books, a baby shower with no baby, a pool party with no water, a New Year's Eve party in the middle of the year, and a wedding for two people who are obviously *not* getting married."

"And I'm coming to all six of these parties?" Kathleen asked. "Why?"

"You'd stand out in the pictures if you're only at the wedding. It's plausible deniability," Mel said for the third time.

"Who's taking these pictures?"

"Lots of people, probably. Everybody's got a cell phone with a camera."

"Are you going to show me how to use the camera on my cell phone? I want pictures, too."

Mel sighed. "Sure, Mom."

"Well that's fine, then," Kathleen said, sounding enthusiastic if still a bit confused. "Nikki, dear, what will you be wearing?" she asked, turning her attention to the most interesting details. "We should coordinate for all these shindigs."

Mel kissed Nikki's forehead and left her to talk clothes with Mom, opting to wash dishes rather than try and fail to follow that conversation. Mel and her mother got along well in their own way, but Mom had always wanted a girly-girl to do girl stuff with. Mel was proud to have found one for her. Nikki could name more words for colors than Mel ever knew existed, let alone all the different fashion terms about cut, style, and fabric. Nikki had been a seamstress in the years before her joints got too painful to handle a needle. She'd also been a mama's girl all her life, until her family had abandoned her, fleeing the supposed burden of Nikki's chronic pain.

Warm water from the kitchen tap rinsed away the disgust that had bubbled up when Mel thought about those people. There was nothing to get riled up about, she reminded herself. Nikki was with her now, and with Mom. Mel could hear them both in the other room, voice to voice, laugh to laugh, heart to heart. It was always going to be this way, for as long as they all should live.

Plus, Ruth was going to let her play with the fire extinguisher next week. This plan Nikki had devised really was perfect.

* * *

The most obvious sort of fake party to throw was, of course, an un-birthday party. Mel and Nikki reserved the biggest common space in the apartment building and spent a month gathering mismatched tea sets from the thrift store, one cup at a time for a quarter each and a dollar for teapots, to support the *Alice in Wonderland* theme. It took a week to repair one of Mel's half-broken printers well enough to print flyers for the building, but she managed it. Nikki secured an invite/plausible excuse for their friend Owen by asking him to curate the music for every party.

Mel posed the only question that stumped them both a few days before the party. "What are we gonna write on the cake?"

With no ideas forthcoming, they decided to consult an expert. The bus let them off at the grocery store and they approached the bakery with giggly excitement.

"Hello!" Nikki called, and the baker peered over the glass case at her. "We need half a dozen sugar-free cupcakes and the wrong birthday cake for Saturday."

"Wrong how?" the baker asked.

Mel and Nikki looked at each other, then shrugged.

"Surprise us," Mel said.

The baker, possibly too confused to respond in any other way, agreed.

They bought the rest of the supplies they needed, packed them carefully into exactly six bags, because no more than that was allowed on the bus, and rode home.

On Saturday, Owen presented them with the half-sheet cake he'd picked up for them, which said, "Happy Birthday Mark," and a fifty percent refund from the bakery for accepting someone else's rejected product.

"Apparently the kid's name wasn't Mark," he explained, "so the baker figured that's the kind of thing you guys would want. Are there any Marks at this party?"

"I don't think I've met a single Mark in my life," Nikki said.

Mel agreed. "It's perfect."

"You know what else has to be perfect? The officiant at your wedding," Owen said, setting the cake in its place among the teacups. He'd been dogging Mel and Nikki for details ever since they'd told him about the plan.

"We ruled out using any real ministers. It's too obvious and not silly enough," Nikki said.

"I figured we can just go to the lake and flag down someone with a boat," Mel added.

"I don't think that meets the sea captain requirement for officiating a marriage, babe, but I like the direction it's going in."

Owen nodded. "A nautical theme might be fun. We'll workshop it."

He opened his mouth to say more, but the alarm that reminded Mel to test her blood sugar went off. Ruth dropped the movie projector on the floor with a squeak and a bang, and Kathleen's hearing aid wailed, "Low battery!" so the issue was set aside.

Once the projector was taped back together, the rest of the party was, as all the guests agreed, right on the mark.

* * *

"We spent $22.50 on the tea sets and $34.08 on the baked goods. All the tea came out of the community room stash, so that's no issue. There's decorations left over, so we can add half of that…" Mel tapped the numbers into a calculator, then sighed. "It's about seventy dollars, rounded up. We could push it to eighty if we need to, but we should try to keep the price for each party relatively consistent."

"How do we have a wedding with a budget of eighty dollars?" Nikki whined. "We need flowers, and dresses, and shoes…"

"I have a suit and Mom's buying you a dress because she forgot the entire existence of Christmas last year. Can't you wear some shoes you already have?"

"I don't have shoes that really suit the dress Kathleen and I are looking for, one like Hepburn wore in *The Philadelphia Story*. Besides, it's our wedding. I'm buying shoes."

Mel almost conceded, then she stopped short. "Doesn't that dress go all the way to the ground?"

"When you're standing up, yes. I have no intention of doing that, so the right shoes will be both visible and important."

They agreed to study their individual budgets for miscellaneous funds before making any final decisions, which they both knew was going to work out in Nikki's favor.

* * *

Two months later, they hosted a pool party, complete with boogie boards, floaties, mandatory sunscreen for all who could safely apply it, and not a single drop of water. "Bring your own liquids," the flyer specified. The baker made them a cake that looked like a pool table, with the sugar-free cupcakes numbered like billiard balls.

"That was brilliant," Nikki told her when she went grocery shopping that week. "Can I write up a comment card or tell your manager about it or something? Your cakes are really pulling these parties together."

"You can do a survey on the store website," the baker said, writing the site address on a scrap of receipt paper. "My name's Sandy."

Nikki tucked the paper into her breast pocket and grinned. "And are you allowed to tell me how you make such good sugar-free frosting, Sandy?"

"We use canned stuff from corporate, but I'll tell you what my cousin does—she's diabetic, like your friend. She puts three-quarters of a cup of Splenda and a teaspoon of cornstarch in a blender."

"That's it?" Nikki said.

"That's it. Doesn't have to be fancy to be good." Sandy winked. "I'm looking forward to the next challenge."

Nikki filled out the survey while she and Mel ate leftovers straight out of the Tupperware. When she popped her disjointed knee back into place with an audible crack, Mel brought her the sock full of rice they kept in the freezer to ease the swelling.

"Thinking about party food…will our budget cover steak and lobster for dinner on our wedding night, like we had on Thanksgiving?" Nikki mused. "Just for us, obviously, and maybe your mom and Owen."

"Definitely not, but we could get pork dumplings for everyone. That'd be nice."

"Oh, or what about something with honey, as a joke about honeymoons? Honey buns are cheap…"

Mel sighed wistfully. "Now I want dumplings and honey buns. Chinese tomorrow night?"

Nikki readjusted the ice pack on her knee and coaxed Mel to cuddle close to her.

"Definitely Chinese tomorrow night," she said.

* * *

The Silver Phoenix was only three blocks away, and they kept their ramp and entryway clear, which meant Mel and Nikki ordered takeout from there constantly. Almost everyone who worked there knew them by name. Even the new guy, Kevin, who had just started working in the restaurant while he earned his astronomy degree, greeted them by their habitual order when they rolled through the door.

"Miss Shrimp Fried Rice! Pork Dumpling with side of veggies, which no one else ever asks for!"

"Hi, Kevin. Did you remember to put chopsticks in the bag this time?" Nikki asked.

"Of course I did," Kevin said, quickly pulling chopsticks from a box. "I also packed a gift for you, Pork Dumpling. My computer is running like dreams."

"That's good to hear," Mel said, reaching into the bag.

She pulled out a red paper flower.

"Oh, Kevin, it's lovely. Did you make this?"

Kevin tapped a set of chopsticks on the counter, blushing. "It's nothing."

Mel's and Nikki's eyes met over the delicate top of the curled paper petals.

"Are you thinking what I'm thinking?" Mel said.

Nikki nodded. "They're perfect. I bet we could braid them into crowns and tie them to the spokes of the chair, too."

"You're a genius." Mel straightened and asked, "How much would we need to pay you to make, say…a hundred of these?"

Kevin fumbled the chopsticks he'd been fiddling with. "Pay me? No, it's really nothing. I'll show you."

He pointed them to an empty booth, slid in, and unfolded a napkin from the holder on the table. His quick fingers folded, then rolled the thin paper, starting tightly at the bottom, then unfurling into a rose at the top. It took him less than a minute, and he was obviously going slowly so Mel and Nikki could watch and learn.

"See, easy!"

Again, Mel and Nikki looked knowingly at each other.

"I don't think I can do that," Mel said, holding up her hand in front of her. It trembled, then jerked sharply.

"My finger joints dislocated just watching you," Nikki said.

Kevin slapped himself gently on the forehead. "Not so easy, then. But you wouldn't have to pay me. I can make them while I listen to a lecture or something. Now that my speakers work on my laptop, why not? But hey, what do you need a hundred of them for?"

"A party," Mel said.

"Why not ask the guests to make them?"

Nikki started to explain that it wasn't that kind of party but Mel stopped her.

"We have a lot of friends who can't come to our…party. What if they made the flowers and sent them to us? That way they could be part of it without having to travel."

Nikki reached out and rested her hands in Mel's shaky ones. Kevin passed them each a napkin to dry their eyes.

* * *

"If I bought a boat, what would I name it?" Owen asked suddenly while they were watching *Queen Christina* one night.

Nikki didn't look away from Greta Garbo for a second, but Mel tipped her head back and chewed the question.

"Is this a riddle? Like, the boat is a leaf in a storm drain and we're supposed to guess what kind of tree it is?"

Owen scoffed. "What kind of riddle would that be? No, I'm looking for suggestions."

"Why would you buy a boat?"

"I'm not saying I would. It's just that people make a big fuss about naming a boat, and you can never change the name, so you have to put a lot of thought into it."

Mel scratched her temple and frowned. "Is it a fishing boat or pontoon boat?"

"Fairly certain you can fish off a pontoon boat, and you're still missing the point. The point is—"

"The Bela Lugosi," Nikki said, not taking her eyes off the movie. "Because boats are pretty and you go to sea on them."

"Well now you have to buy a boat," Mel said.

Owen muttered, "I just might."

Later, while Nikki settled herself on her mountain of pillows in bed that night, she asked, "Do you have any idea what that was about?"

Mel kissed her, then wrapped herself around the body pillow that kept her from jostling Nikki while they slept.

"Nope. It reminds me that we need to find an officiant, though."

Nikki started reciting the full wedding plan checklist, and she didn't stop until Mel told her to Bela Lugo-to-sleep.

* * *

By the third party, the book signing ("Bring a book, any book! We'll sign it!"), all the wedding plans were settled except the officiant, and the bimonthly celebrations had a steady rhythm to them. None of the neighbors showed any sign they thought these parties were suspicious. Some of them had begun to invite friends or come up with fake party themes of their own, eager to share in the fun, and one person had even suggested a silly wedding. Hiding the truth was going to be a piece of cake.

Friends online weren't so easily fooled, but they were happy to discuss the party instead as a form of protest. A fund in honor of Mel and Nikki being legally single forever raised almost two hundred dollars for the National Council for Independent

Living, a disability advocacy group. Mel and Nikki plausibly denied their participation in the fundraiser by handing cash to Owen so he could make a donation for them.

Mel and Nikki were packing up the remains of Sandy's third creation, a marble cake cut and iced to look like an open book, when reality finally set in.

"We're gonna get married in two months," Mel whispered. "Does that feel real to you?"

"Definitely not," Nikki said.

And as long as the Social Security Administration agreed, that was all that mattered.

* * *

"Hi, could I get that survey site address again?" Mel asked when she came to the bakery to order their wedding cake.

Sandy wrote the site down and asked, "What'll it be this time? An armadillo, a big duck and little cupcake ducklings? Don't ask for a penis. I don't make those."

"I really want the ducks now, but hopefully what I'm going for won't be that hard. Can you make a tiered cake with these colors?"

Mel showed her the color swatches Nikki had chosen to match her dress, labeled "slate sky blue" and "cranberry red."

"They're not standard but I can probably mix a little batch up with what we have. And you want it tiered?"

"Yeah, like a wedding cake."

"Someone's getting married, huh? Any requests for the groom's cake?"

"I trust you," Mel said.

* * *

There was no way to mail paper flowers that was both safe and cheap, so Kathleen suggested their friends could write messages on napkins, mail those, and then she and Owen could make the flowers themselves during the week before the wedding. The word was spread subtly to their friends far and wide. Nikki bought and mailed out napkins in the exact shades of dusty blue and cranberry red that best suited her dress, because she wouldn't entrust such a crucial detail to the judgment of others. Mel added a stamp with Sally Ride on it to each envelope to cover return postage.

The message-bearing napkins arrived rapidly over the next several weeks, and Nikki stored them in a shoe box until the day Kathleen and Owen planned to begin their flower assembly. An hour before they arrived, Mel and Nikki sat down with the box between them on the couch and carefully opened each envelope. They read each message aloud to each other, then photographed them to keep after the napkins had been twisted up.

"You know better than anyone how to make the best of things, so I'm sure your wedding will be the best, too!"

"Didn't I always say you'd be a good secret agent? Good luck being under (the) cover(s)."

"We're so happy to have known you online. Distance doesn't stop us from being close to you, and we'll be keeping you both close to our hearts on your not-wedding day."

"What exists between your spirits needs no witness and no approval."

So went the tender messages penned on delicate, sometimes slightly ripped or wrinkled napkin paper. Mel and Nikki were still weeping openly when Kathleen arrived, and she was crying too by the time Owen got there.

"Don't tell me you asked her to marry you," he said when he saw the three women's blotchy faces.

"I haven't done public speaking since I puked on my debate teacher's shoes in tenth grade. I'm the ring bearer," Kathleen said solemnly.

"Says who?" Mel asked.

"Well I'm going to be someone! And says your mother, that's who."

Nikki offered, "You could be the flower girl!"

"The flowers are paper," Owen said, pulling snacks out of a bag he'd brought and sitting at the table for two. "What would the flower girl throw? Shredded napkins?"

Mel frowned. "Ruth said confetti's not allowed. It's a fall hazard, apparently, because someone could slip on it."

"Safety McGee is she," Nikki said. "She probably wouldn't love us bringing a random boat captain into the building."

"Wait, you girls think a boat captain can marry you? That's a myth," Kathleen said.

"No, it happens all the time!" Mel protested.

"Where, besides *Gilligan's Island*? How'd you hear of it?"

"*The African Queen*, a Hepburn movie," Nikki admitted.

Owen and Mel considered for a moment, then replied simultaneously, "*Star Trek*."

"See? It's a TV trope. A captain can only marry you if they're also ordained as a minister, and you decided against a minister."

"Unfortunate news, given I've gone through all this effort," Owen said.

He plunked his bag onto the flower assembly table and pulled out a laminated boating license and a foot-long wooden sailboat. The boat's name, written in silver Sharpie, was The Bela Lugo-sea.

Fresh tears pricked at Mel's eyes. "You're already doing so much."

"As if you could ever ask too much of me. Besides, you know I'm one of those people who didn't get enough attention as a child. I love public speaking!"

"You also love questionable online certifications," Mel choked out as tears and giggles both overcame her.

"A minister accreditation is easy to get and very questionable," Nikki added. She passed a clean cranberry-colored napkin to Mel.

"Don't blow your nose on it," she said. "Sentimental tears are a cute memento, snot is not."

Mel wiped her eyes gently with the napkin. Kathleen made the first rose out of it, and assembly proceeded steadily from there.

* * *

The night before the wedding didn't make the top ten worst nights Mel and Nikki had shared, but it wasn't great. Ruth helped them get the community room set up and decorated and then they retreated to Nikki's apartment to finalize the flower arrangements. Mel wrapped flowers onto the wheel spokes and together they engineered a method of hanging a tapestry of paper blossoms on the back of the wheelchair without unsettling Nikki's back when she leaned against it.

"We should run through the dance one more time now that the chair's decorated," Nikki said.

"Are you sure you're up for that?" Mel asked. "It'll probably be fine. You don't need to push yourself."

Nikki swallowed the whisper of nausea that still clung to her. The anti-nausea meds she'd been taking for the past week had brought her back from the brink of being unable to keep down water. She was still a little dehydrated, but the rib that had dislocated during the worst of her vomiting had moved back into its proper place, and her pain had declined to a manageable four out of ten. She was as "up for it" as she was going to get.

"Just one more time to test it," Nikki said.

She placed her flower crown atop her head as if she were coronating herself. It clashed with her ragged sweatpants and flannel shirt, but it brought out the radiance in her eyes.

Mel couldn't refuse her anything when her eyes were that beautiful and determined.

The tapestry didn't get crushed against Mel's thighs when she pulled Nikki close to her. Nikki was able to grip the wheels without decorations getting in the way, even when she reached low on the wheel for a sharp, dramatic turn. Each step flowed naturally, as if they'd been dancing together all their lives and would do so every day from now on. All was well until Nikki popped a wheelie for her second-to-last move.

The flower crown fell off and she tried to catch it. The sudden motion disrupted her balance, and she started to tip too far backward. Mel, who had stood back to avoid stepping on the fallen crown, lurched forward to catch her, but the sudden impact of her grabbing the chair, then the chair hitting the ground, jostled Nikki's right hip and knee out of place.

Pain was so familiar to Nikki, she rarely screamed, but now she did.

"Oh god, baby! What's hurting?" Mel said, reaching out but not touching her with ever-trembling hands.

Nikki only whimpered in answer.

"Should I try to move you somewhere more comfortable?"

"No," Nikki ground out between her clenched teeth.

She breathed deeply and Mel matched her breath for breath. She sat on the floor next to her, calm and quiet, during the full hour it took for Nikki's muscles to stop spasming and allow her to relocate her joints. She didn't move an inch, even when the alarm to test her blood sugar went off.

At last, Nikki panted, "Can you bring me the ice packs?"

Mel didn't answer. Nikki reached down to shake her arm, hoping she'd simply fallen asleep, but she was soaked with sweat when Nikki touched her. Another deep breath brought the smell of it to Nikki's nose.

Nikki wheeled herself slowly, achingly, into the kitchen. Mel listed to the side without the wheelchair to lean against. She was probably too far gone to risk trying to get her to drink anything, so Nikki pulled a can of frosting out of the cabinet instead.

She used a spoon to scoop out a small heap of it, then waved it under Mel's nose, commanding, "Mel, open your mouth."

Mel opened her eyes, which was a good sign, but she didn't loosen her jaw. Nikki tickled her chin until Mel opened her mouth to laugh and slipped the spoonful of frosting in. Stubborn as ever, Mel refused to swallow, but the sugar soaked into her bloodstream through the lining of her cheeks. Her gaze regained its focus, and the second she was able to stand, she made herself a sandwich to continue stabilizing herself. She pulled two Gatorades out of the fridge, opened them, and passed one to Nikki. They both needed the electrolytes.

"On the plus side," she said, "this happened now instead of tomorrow afternoon."

"Ugh. We're gonna be a mess in the morning."

"That's why we scheduled the ceremony for the afternoon!"

Nikki needed the bed to herself, but she worried that Mel's blood sugar might drop again during the night, so Mel slept on the couch. It was a damn comfortable couch. They'd picked it out together specifically for nights like this.

In the early morning, Mel ate another sandwich, helped Nikki to the bathroom, and opened another Gatorade for them to share. They spent another few hours in bed together, holding hands and whispering their private vows to each other while they rested. A church down the road rang its bells to mark the time. The sunlight of their wedding morning snuck in around the edges of the cheap blackout curtain over the window. It was going to be a beautiful day.

* * *

Mel and Nikki split up to get dressed, enjoying the comfort and accommodations of their own bathrooms. Kathleen agreed to check in and take pictures with Nikki before she made a fuss over Mel, which gave Mel just enough time to wash up, fix herself a snack, and put her slacks on before she was bombarded with demands to hurry up and get cute for the pictures.

"I brought the makeup and you already agreed to put up with that, so finish eating and get your shirt on so we can get it over with, huh? How long does it take to button a shirt?"

Mel fumbled with a button and growled, "Longer when you can't feel your fingers."

"Well you hadn't told me about that," Kathleen huffed. She batted Mel's hands away and started buttoning the shirt for her. "Your father had that, too. Feet more than his hands, though. Are you keeping your feet clean and looked after?"

"Yes, Mom."

"Are you walking okay? Nikki probably has a cane you can use if—"

"I'm okay, Mom. Everything's okay."

Kathleen popped Mel's shirt collar, then dug the tie she'd bought out of her purse. It was exactly the right shade of red.

Her movements slowed, and there was tenderness in the way she looped the red tie around itself.

"I'm sorry for the fuss. You remind me of him, is all, eating an apple in your suit pants and undershirt, slow as Christmas when you have somewhere to be. I know you're okay. I just...I miss taking care of him. And you."

She pulled the tie tight. Mel busied herself with tucking her shirt in and getting her belt on, searching for another topic to soothe her mother.

"Are you ready to be the ring bearer? Nikki has a nice pillow to put the Twizzlers and the lighter on, and you can take them back down the aisle after I make the rings out of that. You might have to hold the lighter, or Owen can."

"You are not getting married with Twizzlers, Melody Michaela. I'm the ring bearer because I brought you some rings to borrow."

Mel looked up from her successfully buckled belt and saw her mother holding out a pair of gold bands. Kathleen's left hand looked pale and fragile without the wedding band in its usual place.

"I keep your father's in my pocket all the time," Kathleen said. "It'll probably fit Nikki best. They're both so little. Or, she is. He was."

Mel closed her mother's hand over the rings.

"You never take your ring off, Mama. I'll wear Daddy's for the day, but I gave Nikki a ring already. Forget the Twizzlers, we'll use that."

Kathleen smoothed Mel's hair back, then grasped her tenderly by the chin. "These rings belong together, Melody, and you'll use them for what they were made for: to say you and Nikki belong together, too."

There was no way to say no to that and Mel didn't want to. She threw her arms around her mother, almost knocking them both into the wall.

"You better be glad you made me cry before my makeup got done, or you'd be in trouble. I'm not putting it on twice," she said, because there were no words to say how she felt.

The doorbell rang a few minutes later and Mel let Nikki in. She was resplendent in the long white and gold Katherine Hepburn gown, with gold traction gloves and strappy shoes to match. The heels were six inches tall.

Mel teased, "I almost asked how you walk in those, but—"

"You can have a lot of fun with shoes when they're purely decorative!"

"She spent almost as much on those things as we did on the whole wedding, if you can believe it," Mel told her mother. "They cost forty dollars!"

"Only forty? You have to tell me where you find your heel deals," Kathleen said to Nikki.

Mel asked, "How will you walk in them?"

"I won't! I'll sit somewhere pretty, change into the shoes, and my entire presence will be purely decorative."

"Like an art installation," Nikki said.

"See, you understand! Now, let's get my daughter into some makeup before she wriggles out of it."

Kathleen charged off to the bedroom where the light was best, but Nikki held Mel back.

"You don't have to wear makeup if you don't want to, really."

"You and Mom are getting makeovers, and I want to spend all day doing stuff with you. Besides, when people see the photos, they'll never believe it's even me, let alone that it's a real ceremony. It helps the scheme."

Kathleen had to scold Nikki twice for looking in the wrong direction while she applied eye shadow. Nikki didn't want to waste a second not looking at her soon-to-be wife.

* * *

Mel met Owen in the community room thirty minutes from the start of the ceremony. He was leaning against the music stand Ruth had draped in a tablecloth, puffing on a fake pipe. The buttons on his long coat gleamed, and he tipped his sea captain's hat to her.

"That doesn't match the color scheme at all," she said.

"It's black. It matches everything. Now, where do the candles go?"

Mel pointed him to a low, round table and he set out three large, tin candlesticks that he'd modified with Silly Putty so they could hold tiny birthday cake candles. Larger candles were prohibited in the community room. Then he pointed at the cakes.

"Both masterpieces, of course. The custom colors really came through."

They really had. The rich cranberry red decorations stood out against the impressively appetizing blue-gray frosting, and all three tiers were dusted with edible gold sprinkles. The groom's cake matched, and Sandy had lovingly written in cursive, "Congratulations, Adam and Steve."

"Nikki's gonna pop another rib," Mel gasped.

They went through the paces of the ceremony again for Owen's benefit, checked the speakers and microphone twice, then started up the organ music. Residents filtered in and filled the rows of folding chairs, chatting among themselves and grazing on the nuts and chips set out next to the cake while they waited for the ceremony to begin.

A few minutes after three, Kathleen strode in and announced, "Dear, gentle guests, please be seated! The bride is on her way!"

When everyone was seated, Kathleen made her way down the aisle, offering everyone tissues from an opened box she carried, then sat in her reserved chair next to Ruth in the front row. Owen changed the music, and the crowd turned eagerly to see Nikki arrive.

Mel had teased her before, but watching Nikki wheel down the aisle, vibrant in her red and blue and gold, was magnificent. They'd both wondered if it would be odd for her to do this part alone, but anyone else would have blurred into the background anyway. She was perfect exactly as she was, coming down the aisle and turning to sit in front of Mel with a jittery but satisfied smile.

The music stopped a few seconds too late, and Owen made everyone wait instead of cutting it off. Finally, he tucked his pipe into the massive pocket of his coat and began.

"Dearly beloved, we are gathered here today to join these two gay nerds, who have never had a serious relationship in their lives, in holy matrimony, which among other legal and social benefits, entitles them to each other's very generous estate of two thousand dollars maximum in money and assets at any one time."

Mel and Nikki snickered. Some of the audience joined them, though there was also an audible squeaking of chairs as some people squirmed.

"Hold hands and look into each other's eyes," Owen instructed.

Mel and Nikki did so.

"Keep looking," Owen said. "Hold that eye contact until it gets weird."

It was a struggle but they managed to stare, almost unblinking.

"Weirder!"

Nikki cracked first, snorting in her effort not to laugh. Mel looked away entirely while she giggled.

"There we go! Now Mel—and dearly beloved, this is my favorite part, because I can make her say anything—repeat after me: I, Melody Sanders..."

He led her, then Nikki, through the vows the two of them had edited together.

I take you to be my wife, in good times and in bad, in varying degrees of sickness and a liberal definition of health, and in all the joy each day may bring, regardless. I pledge to love, respect, support, and honor you for all the days of my life.

They exchanged the rings Kathleen had lent to them and sobbed when they fit. Ruth took several of the tissues Kathleen offered her and blew her nose loudly. Kathleen brought the box up to the music stand-turned-pulpit for Owen, too.

"We need to pull it together," Nikki whispered. "This doesn't look like fun and games."

"Oh, ye of little faith," Owen whispered back.

He cleared his throat and shooed them over to the candles. Kathleen flicked on a lighter and stood between them so they could each put their hand on it. The three of them lit the two candles on the side while Owen explained.

"These two candles represent the individual lives you've led together until today. Now, please raise them and light the central candle."

Mel and Nikki obeyed, surprised at how easy Owen had made it for them to do so. The candle sticks were large enough to grip comfortably and light enough to lift easily. The third candle sparked faintly as it ignited. They thought nothing of that, but they both noticed Ruth staring.

"This central candle represents the life you now share together, as one. Please blow out your individual candles."

Both of them hesitated. Owen hadn't told them about this part. They looked at each other for a moment, then out at the audience before deciding to follow through.

The candles winked out, but Owen said nothing. Everyone waited through another seconds-long pause.

Then the candles flared back to life again.

"Individuality is important!" Owen declared. "You made that flame, why would you want it to go out? And now there's three candles, which is more fire for everyone! Bring all the light you can into the world, my now-married friends. Spread the fire of—"

Ruth burst out of her chair like it was spring-loaded and snatched up all three candlesticks.

"No! Nope, do not spread the fire in this building, please! I'm gonna go put these out now. Sorry about your metaphor."

She hurried down the aisle with the still-lit candles and everyone watched her go. Mel and Nikki took a moment to contain their startled laughter before waving at Owen to continue.

"As I was saying—"

Owen was interrupted by the whoosh of a fire extinguisher. Several people, including Mel, darted to the windows to watch Ruth douse the three offending candles in the front lawn, where the wind blew some of the airborne foam back at her. Nikki convinced a guest to take the poor woman a water bottle.

"That was better than anything I could have scripted," Owen admitted, setting aside his cue cards. "Let's just get this party started with our lucky couple's first dance, shall we?"

He swung the music stand over his shoulder and cued up the first song as he made way for Nikki and Mel to take the now-empty floor.

The dance was about a half-step too slow, and they omitted some of the flashier flourishes, but the audience oohed and ahhed all the same. When Mel and Nikki opened the floor to everyone, people jumped to their feet, took the brakes off their wheelchairs, or grabbed their canes and rollators with all the joy a wedding inspired.

They all persisted in celebrating until dinner time, which left a much thinner crowd for the "honeymoon" after sunset, because so many had worn themselves out. That was fine with Mel and Nikki. They were tired, too. Kevin from the Silver Phoenix had set up a telescope, but the newlyweds left that entertainment to others. They took their tea with honey and settled on the lawn to admire the full moon alone.

Despite her use of the word "borrow," Kathleen had refused to take back the wedding bands. Tomorrow, Mel and Nikki would have to start carrying them in their pockets, like Kathleen had carried her husband's ring for all the years since he'd been gone. For now, though, they held the rings up to the moonlight and admired the way they gleamed side by side, exactly as they were meant to.

TROUBLE IN MIND

Louise McBain

Baggage claim two is packed with passengers from Tulsa. My plane isn't listed on the monitor yet but I recognize people from the DC flight so I know I'm in the right place. Atlanta's Hartsfield-Jackson International Airport is huge and surprisingly easy to navigate. Katie, one of my BFFs, was shocked that I've never been through here before, but the South doesn't interest me. There's enough yokel flavor in my own backwoods upbringing to last me a lifetime.

This place feels like a futuristic city, with its long moving sidewalks and sleek indoor train. My arms are bare after taking off my hoodie on the plane and no one seems overly shocked by my ink. Sure, I'm getting a few looks and I caught one old bat fumbling with her phone to take my picture, but I expect that. The horrific injuries I suffered in what the Army referred to as "the training incident" now look like intentional body art. Pits and pocks from being dragged on the gravel are moons and stars and the road burn a celestial fantasy. The effect is arresting, so people stop and they stare. I'm almost used to it.

I turn off airplane mode and there's a text from Katie.
LaGrange, GA has a population of 31k. 41k fit inside Nat's Park. Just saying.
I type in a reply and we go a few rounds.
I'll try to drop that into conversation when I meet Nancy.
Who's Nancy?
Spencer's mom.
I'm worried that you've never met Nancy!
All the things that worry you will NOT fit inside Nat's Park. Just saying. Text you later.
Haha

I can hear her laughing and it makes me smile. God, I wish Katie was here. Spencer's family are going to think I'm some kind of loner freak when I show up by myself, which is only half true. But the guest list is much bigger than I anticipated. When Spencer said the wedding would just be friends and family, I imagined a group that might be satisfied by a single turkey at Thanksgiving dinner. When two hundred response cards came back checked "yes," I realized that if there's going to be turkey on the menu this weekend, it's me.

We're getting married in Spencer's hometown of LaGrange, Georgia. Katie and Luce both think I'm crazy and they rarely agree on anything. I don't give a fuck. I've only known Spencer six months, and I've never been more certain of anyone in my life. Wedding week kicks off tomorrow afternoon with a cocktail party at her mom's house and I've come a day early to surprise Spencer with a midnight booty call. I need an unscripted moment before the hullabaloo begins because this is kind of a lot—and I'm more than a lot nervous. Katie's been calling it Georgia wedding camp. I wish I could have invited her but I thought Luce was coming and they can't be in the same room. Luce is my tattoo artist and Katie's ex. It's their rule, not mine. My own family isn't coming because they don't know I'm getting married, which is my choice. They also don't know me, which is theirs.

My phone buzzes. It's another text from Katie.
In French, LaGrange means the barn.

Merci beau-cool it. I text back, and pocket the phone. An old couple is now openly staring at me over the luggage carousel. I could put my hoodie back on but it's June in Georgia, and fuck them. I'll cover the ink when I get to LaGrange where Spencer's mother, I'm fairly certain, will not have chickens in her front yard. The sense I get from the bouquet of engraved party invitations on our refrigerator is that her family skews country club not Country Kitchen.

The arrival of the luggage is announced by a blaring alarm that could stand in as a signal for a prison break. Bags spill onto the carousel and I look for the hanging bag Luce insisted I borrow to protect the pearl-gray wedding suit she helped me pick out at the Saks in Friendship Heights. I'm wearing my usual black to all the other events. Long sleeves, because I don't want the body art to define me. Yes, it's flipping cool but I'm not a sideshow attraction. I'm not the tattooed lady. I'm a twenty-five-year-old bartender from western Maryland named Tate. Nice to meet you.

Clothing-wise my style is more Johnny Cash than Coco Chanel. Spencer digs it and that's all that matters. She's my compass, my sun. The woman walks in pure light with her hand on my back guiding the way. Our forever status started the night we met. Sweet-pea crashed into me like a miracle-stuffed piñata, blessing me mind, body, and soul. People want to know who proposed to whom, but does it matter? Our union was predestined, written in the stars. That's why I'm braving a week in bumfuck Georgia to marry her. I'd marry Spencer in a New York City sewer. I'd marry her in an active volcano. Okay, it was me. I'm the one who proposed. Does it matter? Fuck you.

There's no sight of the hanging bag and the feed is slowing down. I watch people reunite with their families and possessions and feel sorry for myself because neither are showing up for me. I've only got myself to blame. I didn't tell anyone I was coming and I stuffed Luce's hanging bag like a sausage casing because I didn't want to pay an extra luggage fee. It didn't hit the weight limit but it's unwieldy and the attendant at National Airport eyed it like there might be a body inside. I know there's a place reserved for bigger items but have no idea where it is because I'm not the type of person who travels with skis or golf clubs. I'm not the type of person who travels at all.

The feed slows to a trickle and then nothing.

Are you on the Groome yet?

Another text from Katie.

Not yet. I'll let you know.

I booked the four p.m. Groome shuttle to LaGrange. The name has nothing to do with weddings (I looked it up) but Katie's been teasing me about it because it feeds my anxiety that Spencer's family will cast me in the role of a man. I present more masculine than my va-va-voom fiancé, no question, but there's a difference between well-groomed and the groom. The only men in our wedding party are supposed to be Spencer's uncle, Big Clint, and her cousin, Clint Jr. There is no groom. That's the whole point. Spencer is my bride and I'm hers.

The baggage claim office is at capacity with unclaimed luggage and unhappy people. There's no place to stand except for a tiny strip of floor against the back wall. I line up behind a frazzled-looking man and his equally frazzled wife, who studies my tattoos with undisguised interest. I roll my shoulders in a practiced motion that makes the planets ripple and her eyes nearly pop out of her head. She grabs her husband's arm and I pull out my phone to send a quick reply to Katie. Her phone notifies me that she's driving but there's a text from Luce, who has sent a picture of her lunch. I swear, Luce spends half her time tattooing and the other half thinking about food. When she and Katie got divorced, I gained ten pounds chasing the best cheeseburger in DC. I'd kill for one now. I've eaten nothing since the crumbly almond cookies on the plane and my stomach is churning. Maybe there's a vending machine at ground transportation.

"This could take all day."

The frazzled woman is trying to bond but I don't encourage her.

"Let's hope not," I say and turn away. Though, technically, I do have all day—what's left of it anyway. Spencer doesn't expect me here until tomorrow. Right now, she's thirty minutes south of LaGrange in a city called Columbus having final alterations done on her wedding dress. I haven't seen it yet because she's chosen to go traditional. I only know that it's floor-length, off-white and strapless. Oh, and she's wearing her grandmother's veil.

A trolly of luggage is wheeled into the office and my bag is blessedly on it. The frazzled woman looks as if I've let her down but I cannot manage her feelings and won't try. Heaving the hanging bag onto my shoulder like a surfboard, I leave the office at a clip. I now wish I'd told Spencer I was coming in early. If I miss the Groome, I'll have to cool my heels in the airport for a couple of hours to wait for the next one or rent a car. I hate rental cars.

The pick-up location for the shuttle is just outside the airport but the heat is sweltering and I feel like I'm walking through soup. What was I thinking wearing Doc Martens and black jeans? Another two minutes and I'll be stewing in my own juice. And, of course, the van is gone. Motherfucker. Coming here early was a mistake. Walking back to the terminal I feel my body deflate as the hanging bag grows heavier.

Lost in thought, I step out into the street in front of a boat-sized Cadillac sedan and nearly get run over. It happens so quickly I've no time to react and fling the hanging bag on the hood of the car which screeches to a halt a few inches away from the tips of my boots. My knees begin to shake and a big man emerges from the passenger seat looking concerned. In two steps he's in my personal space.

"You okay, Tate?"

"Yes, sir," I say automatically. The muscle memory of manners is always stronger than my compulsion to overcome them. But how does he know my name? "Do I know you?"

He reaches out his hand. "I'm Joe Beck. Spencer's handsome uncle from Oklahoma. Come get in the car. Clint Jr. isn't a bad driver. I think you may have caught him off-guard."

I now recognize him as the gawking man from baggage claim. Laying an arm across my shoulders, he guides me toward the car. "Heard you missed the Groome so we doubled back."

"How did you hear that?" I say. I must be in shock. I'm letting a strange man touch me and put me in a car that belongs in a gangster film.

"Beth called Sister."

Okay. Wow. Spencer's people. I've heard most of their names but have not met a single one in person. I reach for my hoodie to cover the tattoos but it's too late. Joe's arm is on my bare skin. He smiles and I'm reminded of a cowboy actor. I climb into the backseat of the Cadillac and find the old bat who took the unsanctioned image of me. Her smile is tenuous and I'm shocked to see a flash of Spencer.

"Hey Tate. I'm Aunt Sister. Sorry we almost ran you over." She pats my leg while the driver looks woefully back at me. Early thirties with a mop of curly blond ringlets, he is Greek statue pretty and his eyes are so similar to Spencer's that I blink.

"I'm Clint Jr. and I really am sorry," he says and I instantly forgive him because of the resemblance. "Please don't tell Spencer on me."

"It's okay," I hear myself say, though I don't feel okay. Aunt Sister is now stroking my knee like I'm a therapy dog and I'm letting it happen. I'm definitely in shock.

"Say you won't tell her," Clint Jr. begs with Spencer's eyes, and it's like she's in the car. "Can we bribe you with food?"

"Sure," I say and gently remove Sister's hand from my knee.

"What are your feelings on pulled pork?"

"I like it," I say and she smiles Spencer's smile.

"How about ribs?" she presses.

"I like ribs," I say, but I'm so hungry I want to scream, *Where! Where are the ribs, Aunt Sister?*

"We'll need extra napkins," she ruminates as Joe slams down the trunk of the Cadillac and opens the passenger door.

"Everybody okay in here?"

"We're doing fine," Sister answers for everyone. "Clint Jr. says we're having BBQ for lunch."

"Okay with me." Joe nods then turns in my direction. "I married into this family thirty years ago, and I'm here to tell you, the Griffins may have spawned from rednecks and scallywags, but they know their BBQ."

"Oh, Joe." Aunt Sister looks pleased.

"I'm happy to share other family wisdom with you for a small fee." He winks at me. "But if you want the deep knowledge, you gotta ask my wife. She's Griffin by blood and knows where the bodies are buried. Get on Sister's good side and the battle's half won."

"Are we talking about family or war?" The question flies from my mouth before I can stop it. It's the reflexive response of a defensive bartender and rude as hell. What's wrong with me? Clint Jr. barks out a laugh that sounds like *Ha!* while Aunt Sister looks wounded.

"I imagine toxic families and war have a lot in common. What do you think, Joe?" she asks her husband.

"How'd I know?" he jokes. "You know I dodged both."

This time I manage to choke back a nasty reply, but my face must betray outrage because Clint Jr. shakes his head at me in the mirror.

"Uncle Joe's a career firefighter, Tate," he says and his eyes drop briefly to my tattoos.

"Oh." The surge of indignation turns to shame and my cheeks flame. It was a civilian firefighter who first responded to the training incident. I remember how gentle his hands were ministering to my bleeding and battered body. The man was a hero and I'm an asshole. Joe is either polite or oblivious.

"Best years of my life." He flashes perfect white teeth at me. "What can I say? Some like it hot."

I'm absolutely certain this isn't the first time he's used this line, yet I laugh along with Aunt Sister who doesn't seem to be holding a grudge.

"He was Tulsa's Fire Chief for twenty years," Clint Jr. continues. "Risked his life hundreds of times."

"That's really impressive. Fire is no joke," I manage gracelessly. I seriously need to relax, but in my defense, I'm ravenous and almost just got run over by a car. I also didn't anticipate meeting Spencer's relatives without Spencer or my hoodie. Yes, I work with the public. But no one ever has accused me of being a people person.

Sister is rubbing my knee again. Her voice sounds like someone mimicking a southern accent in a movie. I'm never sure which are fake and which are real, though Spencer claims to know the difference. I'm guessing Sister's is authentic.

"Why didn't you tell anyone you were coming today? I hope we didn't spoil a surprise."

"Spencer knows I'm here?" I blurt and her face crumbles. Oh, shit. It never occurred to me someone would tell Spencer I was here before I could. This was not supposed to be a big deal. Now I'll have to think of an explanation that does not involve the words booty or call.

"She does by now," Clint Jr. says and Joe chuckles. Sister's hand flies to the golden cross around her neck.

"I'm so sorry! Did I ruin your surprise?"

"Loose lips sink ships." Joe cranes his neck to wink at me.

"I ruined it!" Sister wails.

"You're going to burn in hell, woman," Joe teases and I surprise myself by shushing him.

"It's fine," I say and it's true. Because if there's one thing I'm sure of, it's Spencer. I'm actually relieved she knows I'm here. Sliding out my phone, I find it's already ringing. The photo on the screen is one I took of Spencer the night she walked into my bar looking for a job. She's wearing a peasant blouse and looks like she could be going to a renaissance fair.

Sister grabs for her cross again. "It's Spencer!"

"It's fine," I say again and take the call. "Hey, Sweet-Pea."

"Hey, Tater-tot." Spencer breathes and her voice is low and scratchy like an eighties disc jockey or a pack-a-day smoker. "I've just heard the most delicious rumor."

"Oh, yeah?" The reaction is just what I expected and I can't help smiling. I know I have an audience and I don't care.

"Everyone is talking about this hot woman hanging around the Atlanta airport. Aunt Sister posted a picture on the family group chat and then Aunt Elizabeth called me from the Groome."

"Not the famous Aunt Elizabeth?"

"Yes. She saw your name on the passenger list and called me immediately."

"She recognized my name?" The knowledge makes me inexplicably happy. Although I'm only hours away from seeing Spencer, so this may have something to do with my mood.

"Did you think you could just sneak into my home state and not have me find out?"

"I should've known better."

"Well, you're going to pay." There's laughter in her voice. "Mama knows you're here. Clint Jr.'s supposed to drive you straight to the house after y'all get the BBQ."

"You know I'm in the car with Clint Jr.?"

"Don't underestimate me."

"I wouldn't dream of it," I say, and it's true. Spencer is a force of energy. Six months ago, I hired her to work at the bar and became her boss. Within six weeks, she owned my soul. She's two years younger than me and leagues ahead emotionally. Some people see us as an unlikely pair. I say, fuck those people. Let them chase down their own happily ever after. I got mine and I'm holding on with both hands.

"Be careful, or Mama will put you to work polishing silver for the party tomorrow."

"Really?"

"Yeah, I spent all morning picking up catering tables and folding chairs from the neighbors. Mama won't pay for anything she can borrow from a friend."

"That sounds smart," I say, though the information surprises me. I thought fancy people hired out for everything. "Will the caterer bring the linens?"

"Caterer?" She snorts and I can picture the look on her face. "When I left the house, Mama was rolling out biscuits and my nieces were ironing a pile of lace tablecloths she'd begged off members of the garden club."

"Lace?"

"They are heirloom gorgeous and were probably at six other events this year. That's how Mama's crowd does it. I've still got to pick up Paw-Paw ferns. Mama's texted me six times."

"They borrow houseplants?"

"These are hanging ferns, and they are magnificent, but yes."

"I can go with you."

"Okay. I'll be home just before dinner. Miss Elaine gave us the friends and family rate so I can't rush her. Gossip's a line item in the budget." She lowers her voice. "I'm so glad you're here."

"Me too. Text me when you're on your way?"

"Okay. I love you."

"I love you, too."

I pocket my phone and see that Sister is tapping away at hers. Who is she texting now? I'm not used to this level of connectivity, though I must concede it isn't without merit. I'd still be at the Atlanta airport right now if Aunt Elizabeth hadn't snooped the manifest, remembered my name and called in the calvary. It's impressive when you think about it.

"Why didn't Elizabeth ride with you?" I ask no one in particular and Clint Jr. answers.

"There wasn't room. She and Uncle Alex brought the dogs."

"Gotcha."

Elizabeth and her hippie husband, Alex, are Spencer's godparents. Spencer claims the reason that she's so comfortable in her own skin is because they gave her room to move around in it. When Spencer came out, her mom sent her to spend the summer with the free-thinking, childless couple and she learned how to make veggie burgers and smoked clove cigarettes. When I came out, Daddy drove me to the Army recruiting center in Rockville. Two weeks into basic training, I was forced to jump out of a truck at gunpoint by a misogynist yee-haw corporal and dragged a hundred yards along a gravel road. I won a big settlement in a civil suit but received nothing from the Army besides an honorable discharge. It's more than Daddy got.

"We don't eat there because of politics." Sister points to a billboard for a popular fast-food chicken place known to support conservative action. "Joe loves waffle fries but you can get 'em at the grocery store now, so why support assholes? That's what that A stands for, you know?" She gives me a mischievous look and I can't help smiling at her.

"I agree."

"Yeah," Joe joins our conversation. "One of the store brands has a zesty option that tastes better. I love zesty."

"Some like it hot," I say, and they all laugh like it's the funniest thing they've ever heard. Even Clint Jr. smiles. These are nice people. I want to like them. I do like them. It helps, of course, that two of them look like Spencer.

"Is Amy still teaching third grade?" Sister tugs on one of Clint Jr.'s curls. It goes straight and then springs back into a perfect ringlet.

"Yes, ma'am. She's swimming at Paw-Paw's with the cousins right now. Kids didn't want to go over there alone."

Sister puffs out a breath. "Oh, Daddy's not that bad."

"He's bad enough." Clint Jr. makes eye contact with me in the mirror. "Has Spencer warned you about Paw-Paw?"

I search my brain and come up with a picture of a fruit tree. "Not really. What about him? She said that we're staying in his pool house."

"Now, the pool house is nice and so is Bertha." Clint Jr. pats the steering wheel of the car. "But I'd never describe Paw-Paw that way."

"Stop telling stories. He's your granddaddy," Aunt Sister scolds but Joe is nodding his head.

"Paw-Paw's mean as a snake."

"Joe!"

"I'm sorry, honey. The older your Daddy gets, the nastier his mouth. Hope you got a thick skin, Tate," he says and then looks horrified. "I didn't mean to suggest…"

"You're fine," I say and look out the window. Spencer didn't say anything about a mean grandfather. But Spencer doesn't use words like mean. Now that I think of it, I remember her saying he was unhappy, which may be social worker code for dick. I doubt he's any nastier than my own daddy, who used to lock us in the tool shed overnight if we broke curfew. Let Paw-Paw bring his best; he just better not come for Spencer.

I wonder what she's doing right now. Is she trying on the dress? Is she in her underwear? It's been too long since I've had my arms around her and the thought of her undressed heats me in a different way than the Georgia sunshine. Dinner can't come quickly enough and neither can I.

We roll into the parking lot of the BBQ restaurant and Clint Jr. parks the car. There's a cut-out pig on the sign and Joe nods his approval. "Griffins know their BBQ."

"Mama loves this place," Clint Jr. says then turns to me. "Come with?"

"Sure," I tell him, though I'm surprised to be asked. Does he want me to split the check?

"Wait, y'all!" Sister jams a hand in her purse and pulls out a Louis Vuitton wallet bulging with cash. "We got this."

"Yeah, we do." Joe pushes a money clip at Clint Jr. who refuses to take it.

"Aunt Nancy already paid the bill. Called in her Mastercard."

"Damn, she's good," Joe mutters and Sister looks like someone has stolen her lollipop. She returns the wallet to her purse and I step out into the heat where Clint Jr. is waiting by the entrance holding the door. Katie can't stand it when a man opens a door for her but she's from California. It's not something that's ever bothered me. Sometimes I worry it should.

Inside the restaurant, it's cold and my arms prickle over with goose flesh. A few patrons look our way and one does a double-take at my tattoos and gives me a thumbs-up. Confused, I hug my arms to my chest.

"Some like it cold," Clint Jr. says. He unwraps the half-zip jacket he has tied around his waist. "Want my coat?"

I'm not sure if he's embarrassed to be seen with me or just being gallant. "I'm good."

"Okay." He doesn't push. Our order isn't ready yet so we move into a small area near the register to wait. Clint Jr. leans against the wall and looks at me with Spencer's eyes.

"Tell me about yourself. How did you meet my cousin? How long have y'all been together?" He's too polite to ask why we're getting married so quickly but the question is implied. And it's fair.

"I met Spencer when she walked into my bar looking for a job."

"You own a bar?" I can tell he already knows the answer. There's probably a laminated fact sheet on me at Spencer's mother's house. But Clint Jr. is taking the time to ask me the questions himself. It's like an interview for a job I already have but this doesn't make the answers any less important.

"Yes, I opened it when I got out of the Army. I got a chunk of change from a civil suit I'm not supposed to talk about."

He nods and I'm certain he's familiar with the story. This works for me, as I'm legally bound not to discuss the incident and it's my least favorite topic.

"I didn't have a job or a place to live so I bought a bar with an upstairs apartment."

"Two birds, one stone. I like it." He nods his head and the ringlets bounce agreeably. "What's the bar's name?"

"The Only One," I say, and smile like I do every time I answer this question. "I kind of named it after the Melissa Etheridge song, but also because it's the only damn lesbian bar in the area."

"Really?"

"Unfortunately."

"Sounds like good business."

"We do okay."

"No offense, but why was Spencer looking for a job at a bar? She has a Master's degree in social work. Wasn't she running a women's shelter?"

"She's their intake director," I say proudly. "But she's got this thing about designer purses…" I let my voice trail away and he laughs.

"How could I forget? Spencer's always had a hard-on for high-quality goods."

"I'll take that as a compliment."

"You should."

"We weren't hiring but I took her on anyway."

"You're kidding?" he says and I smile because I've never told anyone this detail of the story. People know I hired Spencer but they don't know I made up a job.

"I couldn't tell her no."

"Terrible precedent, just terrible," he says but his eyes are dancing.

"She didn't have a place to live either so I gave her the extra room in my apartment."

"This is starting to sound like a Netflix movie."

"So, you know how it ends," I joke.

He nods thoughtfully. "I guess I do."

"Things moved really fast with us."

"Still moving pretty fast."

"I don't care," I tell him. "Spencer is the best thing that's ever happened to me. I mean, she's a bright, shining star and makes me want to live my best life, be my best self." I know I sound corny but his face is inscrutable so I barrel on. "I shouldn't have to tell you this, man. She's your cousin. Spencer is kind and smart and sweet and beautiful. I'm lucky to even know her." I feel sheepish ranting, but Clint Jr. is the closest thing Spencer has to a brother, and he needs to know I'm serious.

He looks at me for a long moment and then his mouth twists into a smile. "I do know it, Tate. Glad you do too." He lifts his gaze to the ceiling and lets out a low whistle. "Damn, these beautiful women, got us on a string, don't they?"

"No place I'd rather be," I say truthfully. "How long have you been married?"

"Almost ten years." He pulls out his phone and shows me a photo of a tiny redhead. "I got super lucky. I met Amy freshman year at Georgia. We dated all through school." He squints at me and there's a new question in the air.

"I never went to college," I tell him and feel the familiar shame. "I went straight into the service and then almost straight out again. There was a lot of rehab after the incident." I indicate the canvas of ink that is my arms, chest and shoulders which gives him permission to truly look. His eyes follow the line of planets snaking up my right arm to the sun across my chest and the asteroid field on my left side.

"Your tattoos are incredible. I've never seen anything like it. And I didn't mean to suggest that you should go to college. That's just where I met my wife."

I appreciate his candor and open up more than I usually do. "That's okay. I may still go one day. Who knows?" This is something else I've never told anyone. Not even Spencer.

"I didn't have a choice. Everyone goes to UGA in both our families. My wife's mom was roommates with Aunt Nancy when they were in Athens. It can be a small world down here."

"I haven't met Nancy yet."

"We call her the general because she likes to put people to work. Don't be surprised if she asks you to mix drinks tomorrow."

"Griffin!" Our order is called and we approach the counter to find eight bags of food stacked two-deep. The server smiles at us. "Y'all feeding an army or just want to make sure you got you some leftovers?" Clint Jr. tells her I'm getting married and she gives me a free Rice Krispies treat.

We climb into the Cadillac and he continues our conversation from inside the restaurant. "I was just telling Tate that Aunt Nancy might put her to work."

"Count on it," Joe warns me. "First time I met Nancy she made me man the grill. I was so scared I was going to burn Paw-Paw's T-bone I sweated through my new golf shirt and had to borrow one from Big Clint."

"Nancy's always been bossy," Sister explains. "When Spencer's daddy died, she got worse. It's just her way of moving through the world. But she gets things done and never asks anyone for a dime." By the set of her jaw, I can tell this is high praise. "When Michelle got married, Nancy planned the whole thing and cooked most of the food, too. It was beautiful."

"It was," Joe agrees.

Michelle is Spencer's older sister, yet another Griffin I haven't met.

"Good thing I know how to follow orders and keep my mouth shut," I say to no one in particular and Joe nods.

"That is good. That's a very good thing, Tate."

We're now off the highway speeding down a well-paved, two-lane road. I breathe in the heavenly scent of the BBQ and my mouth waters. There's no way to eat a Rice Krispie treat on the sly so I ask if anyone would like a bite. They all decline and I jam half of it in my mouth like I'm worried they'll change their minds. Chewing greedily, I study the lovely but modest houses of LaGrange. Spaced far apart with large yards and open carports, they remind me of the town where I grew up. Political signs reflect the same conservative values but Spencer has assured me that her family won't give us any trouble. Everything I've seen so far backs up this statement. I need to relax. In four days, I'm going to marry the woman of my dreams and in four hours I'm going to see her naked. The looming threat of Paw-Paw and General Nancy aside, this might not be the nightmare I've anticipated.

"Tate?" Sister lays a hand gently on my forearm. "We're almost to Nancy's house."

Clint Jr. is turning the Cadillac into the golfing subdivision where Spencer grew up. The houses are bigger with rolling, landscaped lawns. There are no cars on the street and no people either. I imagine everyone's inside enjoying air-conditioning and sweet tea. We pull into a large circular driveway in front of a classic mid-century modern ranch house and Clint Jr. stops the car. Before I can reach the door handle, it's opened from the outside and a small boy pokes his head in and screams, "Grandma!" scaring me to death.

"It's Harris," Joe yells and jumps from the car. The boy is now on the other side of the Cadillac embracing Aunt Sister who's smothering his towhead with kisses. Harris must be her grandson. That makes him Spencer's first cousin once removed and my new kin after Saturday.

"Harris and his parents flew in from Japan this morning," Clint Jr. tells me and gets out of the car. Several people have come out of the house and are waiting for us by the front door. Two women in pretty flowered dresses, one older and one younger, who I assume are Nancy and Michelle, stand with a fit-looking, older man and a young boy. I want to put on my hoodie but what's the point? Aunt Sister already showed my picture to everyone and it's got to be a hundred degrees outside. I get out of the car and fall in step with Clint Jr. up the hill.

"How much you want to bet Aunt Nancy's got a chore for me?"

"I'm not taking that bet but I'll help out."
"That'll win you points."
"I'll take any I can get."
"You're gonna be fine."

He punches my arm and we walk the short distance to the front door where Michelle launches herself at me. We've only met over Facetime but she wraps her arms around my neck like we're old pals and gives me a squeeze. Her frame is similar to Spencer's but she smells different.

"It's Tate! Finally!" she says and then grabs on to Clint Jr.

"My turn!" Nancy yells and follows Michelle into my arms. I cradle Spencer's mother gently and say hello over her shoulder to the older man who can only be Big Clint. His hair is curly like his son's but close-cropped and light gray.

Thankfully he doesn't try to embrace me but sticks out an elegant hand. "I'm Clint Griffin, welcome to the family."

"Thank you, sir. I'm Tate." I take his hand.

"It's wonderful to meet you," Nancy says and smiles Spencer's happiest smile. "We're so glad you're here." She pats the cross on her neck and I wonder if it's a family trait. "Spencer left Miss Elaine's ten minutes ago. She'll be here after she stops to pick up some ice."

"I'll get the ice, Aunt Nancy," Clint Jr. says and winks at me.

"Oh, honey, I've already got a job for you. Spencer didn't have time to walk the ferns over from Paw-Paw's."

"Spencer didn't have time? I'm shocked," Michelle says and everyone laughs.

"Why can't we drive them over? Bertha's trunk will hold a dead mule."

Nancy shakes her head. "Paw-Paw wants us to walk them over. We can't crimp the fronds."

"What are fronds?" Clint Jr. wants to know.

"The delicate wispy parts. It makes them beautiful."

"We'll be careful, I promise."

"Sorry, it's Paw-Paw's rule."

"No point pissing off the old man, buddy," Big Clint says, putting an end to the discussion. He reaches out to shake hands with Joe who's just made it up the hill. Sister and Harris are still in the Cadillac where what looks to be a small suitcase of grandma gifts has exploded in the backseat.

Clint Jr. turns to me. "You coming?"

"That's a wonderful idea." Nancy looks excited. "You two get the ferns and Joe can help me reheat the BBQ. Spencer might be here by the time y'all get back."

Joe widens his eyes comically and Clint Jr. gives his aunt a little salute. "Okay, let's go."

"Thank y'all so much!" Nancy gushes and hugs me again.

We make our way down the hill to the street. Waving to Sister and Harris, we walk straight down the middle of the road because there's no sidewalk and no traffic. We turn the corner and there's a steep hill leading down into a cul-de-sac. A pretty woman wearing a bright red bathing suit coverup is standing at the bottom.

"That's my wife, Amy," Clint Jr. tells me and picks up the pace. We meet her in the middle of the cul-de-sac and see that she's hurt her foot.

"What happened, baby?" Clint Jr. drops to one knee and gently takes her heel in his hands. He turns it to the side and a nasty gash is visible.

"It's all my fault," she says and smiles at me over her husband's shoulder. "His mom told me to put on shoes before I came over here, but Aunt Nancy was starting to roll out the biscuits so I ran. I was fine until about two seconds ago when I stepped on a piece of glass."

"Oh, sweetie." Clint Jr. continues to fuss over her foot and she stretches out a hand to me.

"You must be Tate. I've been looking forward to meeting you. I'm Amy."

"Nice to meet you." I squeeze her fingers.

"We should go back to Paw-Paw's and clean this up," Clint says and Amy scrunches up her face.

"Can we go to Aunt Nancy's?"

"Okay." Clint Jr. eyes the big house at the end of the cul-de-sac. "Was he out there with y'all?"

"We never saw him. Your daddy said he might be napping."

"I warned Tate about his mouth," he says and Amy's eyes narrow.

"He won't mess with Tate."

"Probably not. But she deserves a heads-up."

"I appreciate that," I say truthfully. If there's a storm on the horizon, it's better to know.

"I try to stay out of his way," Amy says and tosses her ponytail. "What are y'all doing down here anyway? I was just coming to get ready for supper."

"Aunt Nancy asked us to walk the ferns over." He looks back at the gash on her foot which, upon closer inspection, might require stitches.

"Why don't you take Amy back and let me deal with the ferns?" I say. "It's my wedding, after all."

"No way," Amy says immediately. "Tate can't go to Paw-Paw's by herself. We'll all come back down after dinner."

"Nancy won't like it if we come back empty-handed," I argue. Clint Jr. looks torn.

"How about I grab two now and we'll get the rest after dinner?" I ask.

Amy shakes her head. "I'd be careful."

"I promise."

I'm now perversely curious to meet Paw-Paw. I find it difficult to believe anyone related to Spencer can be that much of an asshole. Between my daddy, the Army, and the bar, I've met more than my share. How nasty can the man be?

Amy and Clint Jr. make their way up the hill and I turn back to Paw-Paw's house, which, upon closer scrutiny, now seems aggressively antebellum. A stately white mansion with a wide front porch and long fluted columns, the house makes a definitive statement about time and place. But the ferns are indeed magnificent. Hanging at evenly measured intervals along the front porch, their delicate fronds lift in the soft summer breeze and remind me of an animated sea monster I loved as a child.

I follow Amy's bloody footprint across the cul-de-sac to the front yard, and climb the steps to the porch. The ceiling is painted a beautiful robin's-egg blue and the floor looks like it's been swept for company but the rocking chairs are empty and there's no sign of Paw-Paw. I test the weight of the nearest fern, and though massive, it's not as heavy as I thought. I can definitely manage two in one trip.

Lifting the plant off the hook, I place it on a small table being extra careful not to crush the fronds. But when I move to get the second, my boot catches on the rail and I pitch forward dropping the fern in the boxwood hedge below. Jesus fuck. I look down, but miraculously, it doesn't seem to be damaged.

"What are you doing with my ferns, boy?" I'm startled by a loud voice behind me and jerk around to find the front door open with Paw-Paw standing in the frame. He has a long bony neck and a face like an apple doll. I've never seen him before but I recognize the hate in his voice.

"Good afternoon, sir. I'm Tate. I came to get the ferns for the party and one fell in the boxwood, but it looks okay." I offer him my hand and he pulls out a shotgun.

"Fell in the boxwood," he sneers and lifts the barrel so it's even with my chest.

When my father got angry a pulsing vein was visible on his forehead. Paw-Paw's angry vein is in his throat. I watch it throb for a moment, and then see his finger tense on the trigger. I hold up my hands as if they can do anything to stop a bullet or an old man's hatred. "Nancy Griffin sent me. I think she's your daughter?"

Paw-Paw takes a moment to consider the new information. My heart is racing and my breath struggling to catch up. When the corporal forced me to jump from the transport vehicle, he had a service revolver. Turns out, PTSD isn't picky about gun type.

"I told Nancy not to bring the car," he grouses but thankfully lowers the gun. "If you put the ferns in the car, you'll crush the fronds." He scowls at me and looks so much like my daddy my stomach roils.

"I don't have your car, sir."

"What do you mean? The car's right there." He points a bony finger over my shoulder. I want to keep my eye on the gun but a noise suggests something is indeed behind us. Turning, I see Spencer jumping out the passenger door of the Cadillac. Her long blond hair is stuffed into an old ball cap and she's wearing workout clothes I've never seen, but the expression on her face is one that's etched in my soul. I'm surprised to see Nancy in the driver's seat, but don't have time to ponder it because Spencer is sprinting across the yard. Taking the porch steps two at a time she flings herself into my arms. I squeeze her too tightly and she breaks contact to search my eyes.

"What's wrong, baby?" she asks.

I shake my head. Still trembling, I can't articulate what just happened but nod toward Paw-Paw who's trying to hide the gun behind his leg. Spencer's eyes widen.

"What are you doing with that thing?" Releasing me, she steps forward and takes the weapon from his hands like it's a plastic toy.

"You know it ain't loaded," Paw-Paw replies, but he's looking over her shoulder at Nancy who's suddenly beside me on the porch.

"Tate doesn't know that, Daddy," she says before laying a hand on my shoulder. Her eyes are pure warmth, which makes me tear up. "Oh, honey!" For the third time that day Spencer's mother pulls me against her body.

"Tater!" The gun clatters to the ground and Spencer joins us. For a moment I'm sandwiched between them.

"We took away his bullets when Obama got elected," Nancy whispers into my ear. "He's a loudmouth but you never know." Giving me a squeeze, she pulls away to address her father.

"I sent Tate over here to borrow ferns, not trouble. You've embarrassed me and owe her an apology. I'd hate for you to have to miss the BBQ."

"Sorry, Tate," Paw-Paw says, now looking abashed. "You caught me by surprise."

I manage a nod but don't say anything.

"Thank you for being so gracious." Nancy pats my shoulder again. I've never been touched by so many people in one day. "I'm going to help Paw-Paw pick out a tie for dinner. See y'all back at the house?"

"Yes, ma'am," Spencer says.

The door closes and she takes me in her arms. Stroking my back in long slow movements, she soothes me. "Did that trigger you?"

"A little," I admit and sink into her.

"Oh, baby. Paw-Paw's an old meanie but he's harmless."

"Not all meanies are harmless," I croak and she pulls me in tighter.

"I know, baby. I'm sorry."

We stand there rocking for several moments until we're interrupted by shouts from the street.

"Aren't they adorable?"

"Y'all get a room!"

I peek over Spencer's shoulder and see Clint Jr. and Michelle walking across the yard.

"We came to help with the ferns," Michelle says, her attention focused on the one laying in the boxwood. "Seems like you may need it."

Clint Jr. holds a hand to his throat in perfect imitation of his aunts. "Did you crush the fronds?"

"I think the fronds are mostly intact," Spencer says and squeezes my hand.

"Did Paw-Paw go after Tate?" Clint Jr. asks. Mounting the steps he picks up the discarded gun.

"Yes, but Mama told him off and now they're inside choosing a tie."

"Sounds like par for the course. Sorry about that, Tate. I shouldn't have let you come alone." He frowns and it's suddenly clear he isn't just here for the plants. I tell him it's okay, and five minutes later the four of us are walking across the yard, each holding a giant fern.

"Hold up a second." Spencer stops short and hooks her free arm around my waist. Gently she kisses my lips, causing a familiar flutter deep in my core and my mood miraculously lifts. But that's the magic of Spencer. Like a powerful magnet she brings me back to center.

"Dinner's not for a little while. Can I show you my childhood bedroom?" she says and I laugh.

"Yes, please."

"We can hear you," Michelle says from behind her plant and Clint Jr. hoots.

"Here come the brides!"

Spencer smiles and kisses me again. I am humbled by her love. Luce fixed my physical scars and Spencer is doing the same for my spirit. Her family isn't what I imagined, but I'll need to adjust my expectations. This is why she's perfect for me. The further I refocus my lens to see the world through her eyes, the closer I'll get to whole. It's what I want, and I plan to love, honor and cherish her for as long as she'll have me.

Clint Jr. steps out into the cul-de-sac. The sun is setting over his shoulder and shining through his curls. "Y'all ready?"

"Yes," we say in unison and Spencer squeezes my hand. Walking up the hill we turn the corner and go home to prepare for the coming party.

OUT WITH THE OLD

Tagan Shepard

The wedding was perfect.

Sophie was stunning in her off-the-shoulder dress and flowing veil. Caleb's tux looked like it had been designed just for his slim frame. Their vows were poetic. Everyone cried. The cocktail hour had been just long enough that the hors d'oeuvres and signature drink lasted. Dinner service had been so well-timed it was almost prescient. The sunset had crowned the couple as they cut their towering masterpiece of a cake. Now night had descended, crisp but not too cool. Light from strings of twinkling bulbs spilled to the edge of the tent, leaving the fireflies to illumine the gardens beyond.

The only sour note of the whole evening was me.

I shouldn't have been there.

"What were you thinking?" I whispered to myself, my words swallowed by the water glass I'd raised to my lips.

Everyone around me seemed to be having a great time. I hadn't heard that much laughter in one place in a long time. That shouldn't have surprised me. After all, this friend group had always been one of the liveliest, happiest bunch of people I'd ever met. I missed that. I missed them.

Rachel Danvers, a college friend of Sophie's that I used to brunch with twice a month, spun as she danced and made eye contact with me. My breath caught as, for a wonderful moment, I thought she was smiling at me. Maybe she'd come over? Or at least wave? Acknowledge that she and I had once shared the same unrestrained laughter she enjoyed now.

She didn't, of course.

Her eyes narrowed to beady slits and the grin melted off her face like ice cream on a hot summer day. After she was certain I'd fully absorbed her dirty look, she whipped around to face her girlfriend, laughing ostentatiously. The girlfriend, whom I'd never met and might've given me the benefit of the doubt, mirrored Rachel's grimace before looking away.

So much for first impressions.

It wasn't only Rachel and her girlfriend. I scanned the party from my position at its outer reaches. There were no friendly looks coming my way. A few were disinterested. A few perplexed. Most openly hostile. The worst was Sophie and Caleb. They looked like they wanted to flay the skin from my bones and hang it up next to the fairy lights lining the tent.

The one person who'd been happy to have me here tonight was nowhere to be seen.

"Time to make my getaway," I mumbled, setting my water glass down.

"Excuse me for bothering you." The voice, an intoxicating blend of low rumble and smooth, buttery notes, came from over my left shoulder. "I've lost my phone number. Can I borrow yours?"

A cheesy pickup line? Seriously?

I turned on my heel to level an indignant stare at the newcomer, but my first glance made me trip over my ballet flats. The woman's hand shot out and grabbed my elbow, setting me back on my feet.

"Had one too many of those, huh?" she asked, cutting her eyes at my sweating water goblet.

Then she smiled at her own joke.

Whoa.

I mean—seriously—whoa.

It was the Maid of Honor. I'd noticed her during the ceremony because she was the only member of the bridal party wearing a suit. And boy was she wearing that suit. It was identical to the royal blue jacket and dress pants, gold vests, and blue and gold striped ties the groom's party wore, but it was better suited to her lean frame and small chest. Her skin was tanned almost as golden as her tie, but pale skin showed through the close shaven sides of her haircut. The rest of her hair, a deep, earthy brown, was pulled into a messy topknot. Even sexier than her clothes was the confident, almost-cocky half grin. It sat well on her wide face and prominent jaw.

I wanted to be mad at her. Mrs. Bell, busy playing the magnanimous mother of the bride all night, had finally vanished and I could've escaped. I could've stepped out of the tent into the enveloping darkness and slunk off to forget this night ever happened. It would've been so easy if this woman and her bad pickup line hadn't interrupted me.

I couldn't be mad at her, though. Not with those pale, washed-out green that might've been blue eyes. I couldn't really tell in the dark, isolated corner of this tent. There was a depth to those eyes I could get lost in, a kindness lightly frosted over with confidence.

"Has that line ever worked for you?" I asked, an unwanted smile growing on my lips.

"Nope," she replied, taking a step toward me. "But I have a bunch more. Let me try another?"

I'd been wrong about the cockiness. I might even have been wrong about the confidence. Hope swirled in those pale eyes now, hope and the slightest hint of longing. Damn she was charming. I nodded before I could stop myself and was rewarded with a dazzling, full smile and another half step forward. She smelled good. Like fresh cotton and oiled leather.

She cleared her throat and cocked an eyebrow. "Do I know you? 'Cause you look like my next girlfriend."

I laughed. It was my normal, obnoxious laugh that was too loud and ended in a snort. I caught myself too late and whipped my head around. Damn. Sophie had definitely heard me. She glared at me and the look was so foreign on her sweet face that I snapped my mouth shut, my teeth clicking. Tears prickled my eyes for the millionth time tonight and I turned back around, my eyes fixed on the ground. The Maid of Honor shuffled her feet, the toes of her two-toned wingtips tapping at the grass.

I forced myself to look up at her once I'd blinked away the tears. "You were right to go with the first one. That's worse."

"I thought so."

Her straight eyebrows came together, a wrinkle forming in her high forehead. Her smile faded and she set her champagne flute on the table. "I thought I knew all of Sophie's friends, but I don't think we've met. I'm Mel."

She held out her hand. Her cufflink was the Wonder Woman logo in flashy blue, red, and gold. I shook it because I wanted to know what her hand felt like. It was calloused in odd places and I couldn't stop my mind from wondering what had earned her those rough patches.

"Laurel Chandler."

I should've said more. If we'd been anywhere else, I would have asked a question or offered a nugget of information about myself. But I couldn't. Not here. Not now. I tortured myself with another glance into the crowd. Still full of hostile faces, and now more of them were pointed my way. Or maybe they were looking at Mel?

"Are you…a guest of Caleb?"

I cringed and gave a shrug that sent my shawl toppling off my shoulder. The vintage, flare-skirted dress in pale pink paisley had been too cute to pass up, even if it was a little late in the season. It wasn't too cold tonight, though, unless you counted the other guests' shoulders.

Mel reached over and plucked the shawl up, covering my shoulder again. "Wedding crasher?"

I snorted. "As if."

"Hmm. That's what I'd expect a crasher to say. Pretty sure I could describe you to the cops." She leaned her elbow on the high-top table, making a show of looking me up and down. I didn't exactly hate the obvious joy she took in examining my body. "Five foot six. Slim build. Caucasian. Fair skin. Heart-shaped face. Thin, expressive eyebrows. Am I getting this right?"

"I'm five foot seven."

"Five foot seven," she repeated, a low purr in her voice. *And now I'm blushing.* "Brunette hair, curly, shoulder length. Eyes gray and far too sad if you ask me, but I suspect there are smile lines under there somewhere."

Definitely blushing. And I did have smile lines. I hated how deep they were since I wasn't even thirty yet, but Momma always said never trust anyone without smile lines, no matter how old they were.

"I was right," Mel whispered and that's how I realized I was smiling for the first time tonight.

"I doubt there's anything you can do about the eyes, though."

"Don't count me out yet."

I looked up into her soft gaze and the low-burning fire in them took my breath away. I felt the usual tug that happened every time I met the next person to break my heart. Just like every other time, I didn't listen to the warning. There was something about Mel. She may have a library of bad pickup lines, but I had a feeling she wasn't the player she pretended to be. Too bad I was meeting her here instead of literally any other time or place. From the moment I stepped foot in the church this afternoon, I knew nothing good could come of this day.

Mel cleared her throat and broke our eye contact. She rubbed the back of her neck and fiddled with her champagne flute. "I thought the key to successfully crashing a wedding is acting like you belong? No offense, but you kinda look like you'd rather be anywhere else but here."

"I'm not offended 'cause you're right." I checked over my shoulder again and there was Mrs. Bell, wandering through the crowd and avoiding her daughter's eye. Shit. There went my chance for escape. I turned back to Mel's inquisitive smile. "Look, have you ever…um…accepted an invitation you were supposed to decline?"

"Do people send out invites to people they want to decline?"

"Maybe if they're trying to be polite?"

My eyes were drawn across the room like a kitten who couldn't stop licking a scratch, even when the attention makes the wound worse. Mrs. Bell was arguing with Sophie now. I could see the signs of Sophie about to lose it. She always used to fling her arms into the air like that before storming off for a frustration cry. Please, god, don't let her cry on her wedding day. Not because of me.

"Or maybe if their mother made them invite you 'cause she hasn't quite given up hope."

I turned away from the scene, but Mel had spotted the commotion. It wasn't surprising and I knew she wasn't the only one. The rumble of conversation beneath the music had died away and if I listened hard, I could hear Mrs. Bell raise her voice. I snagged a loose curl trailing along my collarbone and twirled it around my finger, yanking it tight enough to pull on my scalp before unwinding it and twirling again. The repetitive motion normally calmed me, but watching the scene play out as a reflection of emotions on Mel's face was agonizing. Every now and then her eyes would flick back to me and heat would creep into my cheeks. It was inspired in equal parts by the perfect cut of Mel's jaw and my humiliation.

Mel took a sip of her champagne and I watched the penny drop. She flicked her eyes back to me and they widened into huge, pale-green saucers before returning to Mrs. Bell. Fortunately, she turned her head before choking on her drink so I didn't get sprayed with champagne.

"Wait!" It was indicative of how terrible the mother of the bride versus bride scene was that her shout didn't garner us any attention. She continued in a low rumble, "You're the reason everyone is mad at me for the toast?"

Okay, wasn't expecting that.

"The toast?"

"You didn't listen to my toast?" Mel's voice carried a note of accusation.

"I was…" I swallowed hard and closed my eyes to block out the memory of that second, or was it third, escape attempt. "In the bathroom."

She squinted at me like she knew it was the worst lie ever. "I made a joke. It didn't go over well."

"If your jokes are as good as your pickup lines, that doesn't surprise me."

She shrugged and rubbed the back of her neck again. I spotted the fine lines of a tattoo at her wrist and bit back the urge to reach out and touch it.

"I started my Maid of Honor speech by asking who in the crowd had slept with the bride." My stomach dropped to my toes and I could tell Mel knew why. "I raised my own hand."

My eyebrow shot up. I didn't need the confirmation that she was queer—her suit and flirtation had done that. It did surprise me that she'd slept with Sophie. Mel wasn't her usual type.

"Then I asked who'd slept with the groom."

My stomach leaked out through the tops of my shoes. It was like watching a car accident in slow motion.

"I still got laughs at that one," Mel continued. "Then I asked who had slept with both."

I discovered that I had gripped the tabletop when I heard my nails scraping through the wood. Guess I was finding out why the angry looks had intensified when Mrs. Bell led me back from the bathroom.

"There was this loud gasp," Mel continued torturously. She rubbed her chin and her eyebrows knitted again. "Sophie and Caleb looked at each other and I swear I could hear them screaming with their eyes."

Suddenly I was very glad I hadn't been in the tent when that happened. Mel's eyes were still searching me. I explained, "When I left the bathroom, Mrs. Bell caught me for a chat. I guess I missed the toasts."

"There was only one. The two of them dragged me off the stage and took turns ripping me apart for being an insensitive jerk. They wouldn't let anyone else do a speech."

"Sorry," I groaned.

"Haven't you noticed that everyone here is glaring at me?"

I risked a glance around the party and the same malevolent stares that had tracked me all night were trained on us. There may have been more of them than before, but it was hard to gauge the volume of angry stares.

"I think those are about me, not you," I confessed.

"I'm pretty sure we're sharing them. Wanna tell me why they're mad? Sophie and Caleb weren't in the mood for story time."

I wasn't exactly in the mood for story time either, but Mrs. Bell was still circling and I didn't want Mel to leave yet. I took a gulp of my lukewarm water and a deep breath.

"I started dating Caleb in college. We were together for a couple years. He was nice enough I guess, but it was a rebound from my high school girlfriend. I just got comfortable being with him."

"I've been there," Mel said, rolling her eyes. "Not with a dude, but I know the feeling."

If I tried really hard, I could conjure up the way he used to smile at me. We'd been so young.

"He asked me to move in with him, and I finally…I don't know. Snapped out of it? I didn't want to hurt him but staying would have been worse. He took it well. We stayed friends."

The DJ's voice boomed through the speakers, imploring the crowd to dance. It was the first time I'd heard him in ages. He sounded almost as desperate as I was.

"I met Sophie a few weeks later and we just…clicked."

Mel laughed quietly and spun her champagne flute. She didn't meet my eye and I had the strangest feeling she understood.

"I thought she was the one."

I regretted the pain that flashed across Mel's face. Her voice sounded wistful when she agreed. "Sophie has a way of making people feel that way. She promises you forever in the way she touches you."

All I could do was stare at her and blink. I was quiet for long enough that she looked over at me, her eyes barely touching mine before they darted away again.

"What?" she asked, her eyes fixed on a nearby tent pole.

"Nothing. I've just never thought of it that way."

There was a time when hearing a description like that, especially coming from someone who'd obviously been with Sophie, would have broken me. It would have sent me into a weeks-long tailspin that could only happen to someone who'd been knocked out of Sophie's orbit.

Tonight it didn't make me miss Sophie. It made me curious about Mel.

"I mean," Mel stammered. "I'm over her. She's my best friend. I just…know what you mean is all."

"Same here." The last thing I wanted was for Mel to think I was still hung up on Sophie. "I care about her, but actually being with her is…"

"Exhausting?"

There I was smiling again. "Yes. Exactly."

"Did she ever let you pick the movie?"

"Not once."

"And she's always dragging you to these concerts that are…"

"Bizarre," I agreed. "What even is synth folk?"

"I have no idea." Mel took another step toward me and I couldn't help notice how warm it was this close to her. "But I don't think the bands did either."

"And she always wants to talk about feelings. After a fight, or a good day, or a bad day, or any day. After…"

My voice trailed off as I noticed the sparkle in Mel's eyes. I was in dangerous waters and I didn't want to talk about those particular conversations with her when she smelled this good and stood this close.

She knew exactly what I was referring to, though. Mel winked and drawled, "Especially…after."

I had a vivid and distinctly pleasant image of Mel naked and sweating in rumpled sheets while Sophie dissected the encounter, blow by tantalizing blow. I shuddered.

"Cold?" Before I could deny it, Mel had her jacket off and around my shoulders. "Better?"

Better? I couldn't decide which part was better. The warm, musky scent that clung to the fabric draped over my shoulders or the sight of her in a crisp white shirt, the royal blue vest hugging her in all the right places. I nodded and pulled the lapels tighter around me, afraid she might take it back.

"You were saying?" Mel asked.

I was too busy swimming in her eyes and her scent to figure out her words. "I was?"

Her smile lit up our corner of the tent. "About you and Sophie."

"Oh. Right." I bent my head on the pretext of collecting my thoughts, but really I was gobbling up the scent of her on the fabric. It wasn't perfume, but more of a rich, earthy scent. Something like leather and rosemary mixed with freshly starched cotton. "We broke up before graduation. She was heading to London for her internship and I was off to grad school. It would never have worked. Neither of us had our hearts in it anymore."

"So you stayed friends with her." Mel rolled her eyes as she spoke. "How very stereotypical."

"You're friends with her, too. Don't you fit the stereotype?"

"Sophie and I never really dated."

Don't say it. Please don't say it.

"We hooked up in high school."

Of course she said it. Of course a woman like Mel didn't do commitment.

"She never wanted as much from me as I wanted from her."

That wasn't what I expected.

She continued with a wistful lilt to her voice. "So we figured out our attractions with each other as friends. No broken hearts."

"No broken hearts," I repeated, rolling the words around on my tongue. That's what I'd always aimed for in ending relationships and I thought I'd achieved it but clearly I was wrong.

"Didn't Sophie and Caleb meet at a party right before she left for London?" Mel asked.

"Yep."

Mel's jaw dropped open and she pointed at me. "You introduced them, didn't you?"

"Sort of. We'd planned the graduation party before we broke up. I'd invited Caleb. It never occurred to me that my exes would like each other, but I guess maybe it should have?"

What a strange night that had been. I'd watched their first meeting from across the room and saw the sparks fly. Images of their wedding had flashed through my mind when I walked in on their first kiss. It hadn't looked like this. It had been a happy affair with all of us great friends.

"I don't get it," Mel said after draining her glass. "Shouldn't they love you for bringing them together?"

"They do."

"Umm." Mel hooked her chin toward the dais where Caleb and Sophie were trying to eviscerate me with their eyes. "Sure about that?"

"It's all Mrs. Bell's fault. She…likes me."

"Oh god, please don't tell me you slept with the mother of the bride, too?"

Her laughter was low and rumbling and it made my stomach squirm pleasantly when I said, "You're laughing, so I won't slap you, but it's not funny."

"It's a little funny."

I rolled my eyes but I couldn't stop myself from smiling. How had I never met this ridiculously charming woman?

"No, I didn't sleep with her. She just likes me a lot. We bonded over *Golden Girls* when I was dating Sophie and we've been close ever since."

"Even after the breakup?"

I nodded, though my naivete made me want to crawl under the table. "We have lunch every week. She's been hinting since the engagement that I should try to get Sophie back. I've told her a million times that I don't want her back and that Caleb is a great guy and they're in love, but she won't listen."

"She's always been like that," Mel grumbled, making me curious about her history with Mrs. Bell.

I lowered my voice. "A few weeks ago she invited me over for dinner. Turns out she'd also invited Sophie."

"Wait." Mel's eyes went wide and she looked at me with something like awe. "That was you?"

"You know about the dinner?" I practically screamed the words, aware that every eye was on us now. But if Mel knew, how many other people here knew about that horrible night?

Mel must've read my mind, or perhaps my shriek was enough to clue her in. She reached out, laying her long, slim hand over mine and giving it a little squeeze.

"Sophie came to my place the next day sobbing." My stomach lurched, but Mel's voice was soft, a comforting tone that, mixed with the weight of her hand on mine, actually helped rein in my guilt. She continued, "I'm sure she didn't tell anyone else. We've been BFFs since middle school gym class."

It was far too much to hope that she was right, especially since the angry glares from every corner of the tent belied her reassurance.

"What did she tell you?" I asked. I didn't want to have to say it myself.

"That her mom invited over one of her exes in the hope that she'd stop the wedding. Pull one of those movie moments by sweeping the bride off her feet at the last moment."

"I told her no!" I was so close to sobbing that my intended scream came out more like a whimper. "I defended Caleb and their relationship."

"Really? 'Cause I don't think Sophie got the memo."

"I know that now. I thought I'd get a chance to explain myself to Sophie today, but..."

"But it's her wedding day and she's got it planned down to the last second."

I nodded and mumbled to the table, "I should've thought of that."

"Don't take this the wrong way, but why did you accept the invitation after that night?"

That was the exact question I'd been asking myself all day long.

"Mrs. Bell said she'd smoothed things over. She said they still wanted me here." I should've known better. Of course they didn't want a reminder of that night on their wedding day. I buried my face in my hands, an action I immediately regretted because it took away the buzz of Mel's touch. "I'm an idiot."

"No, you're not."

"She expected me to object during the ceremony," I groaned.

It was quiet so long I chanced a peek through my fingers. Mel's jaw was literally hanging open. When she saw me looking she snapped her teeth together with an audible click.

"Okay yeah, you definitely should've declined this invitation."

My forehead hit the tabletop with a clunk. It hurt. A lot. But then Mel's hand settled on my shoulder, heating my skin far more effectively than the flimsy shawl.

"I know," I groaned into the table and then pushed myself up. It was time to put on my big girl panties and do the right thing. Mel met my determined stare like a woozy boxer. "I need to get out of here but I can't get past Mrs. Bell. Can you help me sneak out?"

Mel was watching my lips move and nodding. Then she seemed to snap out of it. "No way! You're staying."

"I can't." As much as I wanted Mel to be into me, now was not the time. "I've already ruined their wedding day."

"You haven't ruined anything. Mrs. Bell did that. She used you. It's not your fault."

She had stiffened her spine and her eyes blazed. It was actually really hot, but I didn't have time for hot tonight. "You're sweet, but I think it's best if I leave."

I turned to go, making it three steps before remembering I still wore Mel's jacket. That was fine. I'd hang it from a tree on the way out. All I had to do was ignore Mrs. Bell and keep walking. Hopefully she wouldn't force me to run over her in the parking lot.

Mel whipped around in front of me, her smile full of the same mischief she'd approached me with. "I have a better idea. Tell me something about yourself that would make all these people like you."

A burst of laughter escaped my lips before I could stop it. Damn, did she have to be so charming?

"What?"

"Tell me something great about you. Here, I'll go first. I can't watch *The Little Mermaid* without singing along to every song."

Her smile washed over me like a warm wave. "That is kinda cute."

This time I was sure she was blushing and I was even surer because I sorta called her cute.

"I watch it like three times a year. I can't get enough."

I could picture her, curled up on a soft couch with a mug of hot chocolate, singing those classic Disney tracks without a hint of self-consciousness. I wanted nothing more than to snuggle up into that couch with her.

"I'm a really bad singer, though." Mel's blush had deepened with my silence and she was rubbing her neck again. "I was kicked out of chorus in middle school 'cause I ruined every concert."

"That makes me want to hear you sing *Little Mermaid* even more."

"We can arrange that," Mel said, her cocky half smile back in place. "Your turn. Let's hear it."

"No."

I took a step back to emphasize my point, but the crowd was closer than I thought so I couldn't actually run away.

"Come on. It can't be as embarrassing as mine."

"Yes, it can." I sighed and mumbled, "I knit with my granny."

"What was that?"

"I knit with my granny every Saturday. She taught me when I was little and she gets lonely at the assisted living place, so I go knit with her and her roommate. I'm twenty-eight and I spend half my weekend knitting hideous sweaters with old ladies."

"Awwwww!" She drew the sound out in this long, adoring way, not condescending like my last boyfriend when I told him, but like she genuinely thought it was cute. I tried to remember the last time someone reacted like that if I even trusted them enough to admit it in the first place.

There was also the fact that she was grinning like a human embodiment of the heart eyes emoji. I laughed and this time it was the full, honest, unabashed laugh that sounded like me. It felt really, really good to laugh like that.

Mel shifted back to her serious look and said in a low voice I could barely hear, "You have a great laugh. I'm glad I got to hear it."

"I'm glad you got to hear it, too. It's been...like maybe the worst night of my life."

"I'm sorry to hear that 'cause it's been a pretty great night for me."

"Even with the disastrous speech and your best friend mad at you?"

She reached down and took my hand, entwining our fingers. "Even with all that."

I could feel my body leaning toward hers. My mind screamed for me to stop. This wasn't the place and it would only make everything worse. But I didn't want to stop leaning in. I wanted to keep leaning in all night and let Mel catch me before I fell.

Her eyes flicked away from mine and a crease formed between her eyebrows. It looked like a well-worn path and I wondered what a woman so young and confident could have to worry over so often. As I told myself over and over not to reach out and smooth the crease away, Mel's lips curved into a slow smile.

Her eyes flicked back to mine and she whispered, "Bet I can make your night better, too."

"Your pickup lines are getting worse and worse."

She chuckled low in her throat and my heart skipped several beats. "Not what I meant. Follow me."

Mel didn't leave me much choice. She pulled me by our joined fingers and I followed without hesitation. A pair of long strides took us out of the tent and into the dark garden. A weak splash of moonlight provided just enough light to prevent me from tripping, but I was glad I'd decided against heels.

The night air, previously blocked by the tent, washed over me now, crisp and fresh and so much easier to breathe. With each step I took away from the party, the less I ever wanted to return. The weight of all those eyes left me and I felt like myself. Mel's hand, entwined with mine, was a connection to the earth while the rest of me floated. It was easier to think out here in the night, easier to enjoy the firm hand of a beautiful woman leading me into the darkness.

"Hey, Mel?"

"Hmm?"

"Why weren't you at the party?"

She stopped at a break in the line of bushes and peeked around the corner. "What party?"

"The graduation party. When Sophie met Caleb." We started walking again, this time on the other side of the wall of bushes. "How come we haven't met before tonight?"

"Oh, that. I was being all that I could be."

"What?"

"I enlisted in the Army right out of high school."

She was getting better and better. Nothing sexier than a woman in uniform. "So were you in Iraq? Afghanistan?"

"Worse," Mel replied, turning a grim look on me. "Fayetteville."

When I giggled she shot me a wink that could've melted the polar ice caps.

The deeper we wound through the shadows, the more I assumed Mel was leading me out here to find a quiet place to make out. It wasn't my normal style, but I wasn't opposed to moving fast this one time. She kept scanning the night, peeking behind trees and around shrubs. I was about to tell her that I thought we were far enough from the reception to be safe, when she lurched to a stop. Caught off guard, I rammed into her and she caught me with an arm around my waist.

My breath caught when her hand settled on the small of my back. I looked up into her eyes, her irises glowing in the soft moonlight. They really were incredible eyes—the eyes of a soft butch who would flirt hard in a club only to bring you home and recite poetry from memory while she undressed you. Then my gaze wandered from her eyes to her mouth. Her lips were pale and plump, the bottom slightly poutier. They looked as soft as her grip on my back. I wondered how she would kiss. Would she start slow? Seeking permission from an equal partner or would she lunge, taking what she wanted and giving just as much? My mind spun with the possibilities and my body ached with anticipation.

Mel dropped my hand, letting my fingers swing free for the first time since we'd left the tent. As cold as they were without her touch, my heart leapt as her hand moved toward my face. I gripped her bicep hard, waiting for her fingertips to brush against my cheek. I tilted my chin up, putting my lips into the perfect kissing position, and waited for her to make the final move.

She didn't kiss me.

She didn't cup my cheek or brush away a curl from my forehead like some romantic film.

She pressed her pointer finger to her own lips. Disappointed as I was, I didn't need the admonition to be quiet. Now that we were still, I could hear voices.

It was Sophie and Caleb. Worse, it was Sophie and Caleb, their voices raised and angry. Every muscle in my body wanted to run screaming from this place and I yanked hard on Mel's arm, trying to pull her away. The only way I could make this night worse would be to walk in on them fighting.

Mel teetered from the force of my pull, but she didn't release me or move away. Instead she leaned in close, bringing the smell of her skin and the warmth of her breath on my neck. Pressing her cheek against mine, she whispered into my ear, "Trust me."

I found that I did, in fact, trust her. I didn't have any reason to, other than her kindness and her bewitching eyes, of course. But my gut told me that this woman would never steer me wrong. We crept closer to the massive, gnarled trunk of an oak tree. It was wide enough to conceal us both if we stood close and she seemed as willing as I was to share the tight quarters. When we both tried to peek around the trunk, Mel's jaw came into painful contact with the side of my skull. She screwed up her face in pain but didn't make a sound as she rubbed her jaw. Stifling a giggle, I brushed her hand away and pressed my lips to the spot.

As I'd suspected, her cheek was smooth and soft, with the hint of firm jaw beneath the skin. I let my lips linger long enough to hear her breath hitch, then pulled away to see the result. Her eyes were unfocused and her breathing ragged. I couldn't help preening a little. Unsettling a butch was one of my favorite pastimes. I mouthed an apology before slipping my arm around her. Her eyebrows shot up and it was her time to lean in expectantly.

Let's see how you like it.

I pulled her body with me, leading us both around the trunk so we could see the scene playing out in the isolated garden. All thoughts of teasing seduction fled.

Caleb paced a patch of gravel surrounding a small, tinkling fountain. He ran his fingers through his already messy hair and his coat and vest were both open and rumpled. The last time I'd seen him he'd looked harassed but not disheveled. Not like this. He looked like he'd slept in his tux for a week.

Sophie didn't look much better. She was sitting on a stone bench, her eye makeup badly smeared. As I watched, she dropped to her knees on the stones in front of Caleb and grabbed his hands. He tried to keep walking, but just as Mel had done with me, Sophie pulled him back.

"Damn it, Caleb, I don't care what my mother says. She could throw a thousand people between us and it wouldn't make a difference. Don't you see that? I love you, not Laurel."

At the mention of my name, Mel's arm tightened around me. The weight of her against me, her solid, unmovable presence removed all the sting from Sophie's words.

"I want to be with you," Sophie said, shaking his hands in hers. "And only you."

I'd thought he was angry but he looked at her with desperate fear. He smiled, but it was as weak as any smile I'd given that night.

"Really?"

"Of course, you big idiot. Why do you think I married you?"

His eyes went wide and the guilt-induced fear that had gripped my guts for hours loosened. Caleb reached down and hauled Sophie off her knees. I noted absently the stains on the skirt and wondered if I could find a way to pay for the dry cleaning without starting another fight.

"But what about Laurel?" Caleb asked.

"What about her?"

"You guys…I mean…You're telling me there's no feelings there anymore?"

"None at all." She squinted and poked him in the chest enough to make him stumble back. "Why? Do *you* still have feelings for her?"

"No way." He threw his arms up in surrender, but clearly thought better of it and wrapped them around Sophie. "You're the only one I want."

"Damn right."

She pulled him down into a kiss that was certainly not for anyone else to see. I looked away and caught Mel averting her eyes, too. Her thumb traced lazy circles on my lower back and I was thinking about how to make her groan the way Caleb was when loud footsteps drew my attention back to the garden.

Mrs. Bell had marched into the scene, looking like she was ready to spit fire. Unfortunately, she'd raised her daughter to be just like her. Before Mrs. Bell could get a word out, Sophie had stepped in front of Caleb and started shouting.

"Not another word, Mother. You've said quite enough tonight."

"I only want…"

Sophie cut her off, taking Caleb's hand and shouting, "I don't care what you want. I want Caleb. I'm with the person I love and there is nothing you can do about it. You can either accept that or you can leave."

Caleb looked very much like he wanted to hide behind the stone bench. Mrs. Bell looked like she'd gladly tear the bench apart with her bare hands. Sophie looked like the woman I'd fallen in love with all those years ago, the one who'd run across four lanes of traffic to yell at a man for not cleaning up after his dog in a public park. Caleb had encouraged her passionate nature in a way I never could. It's why I knew from the start they were right for each other.

Mrs. Bell stormed off in a huff without looking back. If I was very lucky, she might be leaving the wedding itself, not just the garden. The moment she was gone, Sophie whipped around and grabbed Caleb by the face, pulling him into a sloppy kiss. My heart soared to see them united and I found that my stomach was finally free of knots. I celebrated by pulling Mel closer, burying my nose in the collar of her shirt to better catch her scent. My hands moved of their own accord, sliding up Mel's sides to her shoulders. Her eyes flashed in the starlight, settling on my lips as her hands settled on my hips.

Every first kiss I'd ever had felt like an obligation, as if a milepost had been met and so it was the next chore to be ticked off the list. I'd wanted those kisses, but I hadn't chosen them. This was a kiss I chose.

I wrapped my arms around Mel's neck and she lowered her face to mine. Our lips didn't meet so much as melt into each other. She tasted like mint and rosemary and her lips were a work of art. They pressed into me with purpose rather than greed. Her arms held me close and safe as her mouth explored mine. A pearl of desire hovered in my chest for the space of two heartbeats before bursting and coursing through my blood. I parted my lips, inviting her in, and she deepened the kiss with a groan. I lost myself in the dance of her tongue against mine. I would have spent all night there wrapped in her arms.

Mel's jacket slipped off my shoulders and fell to the ground. I broke away from the kiss, struggling to catch my breath and the fabric. We both reached for it at the same time and Mel banged the other side of her jaw into my head. Lost in barely stifled giggles, I snatched the jacket as she rubbed her jaw for the second time tonight.

Behind us, Sophie tossed Caleb onto his back but he didn't seem to mind the rough landing on the gravel. I knew my eyes were as wide as Mel's as we shared a look before hurrying off into the darkness to give the couple some much deserved privacy.

We stopped when we reached the edge of the light, the tent a few steps away. I checked Mel's jacket for damage, but apart from a few stray blades of grass, only the white rose boutonnière had suffered damage. I straightened the bent petal as best I could before handing it back to her. She slipped into the coat and I realized that the energy in the tent had changed. Some of the tension had broken, but whether it was my departure or Mrs. Bell's that changed the mood wasn't clear.

"So I was thinking," Mel said, scuffing the ground with the toe of her wingtip. She jerked her thumb over her shoulder toward the dark garden. "That's all figured out. I have a feeling they'll be much more open to forgiving you in about half an hour. Maybe you could stay?"

"I don't have a reason to go anymore," I admitted. "But I'm not sure I have a reason to stay, either."

"Sure you do," Mel said as a slow song started to play. "You haven't danced yet."

I slipped my hand into her offered palm, but I held back when she tried to lead me into the tent.

"What's wrong?" she asked.

The crease formed between her eyebrows again and this time I gave in to instinct and reached out to smooth it away. "Just trying to decide if this is one of those invitations I should decline."

Mel moved closer, a smile spreading across her lips. She held our joined hands against her shoulder and slipped her other arm around my waist.

"No. This is an invitation you should definitely accept."

I rested my cheek on her shoulder and we danced there in the dark grass beside the tent where no one could see us.

QUEEN FOR A DAY

Celeste Castro

Monica raced through the airport as if she carried a cooler with a live organ destined for its transplant recipient. Not really, but she hustled with the same urgency. No way she was missing her connecting flight to London Heathrow Airport.

"Move it!" she yelled as she barreled through crowds. "Coming through. Move! Please! Now! C'mon kid!"

She narrowly missed flattening the little guy. She swore when she heard the *no, seriously, this really is the final warning* announcement from the gate attendant.

"Coming! I'm coming, don't you dare…" she said through clenched teeth and waved her free arm in the air. "You better not leave without me."

"Miss Mercado?"

"Yes." Monica took a deep inhale, her nostrils flaring as she drew air. "It's me. I'm here."

She presented her passport and her ticket and ran down the jetway. The moment she stepped on board the aircraft they shut the door. She met the pissed off glares of onlookers with a wide grin. She didn't even feel bad when she made two people unbuckle their seat belts and stand to let her through to her window seat. Nothing was going to come between her and her once-in-a-lifetime opportunity.

She had begrudgingly agreed to go to a friend's chic fundraiser and begrudgingly spent twenty dollars for a single raffle ticket at the off chance that she'd win, knowing that her chances of winning, statistically speaking, were slim. She couldn't compete with the other people who donated hundreds of dollars for raffle tickets. The prize? Round-trip airfare, three-night stay at a luxury hotel in London, and all expenses paid. And that wasn't even the best part. The experience came with VIP entry to the Historic Royal Places' soft opening of its new digital exhibit with interactive holograms! She would witness the secret wedding of King Henry VIII and Anne Boleyn—a historical event that the world knew little about.

She could hardly wait. She was a royal family fanatic and a huge history buff. She especially loved hidden history, stories that were buried, like the secret wedding of Anne Boleyn.

As soon as they reached cruising altitude and the captain turned off the fasten seat belt sign, she had to pee. Her seatmates glared at her again when she made them move to let her out.

After making her way through customs, Monica hopped aboard the Heathrow Express to her hotel—The Lanesborough, the number one-rated hotel in London. No way she'd ever in her wildest dreams be able to afford to stay there on her public schoolteacher's salary. The photos online in the months, weeks, and days before her trip gave her plenty to dream about. The Lanesborough was the kind of place with twenty color-coordinated pillows on luxurious beds with matching duvets, tea service, and sweeping views of Hyde Park. Not that she planned to spend a whole heck of a lot of time in her room, not with everything she had planned for her three-day adventure.

The hotel was in the perfect location for most everything she wanted to see—Westminster Abbey, Buckingham Palace, Big Ben, and it was a short walk to St. James Square and the interactive exhibit as well as all the pubs and shops and sights in between. The accommodation also came with complimentary food and drink, including dinner for two at its Michelin-starred Céleste restaurant. Who knows, maybe with her newfound luck she'd find a pretty local lady to join her?

She felt like royalty when she entered her hotel. Everyone called her *Miss* or *Miss Mercado*. She could definitely get used to the lifestyle of the rich and famous.

Monica popped awake well before her morning alarm. There was so much she wanted to do before the opening of the interactive exhibit later that evening. She FaceTimed with her mom and showed her every nook and cranny of her suite: textured wallpaper, pillow, wrapped bar of soap, wooden coat hanger, and the espresso machine. She promised her mom that she'd get a photo if she happened to see anyone famous, maybe the Duke and Duchess of Sussex, if they happened to be at the event.

She laughed at the outrageous thought but she'd packed all of her fancy clothing just in case. In the meantime, she threw on a lightweight sundress, grabbed her shoulder bag and stepped into a pair of flats. She headed to her adventure that included the London Eye, Westminster Abby, and a reservation for a historical boat tour along the River Thames.

Monica burst into her room after sightseeing, threw her bags of souvenirs onto her bed, and called for room service.

"A bottle of champagne, please."

"Does Miss Mercado have a preference?"

"Um, well nothing too crazy, price-wise."

"I'll remind Miss Mercado that all expenses are paid."

"Well, then, please send your finest."

"Thank you."

A rapping sound at the door told her that her room service had arrived. The waiter set a bucket of ice with Veuve Cliquot onto a table and poured her a drink. Then he stood there, his gloved hands crossed before him.

"Right," she exclaimed, rummaging through her bag for a tip. "Here you go." She handed him twenty pounds, hoping that was good enough.

He smiled, nodded, and said thank you before taking his leave.

She took her time getting ready, including a luxuriously long shower. She sipped her champagne while swaddled in the puffy cotton hotel robe. She wondered what to wear to the event. She wanted to be comfortable, yet elegant. It was a VIP experience after all. She decided against the formal dress with the plunging neckline, opting to save it for her dinner at Céleste. She was a self-proclaimed voluptuous—*cum*—plump woman and so she decided on her simple, black, sleeveless tailored dress that hugged her curves and made her breasts look otherworldly. She was on the shorter side of life at five-foot something and relied on heels to help her out most everywhere she went. She wore her great mass of black curls in a bun, giving her another inch or two of height. She punctuated her look with dangling earrings, bracelets, and a necklace. She forwent a sweater, since it was late summer and still wonderfully splendid at night.

She gathered only the basics—cash, identification, and her Save-the-Date-themed VIP entrance ticket—and placed them into a small clutch. She didn't apply any makeup, her dark complexion didn't require any, but she applied a good amount of bright red lipstick, a perfect complement to her bronze skin color. She blew herself a kiss in the mirror and left.

Intending to walk, she second-guessed her decision with her heels. She knew it was a good idea when she learned the hotel had a Maserati that delivered her the short distance.

She arrived early to the exhibit venue—The Banqueting House, the only part of Royal Whitehall Palace that had survived the Great Fire of 1698. Since the doors didn't open for another half hour, she asked her driver to drop her off a few blocks away.

She strolled down Whitehall Road, taking in the crowds, the guards on horseback, the beautiful architecture. She imagined what it had been like the morning of January twenty-fifth, 1533, the day when Anne and Henry tied the forbidden knot, back when the road was "foul and full of pits and sloughs," she remembered reading because she thought it was funny. She recollected historical drawings as she gazed upon the area where the palace and the three-story, black-and-white Holbein gatehouse once stood. Not only was it an architectural marvel, but it also served as a passageway, built to connect the two sides of the palace. It allowed the King to move free from prying eyes, especially on his and Anne's wedding day.

And while the Holbein Gate had survived the great fire that destroyed Whitehall, it was deemed a major impediment and later demolished. Though parts of it were incorporated into other buildings in Windsor Park, Monica considered it a loss due to its historical significance—it was inside the three-story Holbein structure that the notorious, secret wedding happened.

Monica was the first in line when the museum doors opened. Someone directed her to a ballroom with tables of food and free drinks. She ate her fair share and had a good buzz before long. She swept her surroundings. No famous dukes or duchesses, just a bunch of well-dressed history nerds collectively gawking over the digital displays.

She joined in on a few conversations and kept locking eyes with an interesting woman, a fair-skinned, black-haired woman who was about Monica's height. She couldn't tell what color her eyes were, she was too far away, but her smile lit the entire room. It was innocent and sultry all at the same time. Judging by the way she dressed—a velvet dress, hoop petticoat with French hood, the entire ensemble studded with pearls and other decoratively beaded jewels—she looked like an employee, part of the catering staff. Her Tudor-style attire made it difficult for Monica to judge her age. She looked older, but her mannerisms and the way she held herself looked youthful.

Monica circulated through the exhibits and stopped to read the placard that described the fire at Whitehall. As soon as she stepped in front of it, an image in a framed mirror appeared before her and began talking. "On the afternoon of the fourth of January, 1698, a Dutch maidservant went about her morning routine and dried her linen sheets on a charcoal brazier in a bedchamber. While it wasn't an unusual practice, or forbidden to dry linens, it was common knowledge not to leave them unattended. It took only seconds for the sheet to ignite—"

"Isn't it always a woman's fault?" a sexy British accent from behind Monica whispered.

"I'm sorry?" She turned, coming face-to-face with the woman she'd been watching all night.

"Blaming the great fire on a woman. So typical."

Monica nodded and smiled.

"It's always the woman's fault. Eve and the apple, Cleopatra and her face."

"Yoko Ono and the Beatles."

"Exactly. Every fire, plague, something bad, blame it on a woman."

"So true." Monica let her eyes linger on the woman's chest for probably too long. But her bosom was right there, almost directly below her eyes thanks to the style of the gown. "Beautiful threads." She hoped that she's saved herself. She bit her bottom lip.

"Threads?" The woman looked at her chest.

"Your costume."

"Oh," she chuckled, "this old thing." She carried a silver tray with a glass of wine on it. "Are you thirsty?"

"Parched." Monica set her empty glass on the tray and took the full one. "You have wonderful timing."

"I'm Andi by the way," she said. "I hope you'll enjoy the show." She left Monica with a gentle smile before walking away.

Monica wore a smile through the rest of the exhibits and continued to exchange glances with Andi.

Finally, the lights dimmed and the presentation began. Andi vanished along with the rest of the costumed crew.

Monica gasped when a woman walked on stage. It was the host of her favorite podcast of all time, *Tudor Talk!* Monica clapped harder than she'd ever clapped before. She hung on her every word and got some good photos and videos for her mom.

"Thank you so much, Natalie," a costumed docent said as he joined her on stage when she was done with her opening remarks. "She never fails to bring history to life. Sometimes I wonder if she's a ghost of the past, given how she's able to paint such vivid details of sixteenth century England." The room laughed at his comment.

"Welcome everyone to our exclusive, interactive historical experience that's unlike anything in the world. Many museums have already started incorporating holograms into their exhibits, but what you're going to experience tonight is like nothing you've ever seen before. Our patented technology brings to life the most realistic, self-learning holographic images, preprogrammed with speech and experiences, and that look and feel so real, you won't believe your eyes.

"I'm willing to bet that most of you aren't aware that you may have interacted with a hologram at some point tonight."

Silence befell the room. Monica's heart thudded in her chest. Had she flirted with a hologram? She whipped around and met Andi's gaze from across the room. Andi smiled and waved a gloved hand.

The room took a collective gasp when the man disappeared from the stage and reappeared a moment later in the crowd. "That's right, I'm a re-creation, part of the show." The room cheered and clapped. "Thanks to the lords and ladies up there." He pointed to the technicians staged in the balcony who waved. Monica breathed a sigh of relief and was once again distracted when Andi approached her with another glass of wine, that she missed most of the details about the holographic technology.

"...which allows them to move freely and which is why I can shake this fine gentleman's hand." The crowd erupted in laughter and broke into hearty applause. "Now that we have your attention, we are pleased to invite you deeper into our story and into a re-created chamber, the secret chamber where King Henry VIII and Anne Boleyn were married in front of an intimate audience that now includes all of you."

They were led into the chamber. They sat in pews. Monica sat toward the back with only two other people. A taller man settled in front of her partially blocking her view. She cursed her short stature.

"Can I sit next to you?" a voice said. It was Andi.

"Of course. Please." Monica scooted over, giving her room.

"I can't wait," Andi proclaimed.

"Me too." Monica cast a sidelong glance toward the woman. "I take it you work for the museum?" She silently berated herself for asking the most obvious question.

"What gave me away?" Andi laughed softly and made a big deal of smoothing her dress. Andi's accent was the most eloquent, soft notes, the finest enunciation she'd ever heard and so different than what she'd heard throughout her time in London thus far.

Monica looked at her surroundings. "You're so lucky you work here."

"I'm on loan. I usually work at Hampton Court."

"Doing what?"

"This and that, catering, guest services, I used to do tours. I go where I'm needed."

"That's the coolest job ever. And to work at Hampton Court. I can't imagine what that must be like being surrounded by history every single day."

"I love it," Andi said. "Where are you from?"

"Carnation, Washington."

"Right. Where's that?" she asked and laughed.

"Northwest part of the United States. Thirty-something miles from Seattle, if you've ever heard of that place."

"You're a long way from home, then. Are you staying long?"

"Three short days."

"I'm glad you're here at this precise moment." Andi's smile made Monica's insides tingle.

"Me too." Monica nodded, catching Andi's eyes all over her body and glad that she wore her low-cut dress that showcased her amazing cleavage.

The crowd hushed as the lights dimmed. Doors on either side of the altar at the front of the room opened. From one door came Anne Boleyn followed by her attendant, Lady Berkeley.

Monica gasped as she observed the two women, following their every move. They appeared no differently than any other bride and maid of honor might be on a wedding day. They shared smiles and whispered to each other. "They're so life-like. Anne is so beautiful, stunning. I wish I could see Lady Berkeley better." Monica tried to sit more upright, stretching.

"She's fabulous, trust me."

"I love their gowns. I love your costume, by the way. It's so accurate." Monica turned to see that Andi was looking at her.

Andi looked herself over and nodded.

"I'd expect nothing less for a lady of Hampton Court." Monica knew she flushed the moment the cheesy line left her lips. She cleared her throat. "Are you of the school of thought who believes that Anne was pregnant at the time of her wedding?"

"Well," Andi stretched her arm along the backside of the pew, drawing closer to Monica and talking into her ear. "I can see how people think that, considering the whole rushing in, marrying in secret thing, but that was all because he was still married. Although the official documentation points to her being pregnant, I don't believe she was. You see, when Cranmer wrote to Archdeacon Hawkyns, I'm convinced he made that part up as a way to tarnish Boleyn's reputation from the start. The woman hadn't a chance. Everyone disliked her from the beginning."

"Interesting theory."

"It's not a theory."

"And you know this how?" Monica asked. There was no judgment in her voice. She had several intense conversations with mutual history nerds all the time. She loved challenging ideas and she'd formed several outrageous theories of her own.

"Perk of the job," Andi whispered into her ear before leaning back. "I get free tickets to all the Historic Royal Places-hosted lectures. I've been to an uncountable number of them, heard every argument there is. I'm convinced she was not pregnant when they married."

"I'd love to hear what other secrets you know." Monica ran her eyes over Andi, settling on her plump lips. "Maybe after this was can enlighten each other, that is if you don't have to work." Monica held her breath awaiting Andi's answer.

"I'd love that."

They shared a smiled and settled into a comfortable silence. A huge beast of a man walked through. "That's him," Andi said. "That's the King."

"I didn't realize how big he was," Monica whispered. "Then again, up until now, I've only seen him in books and paintings."

"I think part of it is his presence, his command of the room, wouldn't you say?"

Monica nodded in agreement and sat up straighter.

Following the King were two members of his privy council and then the chaplain who conducted the wedding. The whole thing took about five minutes.

It took longer than Monica would have thought for Andi to change. Then again, she'd never had to change out of a Tudor-style garment. She remembered all the buttons and jewelry Andi wore and it made more sense. She finally spotted Andi heading toward her. She wore black jeans that were rolled at the ankles, a Historic Royal Places T-shirt and a black blazer that was a size too large for her. Monica missed the open display of cleavage that the Tudor-style gown boasted.

In plain clothes, Andi looked much younger, about Monica's age, early thirties, maybe younger. "I hardly recognized you. And I suddenly feel entirely overdressed."

"Nonsense," Andi said, twining her arm through Monica's and pulling her through a side door. "Let's get out of here before someone catches me and asks me to help with clean up," she laughed. "I've put in enough hours today."

Monica laughed and followed Andi through an array of doors and corridors bypassing people until they were the only ones walking through the hallways and their steps were the only sounds between them. Andi stopped next to a door and tried the knob. It was locked.

"What are we doing?" Monica asked, hesitant to follow her any further.

"Detour way out."

"Cool. Wait. Are you sure it's okay?" Monica protested, wanting to avoid getting caught and slapped with a lifetime ban to the Royal Historical Places. She looked from side to side, making sure no one was running after them if they'd accidentally triggered an alarm.

"Don't worry, this little thing," Andi flashed what looked like a work badge, "gets me into wherever I need to go."

"Well in that case." Monica stepped into the room, instantly silenced. "Beautiful," she hushed as she peered upward. "I can't believe I'm looking at the only surviving in-situ ceiling painting by Sir Peter Paul Rubens." The gilded canvases depicted the *Union of Crowns*, *The Apotheosis of James I*, and *The Peaceful Reign of James I*. "This was one of the last known commissioned works by Charles I."

Andi laughed softly.

"Sorry. I'm acting like a tour guide, that's your job and you probably already know that." She squeezed her eyes and rubbed her temples.

"I do, but you're doing a very good job. I'd definitely buy a ticket to follow you around a museum for a few hours."

Monica thanked the soft lighting for covering her blush, but she couldn't hide her huge smile and the giggle that escaped her lips.

"Isn't it much better when you don't have to share spaces like this with a horde of tourists?" Andi said as she meandered through the room.

"Meeting you certainly has its perks." Monica followed Andi's lead.

"I could say the same thing about you," Andi said, running her eyes along Monica's body leaving Monica no doubt as to what she wanted out of the evening.

Andi cleared her throat and broke eye contact. "My brother got married here."

"He did?"

Andi nodded.

"I can't imagine how beautiful that must have been, set against all this history with all the artifacts and paintings—"

"And ghosts." Andi reached for Monica's hands, taking them in her own.

"And ghosts," Monica whispered, pulling Andi closer to her. "I bet you've seen a thing or two working at Hampton Court?"

"There's not a day that goes by where I don't feel or see something strange," Andi said. She squeezed Monica's fingers before letting them go.

"You've got to tell me."

"Maybe over dinner," Andi asked. "I haven't eaten in ages. I'm starved."

"Shall we?" Monica asked.

"This way." Andi led them down a corridor that opened to another side door that then opened into a crowded street. "Free at last."

"And the night is young," Monica said as she watched Andi take in the crowd. Her eyes sparkled with excitement. Her energy made Monica tingle at what their night beheld. "Where to? You're from here, what do you suggest?"

"You're the guest. I want you to choose. I want to see London through your eyes."

"I wanted to try this place called the Prospect of Whitby. It dates back to the fifteen hundreds. Have you been?"

"It's been a long time."

"We'll have to take an Uber."

"An Uber?" Andi wore a perplexed look.

"Oh, yeah I forgot, they're not allowed in London."

"I'm perfectly amenable to walking and taking in the air." Andi gazed upward and breathed in deeply.

"Me too, but it's a four-mile walk and I'm wearing heels, so we might need to take a taxi."

"Lead the way."

Monica's entire body hummed when Andi smoothed her hand down her arm and held her hand as they walked along the Thames toward the cab stand.

"Most people don't know that Anne comes from a line of troublemakers. Rather, trouble finders." Andi leaned back when the waiter picked up her plate after dinner and topped her wineglass. "Thank you."

Monica focused on Andi's fingers as she twirled the wineglass, her expressive blue eyes and flawless pale skin were a perfect contrast against her raven-black hair that she wore in a loose ponytail that rested at her shoulder. Her appearance wasn't even the sexiest thing about her. Her in-depth knowledge about the life of Anne Boleyn put her into the drop-dead gorgeous category.

"Her great-great-grandfather was always being hauled to court for trespassing, plowing through property boundaries, and taking water from the manor without paying for it," Andi laughed.

"I can't imagine how different Anne's life would have been if she married her Irish cousin," Monica said.

"James Butler, what a quatch. Anne's father hated him. He forbade it only because the decision benefited himself in the long run. What an opportunist, not to mention her mother." Andi rolled her eyes.

Monica loved that Andi peppered old Elizabethan into their conversation the more excited she got in her storytelling. "Do you believe that Anne's mother had an affair with the King?" Monica asked.

"Heavens, no," Andi said with total absolution. "Her mother loved that people thought the King bedded her. But it was gossip, rumors started by a total lubberwort who made the whole thing up. Of course, the fact that Anne's sister, Mary, was the King's mistress didn't help their case. Besides, the King denied it."

"And you believe the King at his word?" Monica laughed.

"In this case, yes."

"I read that later in the sixteenth century, the Jesuit, Nicholas Sander, claimed that Anne Boleyn was Henry VIII's own daughter!"

Andi's eyes grew, she gasped and laughed. "I have not heard that! That's good."

"Did you read Alison Weir's book?" Monica leaned in and rested her elbows on the table.

Andi mimicked her pose. "No. What's it called?"

"*Mary Boleyn, The Great and Infamous Whore.*"

Andi laughed loudly, drawing onlookers. "Fitting, but she's not the whore of the bunch." She coughed lightly and muttered the words, "King Henry VIII," under her breath.

"You're so absolute about your interpretation of Tudor history. I love it."

"Working at Hampton Court, hearing the stories day in and day out, I feel like I'm part of the royal court at times."

"Is there anything else you two would like?" their waiter asked. "Perhaps dessert?"

"We could continue here or take our history conversation back to my hotel. I'm staying at the Lanesborough, and I know for a fact they have primo desserts there, that is, if you're amenable," Monica said.

"Oh, I'm amenable." Andi nodded and bit her bottom lip.

"Check please," they said together.

They reached for it at the same time, resting their hands atop each other's. Andi flipped her hand over and wove her finger in between Monica's.

Arousal shot directly between Monica's legs. She reveled in Andi's touch, her heat. Andi had the softest skin ever, it's pale color a stark contrast against her own. "Did it suddenly get hot in here?" She pulled her hand away so she could pay the bill and get the hell to her hotel as quickly as possible.

"Scorching," Andi said as she drained the last of her wine. "What do we owe the drawer?" She reached inside the pocket of her blazer.

"Don't worry about a thing. My treat in exchange for the fascinating history lesson."

"Well, I have no choice but to accept. I'm a git. I think I left my coin purse at the Banqueting Hall. This is all I have," she said, presenting two twenty-pound notes.

"Oh, no. Do we need to go back and get it?"

"No, it's okay. I'll pick it up next time I'm there. This was a lovely dinner and even lovelier company. I can't wait for dessert."

"Me too," Monica agreed.

Monica smiled when Andi leaned out the window of the cab on their ride to her hotel. Her cheeks were flushed and her black tresses danced on the wind. Her pale blue eyes reflected the twinkling city lights. "Having fun?" Monica asked.

"I haven't had time off in…I don't know how long. It's nice and even nicer in your company." Andi's smile was large and bright. She rolled up her window and turned toward Monica, surprising her with a soft kiss upon her lips. Before she could pull back, Monica held her in place and consumed her mouth, letting her know exactly how she wanted to spend her time off.

The driver cleared his throat and they both laughed and faced forward. Andi rested her hand atop Monica's thigh and slid it between her legs, her entire body flooding with heat.

Their driver pulled up to the front of the hotel. "Here we are, ladies."

"Thank you," they said in tandem as they paid and clamored out of the taxi.

They walked hand in hand through the grand foyer of the hotel that was alive with people and couples enjoying cocktails. They approached a bar and ordered two drinks. "Allow me to pay this time," Andi demanded, while pulling her cash from her pocket.

"Only if we enjoy them in my room. It's much quieter up there and I have a stunning view of Hyde Park."

"What a great idea. Being around all those geeky history nerds does a number on me sometimes. Sensory overload," Andi laughed.

"I know the feeling."

With drinks in hand, they headed to Monica's room. Monica turned on a couple of lamps, creating a soft glow and illuminating her luxurious suite.

Andi waltzed around the room taking it all in as if being surrounded by opulence was something in which she was accustomed. Maybe she was. It didn't matter. What mattered most was knowing that Monica would soon replace the straw that Andi was at present wrapping her lips around. "What lovely quarters," she said.

"It's more than I could afford. The accommodations and tonight's tickets were all part of a prize package that I won."

"What a lucky, lucky woman." Andi's eyes lingered on the bed before heading to the window. "And what of this grand view you promised?" She pushed open the curtains. "Stunning," she gasped.

Monica joined her at the window. "It is."

"Anne used to love visiting Hyde Park and feeding the birds."

"Oh, yeah?" Monica said, setting her empty glass on the table. She took hold of Andi's as well and set it there too.

Andi pivoted toward her. "The squirrels would crawl up her arms." She mimicked the motion along Monica's arm, setting off sparks in Monica's spine.

"Is that so?" Monica asked, closing their distance. She smoothed her hands underneath Andi's blazer, feeling her warmth through her shirt.

"She was an animal whisperer. Most people don't know that about her," Andi whispered against Monica's lips.

"And what would she whisper to these animals?"

"All sorts of things." Andi nipped and licked Monica's lips and pushed against her, guiding Monica toward the bed, stopping when the back of Monica's legs bumped against it.

"What other little, long-lost, Boleyn family secrets do you know?" Monica moaned when Andi peppered kisses and licks along her neck.

"I know more than the average person."

Monica worked Andi out of her blazer, feeling something rough at her neckline. "What's this?"

"Hmm?" Andi said in between kisses.

Monica laughed. "Your shirt?" She felt the familiarity of a shopping tag at her neckline. "You left the tag on your shirt."

She giggled. "Oops."

Monica ran her hands along Andi's stomach, underneath her shirt. She lifted it over her head and saw she wore nothing underneath. She trailed her fingertips over full breasts and pink nipples. They stood at attention, ready for her mouth. She pinched them gently, working them into stiff points, watching Andi melt against her at the attention.

Andi reached behind Monica, feeling, searching. "How does this thing come off?"

Monica guided her hand toward the top of her zipper at her neckline. In one movement Andi had it off. "Clever."

"Designed for easy exit, not like that complicated Tudor number you wore earlier," Monica's laughed.

"You're a beautiful woman." Andi licked her eyes all over Monica's body.

Monica twined her arms around Andi's neck and arched into her when Andi's hands found their way to her bottom. She squeezed a butt cheek. Monica grunted.

"I love your body," Andi growled.

"I'm glad you approve."

They locked lips, teasing, exploring, filling each other with promises. Andi's kisses traveled lower, to her neck and her chest, lower still until a warm mouth met eager breasts. She bathed them, worshipped them with her tongue. They fell backward onto the bed. Andi landed on top of Monica, not breaking their kiss.

"Tell me about your life in America," Andi said, seated between Monica's legs in the jacuzzi in Monica's room, sipping champagne. Andi turned slightly and arched toward her, receiving a kiss on the lips.

"I'm a teacher," Monica said. "Seventh grade."

"Seventh grade?"

"Middle school. Eleven- and twelve-year-olds going through puberty. It's gross." Monica laughed. "But I love them. Their imaginations are at peak level. It's a fun grade to teach."

"And do you live in a big city?"

"No. It's tiny, but we have all the basics. A great library, a community theater, and a history club. I want to know more about you."

"I was born in England and my dad was a sheriff."

"And you have a brother?"

"I have seven brothers and it's exactly as it sounds." Andi laughed. "One of my brothers has done quite well for himself.

We used to be quite close. He lives in Cheshire. He's a landowner, works in politics and historical preservation of a sort."

"Sounds like the love of history runs in your family's veins."

"Quite literally," Andi proclaimed.

"What else about you?" Monica asked and took a sip of champagne.

"Before working at Hampton Court I was a personal assistant."

"To anyone famous?"

"I signed an NDA. I couldn't tell if I wanted to."

"The lifestyles of the rich and famous. It just occurred to me. Am I keeping you out too late? Do you have to leave? I'm not asking because I want you to leave, I just want to be respectful if you have to work or be someplace tomorrow."

"Tomorrow's my day off. I have nowhere to be."

"Then you'll stay with me?"

"You'd kick me out at two in the morning?" Andi laughed and leaned her head against Monica's chest.

"I'd do no such thing." She downed her champagne, set the glass to the side, and submerged both her hands into the steaming, bubbling, fragrant water. She found Andi's silky smooth breasts. She massaged them tenderly. "So, then it's settled," she whispered into her ear. "Do you want to tour London with me? I was planning on touring the London Tower and the Church of St. Peter ad Vincula, where Anne Boleyn is buried."

Andi stiffened. "I have a better idea, but you can say no."

"Tell me."

"Let's go for a ride in the county. I know some people at Hever Castle. How about a private tour?"

"Are you fucking serious?" Monica squealed. "Anne Boleyn's childhood home? I thought it was closed for renovations until next year."

"It is, but I have my connections."

"I'd love that, truly, but on one condition."

"Name it." Andi turned in Monica's lap, wrapping her legs around her waist and her arms around her neck.

"Have dinner again with me tomorrow night. I have reservations at Céleste. It's here in the hotel. The menu is divine."

"Deal," Andi said. "But wait. It's super fancy there, right? I don't have anything to wear unless I go home sometime tomorrow." Worry flashed across her face.

"You can borrow something of mine, granted it might be a little big on you, but we can figure something out."

"Really? Then it's a deal." Andi's worry was replaced by lust. She assaulted Monica with kisses. She inched up slightly, communicating what she wanted.

Monica sucked Andi's breast into her mouth and slid her fingers deep inside, eliciting a moan of appreciation.

They eventually pulled themselves out of bed and down to the concierge desk. They arranged for a personal driver to take them on the two-hour round trip to Hever Castle. When the concierge learned they were going on a day-long excursion, he ordered them a picnic lunch.

"We couldn't have picked a better day," Andi said as she rolled down the window, letting a soft breeze blow through the car.

Monica reached for Andi's hand and kissed her fingers.

"What time is dinner tonight? I have a surprise stop along the way, but I don't want to risk dinner plans. We did get a late start after all."

"Wasn't it so worth it?" Monica asked, reliving their late night and early morning lovemaking. "We have plenty of time. Reservations are at nine."

Since they had time, Andi directed their driver on a scenic route that took them to Eltham Palace, one of Anne and Henry's favorite vacation spots. They spread out their picnic in the gardens and spent a lovely afternoon enjoying lunch and strolling through the gardens before continuing to Hever.

"It was a medieval defensive castle when it was built in the thirteenth century. Imagine a motte and bailey surrounding the entire thing," Andi said as she led Monica toward the castle, hand in hand.

"How did it come into her family?" Monica asked, hanging on Andi's every word, "from the thirteenth century to Thomas Boleyn?"

"He inherited it in 1505, passed to him by his father, Sir William Boleyn. The ironic thing is that after Anne's death it passed to Henry's fourth wife, Anne of Cleves."

"Not Jane Seymore, his third wife, and her second cousin?"

"There wasn't much time for her to do anything to secure her legacy. She died shortly after childbirth."

"Wow." Monica stopped walking, halting their movement.

"Are you quite all right?" Andi looked her over from head to toe.

"I feel like a Tudor insider, like I know more secrets than even the most well-read scholar. You're a great teacher."

"Great?" Andi raised an eyebrow.

"Great. Hot. Knowledgeable."

"I can't say I've had someone hang on my every word quite like you." Andi took Monica's face into her hands and kissed her gently before they continued their walk toward the entrance of the castle.

True to Andi's claim, she knew someone at Hever who permitted them the run of the palace. Monica couldn't believe their luck. What's more, the restoration crew had the day off. Aside from a handful of grounds staff, they were the only ones there.

As soon as they stepped into the historic building, Monica was confronted by the three Tudor monarchs. Portraits of Henry VII, VIII, and VI. She stopped to stare. She placed her hand over her heart in reverence.

Andi pointed to a portrait. "That is the only surviving portrait of Henry's brother, Arthur. It's considered the single greatest acquisition the castle has made."

Monica balanced her attention between the artifacts and Andi who continued peppering in her knowledge as they toured the property. "These are the original timbers from the thirteenth century."

Monica placed her hand on a beam, as if it would take her deeper, closer to Tudor history.

Andi led them through hallways and side rooms where they gazed upon other rare paintings and architectural highlights.

"Here's one of my favorites paintings," Andi proclaimed. "Anne's daughter, Elizabeth, before she was queen. And this one." She held out her hand and stood next to it.

Monica drew closer and read the placard. "Elizabeth of York. A key figure of English history uniting the House of York and Lancaster, solidifying Henry VII's claim to the throne." She turned to Andi. "Isn't it refreshing that history isn't blaming a woman?"

Andi smiled. "Entirely refreshing. Just like you." She leaned in and kissed her. They melted into each other. Monica pulled Andi against her and Andi's leg settled between Monica's, the heat getting entirely out of control. "Want to see Anne's room? Want to fuck in Anne's room?" Andi whispered against Monica's lips.

"What?" Monica gasped.

"Come on," Andi said, not giving Monica time to respond.

Monica held on to Andi's hand, high on art history, endorphins, and arousal. Andi led them through the castle, through the inner halls, and various sitting rooms, seemingly knowing exactly where to go. "How is it that you know this place so well?"

"I used to work here once upon a time, early in my career."

"I'm so in awe." They lingered a long time in the library, admiring the beautiful white-paneled ceiling and sabicu carvings in the style of the famous woodcarver, Grinling Gibbons.

"Wait," Monica exclaimed when they stepped into the Book of Hours Room. "I can't believe I'm here." She ran her fingers along the glass encasing Anne's personal prayer books. "I bet she prayed right here when she was recovering from the flu." She closed her eyes and tried to absorb the history through her fingertips.

"So that whole Anne almost dying from the sweating sickness in 1538…not true."

"You're kidding," Monica protested, knowing the story of how Anne nearly died from a type of influenza that had run rampant during that time.

"Henry was a huge germaphobe. Anne ran hot. Like most women, she ran hot. He freaked out and sent her here as a precaution. It was so incredibly unchivalrous."

"That's. So. Crazy."

"Isn't it just? Although it was serendipitous that she was sent home, because her father became very ill. She helped nurse him back to health with Henry's help, who was kind enough to send his second-best doctor. The first best was *predisposed*."

Monica snorted when she laughed. "What a pig."

"I know."

"Ready for the grand finale?" Andi asked, reaching for Monica's fingers and kissing them.

"Sex in Anne's bedroom?" Monica hushed while peering over her shoulder.

"Uh-huh."

"But don't they have cameras?"

"Luck would have it that they're being rewired as part of the reconstruction." Andi led them to Anne's room.

Monica stepped only one foot inside. A soft cast of sunlight illuminated the room in a warm glow and invited her in. "We're not going to actually, you know, on Anne's actual bed are we?" Monica asked, looking behind her, meeting the eyes of the people in the portraits. She looked away quickly. "I feel like I'm, I don't know, sinning."

"Don't worry, almost everything here is a replica, at least the linens are. Besides, something inside me says she won't mind," Andi said against Monica's lips, leading her toward the bed. She lifted the velvet rope, they ducked underneath it, giggling and kissing.

"If you say so," Monica whispered. She couldn't stop herself if she wanted to. Andi's allure was so intoxicating, her kisses so fucking delicious. It was over when Andi pulled Monica against

herself and they fell onto the bed. Monica remained on all fours.
"Do you think Anne had sex in here?"
"Fuck yeah, she did."
"This is so fucking hot," Monica groaned.
"You're so fucking sexy." Andi played with the weight of Monica's breasts that hung in her face, nuzzling against them. She reached behind Monica, pulling the hem of her dress over her hips. She slid her hand inside the elastic waistband of Monica's silk underwear, meeting wetness. She easily slid through her length. Monica squeezed her eyes shut to avoid the prying eyes of the paintings.

In a sex daze, they righted their clothing as they exited Anne's room and headed out of the castle. They passed through the Queen's Chamber on their way out. Monica stopped in her tracks as she came face-to-face with Anne Boleyn herself, and her sister Mary! She froze in horror, stunned at the lifelike realness of the mannequins on display. She placed her hand over her heart and exhaled as she walked past them and whispered that she was sorry. Their responses—soft, knowing smirks.

"Andi?" Monica said for the third time. She covered Andi's hand with her own. The act broke her from her reverie. Andi wore an exhausted, satiated, and dazed smile. Monica didn't blame her. As soon as they got back to her hotel, they soaked in the jacuzzi, which led to sex, which then led to more sex in the shower and then in the bed. The woke up groggy at eight thirty, leaving them a half hour to get ready for dinner at nine.
"I'm sorry. I'm starting to fade," Andi said. They were one of two pairs left in the dining room. "That and I'm absolutely stuffed," she proclaimed at the arrival of what seemed like their third dessert. Her eye widened. She patted her stomach. "I don't know if I can do this," she laughed. Their dinner at Céleste consisted of seven courses and seven paring wines.
Monica kept her hand atop Andi's and gave it a gentle squeeze but kept her eyes trained on their interwoven fingers. Monica dreaded this part. The inevitable goodbye. She'd had

the time of her life. The most amazing experience. She'd miss Andi tremendously—her laughter, her insights, her beautiful body.

"You okay?" Andi asked. She squeezed Monica's fingers, forcing eye contact.

"I've loved my time with you. I'll never forget this. Thank you for everything, for showing me Hever, and Eltham and..." She stopped and pursed her lips, not wanting to lose it and embarrass herself. "I've had so much fun with you. I just want you to know that."

"Monica, I've had the time of my life, truly. I'll never forget this either. Thank you."

"I bet you say that to all the American girls." Monica smiled.

"Only the pretty ones." Andi pulled her hand away to sip the last of her wine. Monica missed it immediately.

"Come upstairs with me for a nightcap?" Monica asked, barely competing with the notes of the piano.

Andi pursed her lips. "I have to work early. Big day tomorrow. It's the official opening of the exhibit. I don't want to be totally drained of juice."

Monica smiled and nodded. "Then I don't want to keep you." Monica looked at her dessert and ran her spoon through it. "Can I call you a taxi?"

"I'd appreciate that, thank you. But I am going to have to come upstairs."

Monica cocked an eyebrow.

"I suppose you want your clothes back."

"Oh," Monica laughed. "Yes, I suppose I do, but it will be risky."

"I know, but it has to be done."

"Try not to tempt me," Monica said.

"I'll try not to be tempting."

"I can't wait for the challenge."

Andi bit her lip and leaned forward. The light of the candles flickered in her eyes like glistening stars. "Well, maybe I can stay for a little while, for a proper goodbye, that is."

They wrapped up and headed to Monica's room, arm in arm, walking slowly as if they could prolong the inevitable goodbye.

Monica stirred awake to a soft shuffling sound in the room. A faint glow of light filtered through the curtains. Andi was looking out the window.

"What time is it?" Monica said as she joined her. She wrapped her arms around Andi from behind, leaning into her warmth. She kissed her neck.

"Four in the morning." Andi leaned into Monica's embrace and groaned.

"I'm sorry I kept you up so late. I should have sent you on your way right after dinner."

"But wasn't it worth it?" Andi said, turning in Monica's arms, resting fully against her.

"Thank you for staying." Monica smoothed her fingers through her hair.

"Call a taxi for me?" Andi asked.

"Of course."

Andi began rounding up the clothes she'd come with. They dressed together and headed out.

They huddled under a heat lamp while they awaited Andi's taxi, which arrived too quickly.

"Take care of yourself, Monica. Look me up the next time you're in London, okay? You know where to find me."

"Until next time, darling." Monica took Andi in her arms and left her with a blistering kiss.

After a lazy morning of sleeping in, talking to her mom, enjoying room service, and revisiting all the memories she shared with Andi in the shower, jacuzzi, bed, Anne Boleyn's bed—she still couldn't believe that they had done that—she was finally packed. On her last sweep of the room, she found, tucked underneath the bed, something unfamiliar. She turned it right-side-out, spotting the shopping tag. Historic Royal Places blazed across the front. She smiled and held it to her body. Andi must have accidentally grabbed one of Monica's shirts in the dark earlier that morning. Her heart raced and she became a blundering idiot when she realized she had more than enough time to make it to the Banqueting Hall to return Andi's shirt before catching her flight.

She raced out of the room, checked out and caught a taxi to St. James Square. She hoped to God the exhibit was open and that Andi was there. Andi did say that she had to work early, or was it that she had to work late? Monica's stomach knotted at the thought of seeing her again. Maybe they'd sneak off into a side room filled with history for a last kiss and maybe more. Her breath caught in her throat when she spotted someone walking toward the doors of the museum.

"Stop!" she screamed. "Right here! I'll be right back! Thank you! Sorry. I don't mean to yell!" she said to her driver. She nearly fell out of the cab and scrambled toward the person she had seen who was already one foot into the building. "Excuse me?" She raced toward him, waving an arm in the air. "Excuse me, sir?" Finally catching up. "Oh good. So glad I caught you," she panted.

"Can I help you?" He looked her up and down.

She held a hand against her chest. "Sorry, yeah. Phew. There's an employee, Andi. I met her at the soft opening the day before yesterday." She took a deep breath. "I have something that belongs to her. I just wanted to return it." She held out the bag with Andi's shirt inside.

"I'm sure that's fine. Come in, then."

"Thanks." A huge smile grew on her face as she followed him inside. They headed down a familiar hallway, bypassing the ballroom where Monica attended the reception.

"What did you say the name of the employee was?"

"Andi."

"Do you know her last name?"

"Uh, no, sorry." She blushed. "She said she usually works at Hampton Court. She was on loan, or something, working the soft opening with a few colleagues. Catering department."

"Right. Of course. Let me find Peter. He's from Hampton as well. He'll know. This way."

"Mr. O'Toole?" a worker interrupted them. "We're starting soon. Are you coming, or…" He ping-ponged between the two of them.

"Right." Mr. O'Toole consulted at his watch. "Do you know where Peter is? The tech from Hampton Court? Is he here yet? One of our guests needs to return something to a colleague of his."

"He's in testing, last door on the right." The worker pointed down a hall toward the replica wedding chamber.

"Thanks." Monica headed toward the room before they could stop her.

She peered into a dimly lit room. There was a huge window looking into the replica chamber where the wedding had taken place. She didn't remember seeing the window at the time. She'd been so enthralled with the holograms and Andi. A couple of people wearing headsets were inside the wedding chamber. Three people hunched over laptops in the dimly lit room. From the surprised looks the trio gave her, it was clear she was interrupting.

"Can we help you?" someone asked. He got up from his chair and mumbled something into his headset. The people on the other side looked through the window.

"Sorry to bother. I'm looking for an employee. Her first name is Andi. I don't know her last name. We met at the soft opening the other night. I have something that belongs to her." She held out the bag as evidence. "They said someone by the name of Peter knows her or works with her at Hampton Court."

"I'm Peter," the guy said. "Andi, you say?" He took off his headset.

"Yep."

The guy pursed his lips. "I don't recognize that name. Maybe she's a volunteer?"

"She said she worked there. Catering."

"Sorry, I don't know everyone that works there and we had a ton of people on hand that night. There's a big staff meeting this afternoon. You can come back then and try and catch her."

Monica hung her head. "I'm about to board a flight back to the United States. Please, is there someone else who might know who she is?"

"The best I can do is deliver a message along with the package. I'll personally make sure she gets it."

Monica clutched the plastic bag against her chest.

"Sorry, but we need to get back to work. You caught us in the middle of testing. We have a big night tonight. You're welcomed to stay and watch for a few minutes."

"Really?" She consulted her watch. She had time to spare. "I'd love to! Cool."

"Brilliant. Take a seat then, wherever."

"Thanks."

Monica found a folding chair and placed it close to the window. She had a much better view than she'd had the other night. The trio of techs turned to their computers and resumed chatting with the people on the other side of the window.

One by one the holograms appeared into the chamber. First, the King, then his chaplain and two members of Henry's privy chamber. Monica still couldn't believe how incredibly lifelike they were and how they reacted to the staff, responding to their questions, moving on cue, laughing even.

Anne Boleyn emerged from a side door, followed by her attendant, The Lady Berkeley—Andi. "Oh," Monica said, standing up. She placed her hand against the window. "That's her. Andi. She's working tech."

"Pardon?"

"Andi." Monica pointed, stood and waved.

Peter followed her line of sight. "I've not heard of her being referred to by that name before, though, we know so very little about Anne Savage, The Lady Berkeley," Roger said.

"No—"

"Right. If you were at the soft launch you wouldn't have seen this model. It's been malfunctioning. Bugs in the programming and we weren't able to use this particular stunning holographic image. The clarity is much better, wouldn't you say? You're lucky you're able to see her in action before you left."

The plastic bag was the first to drop followed by Monica who slumped like a sack of potatoes into the chair. The image before her wasn't Anne Savage, The Lady Berkley. It was Andi, the woman she'd spent the last thirty-six hours with. This had to be a joke. Monica had carried on conversations with Andi. People had interacted with Andi. She touched Andi. She'd... Monica's hand covered her mouth.

"She leaves us speechless too. She's the best of the best, the most realistic, most intelligent, self-learning holographic model on the market." The programmer turned his attention to someone else who entered the room.

Monica dragged her eyes back to the scene to see Andi, or rather Anne Savage, the Lady Berkeley, trusted attendant to Anne Boleyn herself.

Anne—Andi—whispered something to Anne Boleyn. They both turned toward Monica, making eye contact. Monica's eyes grew wide when Andi smiled, gave her a little wave, and winked.

THE MAGIC OF THE COIN

Dillon Watson

"Come on, Robyn, I thought that was all decided." Aaliyah Hamilton swiped her transit card and walked through the open gate. "Besides, you already know I can't tell the difference between green and green, no matter what fancy name you give it." She rubbed her forehead as she listened to her fiancée go on and on about what to her mind was nothing. It should be enough that she'd already lost three hours going over every little wedding detail. But with Robyn it seemed enough was not enough. "Just pick the first thing you said," she interjected. "Listen, I'm about to get on the train. We'll talk later." She slid her phone into her pocket and leaned back against the wall to wait for the westbound train.

This damn wedding was going to get her in serious trouble. Either she was going to die in the next three months or she was going to kill. Might be both.

Who knew there was so much involved in getting married? If she'd known then what she knew now, she'd have insisted they do the Elvis wedding in Las Vegas. Then she wouldn't have to worry about colors for this or colors for that. She wouldn't have to worry about making sure this matched that. She certainly would not be charged with finding a new suit when she had several perfectly good suits hanging in her closet.

Aaliyah blew out a breath and reminded herself the bride was always right. Yes, technically she was also a bride. Just not the main bride. This was what Robyn wanted, so this was what she should want. Relationships were about compromise, and if sometimes it felt like she was always the one who did the compromising, so be it.

Stop thinking about it, she ordered herself. She had the rest of the day free, and she was damned if she was going to spend it brooding over something that was three months away.

As was her habit when agitated, she removed her talisman from her pocket. Twining it through her fingers made her feel calmer, helped clear her mind. The coin could work magic despite what friends and family said. She'd been eight when she found it, out roaming the woods with her grandmother. She remembered that day so well.

"Gram! Look, Gram!" Aaliyah raced back to her grandmother, waving the coin she'd found. "I found a magical coin, just like you said I would!" She thrust it at her grandmother. "Do I get to make a wish now? Do I, do I, do I?"

"I'm afraid it's not that kind of coin, Aaliyah." Her grandmother took the coin and let it rest on her palm.

She scrunched up her nose. "Then what kind of coin is it?"

"The kind that will tell you when you find your one true love."

"Like if a frog is really a prince? I'm going to marry a prince when I grow up. Just like Tiana. Now I won't have to turn into a frog first like she did."

"I don't know if you'll marry a prince. Princes are rare. What you need is to marry a man who'll treat you like a prince."

"You mean how the prince took Cinderella from her mean stepmother, so she didn't have to do all that cleaning anymore?"

Her grandmother patted her head. "Something like that."

Aaliyah reached for the coin. "But how can a coin tell me if it's the right boy? Coins can't talk, can they?" She poked it with her finger, hoping to make it talk.

"It'll give you a sign."

Her eyes widened with wonder. "It can draw?"

Her grandmother laughed. "No, sweetie. Not that kind of sign. When your coin glows, you'll know you've found your true love. That means you have to carry it with you all the time."

"I will Gram, I will," Aaliyah said solemnly.

Perhaps because she had magic on her mind, her gaze caught warm brown eyes. It wasn't possible, but it felt like her heart stuttered and the world stood still. The face surrounding the eyes was light brown and narrow, with a cute nose and full lips—altogether arresting. Her brown hair was worn close to her head, and Aaliyah had a sense the body in a red T-shirt and cargo pants was slim. Her heart yearned.

Before she could think of what to do, the eastbound train pulled into the station. When it pulled out, the woman was gone.

"Damn!" She put a hand to her heart, surprised it was still beating. "What the hell just happened?" Looking around, she saw she was still in the station, still waiting for the westbound train. But she wasn't sure she was the same.

* * *

Skye Sydney Newman-Manns sat on the train, trying to figure out what had just occurred. One minute she was okay, the next she was in another world—a better world that included a tall, beautiful woman with intense light brown eyes, creamy brown skin, and a tail of braids over her shoulder.

She was pulled out of a daze, when her friend, Jacqueline Conley elbowed her. "Huh?"

"I said, you and that stud had a struck by lightning moment."

"You're telling me? One minute I'm checking her out, because you're right, she is a stud. Then the next moment she's looking me dead in the eye, and I'm like, pow." She made the sound of an explosion. "Fireworks." She patted her heart and sighed. "Too bad it's only two ships passing in the night."

"We should get off at the next station, go west and try to track her down. What if she's your one and only? You can't let that go."

Skye laughed, though her first instinct had been to do just that. "Listen to you, getting all romantic. That stuff only happens in movies, Jac. And even if she was my one and only, her type does not do one and only. Not when you look that good. Better to have loved and lost than never to have loved at all, right?"

Jac rolled her eyes. "Only you. You're such a nerd."

"Hey." She scratched her cheek with her middle finger. "Helped you get through high school, didn't it? Considering I came all the way from Portland to visit your sorry ass, you should be nicer to me."

"Trying to get you to go find her was being nice. And anyway, you came for a job interview."

"And to see you, go to Charis. I can't believe they moved to Decatur. They were in Little Five Points forever." Charis Books was one of the few remaining feminist, women's bookstores. She and Jac had discovered it and lesbian fiction in tenth grade.

"I know. It's almost as weird as you considering moving back to Atlanta. What's up with that?"

"Pops has cancer. Colon cancer." Skye considered Pops, also known as James Earl Fisher, her savior. He'd taken her in when her stepfather kicked her out at seventeen for being gay. Though Pops wasn't blood kin, she'd always considered him family. He'd been her grandmother's special friend, and despite her parents' objections, he kept in contact with Skye after her grandmother died. "The diagnosis shook him up. He wants to fight it on his home turf. So we move."

"Will you be okay living here? Being this close to your mother, the Demon?"

"After twenty years, my mother's demonic husband doesn't scare me anymore. As for her? Well, she ceased being my mother when she let him kick me to the curb with only what I could fit in my backpack. Atlanta's big enough to avoid the two of them."

With counseling, Skye had gotten past the abandonment by her mother. Moving back to Atlanta might've brought a tinge of unease at the thought of seeing her stepfather, but in the end this was about what Pops needed.

"It's good you see it that way. You were always too strong for him to brainwash you with that religious bull of his."

"Thanks to the ten years I had with Nana." Skye smiled, thinking about her grandmother, the self-proclaimed hippie who taught her so much. "She was all about peace, love, and strong women taking care of themselves and others."

"And Pops. She was all about Pops and the sweet music they made together," Jac pointed out.

"He's still all about her. You know, if she'd been alive there's no way my mother would've married the Demon. But I guess that doesn't matter. Why the hell are we talking about the Demon anyway? That man is *not* worth our time." She stood as the train pulled into the Decatur station. "Let's go back to our past."

* * *

Aaliyah paced in front of the Indian restaurant. She was waiting for her friend, desperate to have someone help her make sense of what had happened at the train station. There was no way she could settle down until she was able to make sense of that. No possible way.

She forced herself to stand still when she caught sight of Tricia Simon, who had been her best friend since grade school.

Tricia lowered her sunglasses and gave Aaliyah a slow once-over. "You look a lot calmer than you sounded on the phone."

Aaliyah had called Tricia in full-blown panic mode as soon as she noticed the coin was glowing. And she could admit, she hadn't sounded coherent. "I sort of am, but sort of not. I don't know what I am. I feel like I've been abducted by aliens. Without the anal probing."

Tricia grinned, flashing dimples. "That's good to know. So, if it wasn't aliens, what did get you? 'Cause truthfully, you sounded like a lunatic."

"I think I saw the love of my life." She said it so fast the words blurred together.

"What? I got something about love, life. Girl, don't tell me you're freaking out over the wedding *again*. How many times do I have to tell you to chill? I know Robyn is—"

"It's not Robyn or the wedding." She ran a hand over her neat braids. "There was this woman at the train station. This is going to sound off the charts, I know that. Anyway, I saw this woman and my heart did a little stutter thing. Damn, Tricia, it was as if my eyes zeroed in on her and someone hit the pause button. I've never, ever felt that way. Never. Then the train comes, pulls away, she's gone, and I'm standing there all but paralyzed. It was so damn freaky and yet so exhilarating."

"You got your eyes dilated before this happened, right? It's hard to see straight after that."

"I might buy that, but…" She pulled the coin out of her pocket. "My train comes, I sit down, then realize my left hand's warm. I open it and the coin's all glowy and gold. Just like Gram said it would. What else can it be but true love, right?"

Tricia sighed loudly. "Please, not that again. You know it's just a sixpence some British tourist dropped who knows when, and *not* some magical fortune teller. I'll give you there's this notion it brings luck to brides if they wear it in their shoe. I thought we talked this all out when you were thirteen and all worried about crushing on what's her name."

"Zoey Russell," she said and exhaled. About the time she hit puberty, Aaliyah's thoughts turned from princes to princesses. "And yeah, I do know what wedding tradition says a sixpence is for. But come on, this coin is different. It. Was. Glowing. That has to mean something. Has to."

"If we're going to hash this out again, I need food. Let's go get a table because I also need to be sitting down, preferably with alcohol, which I can't because I'm working." Tricia was a fitness coach. Her body attested to her skills.

They placed their orders, got their drinks, then grabbed a table by the window.

"This time it's different, Tricia." Aaliyah placed the statue displaying their order number on the table and took a sip of her Coke. "Nothing like this has happened before. My heart, the coin. Signs. They were signs. How am I supposed to ignore that? God, Tricia, I don't think I can forget that feeling when I saw her."

"Forget and ignore are not the same thing. What about Robyn? You've been together for three years. You're getting married. Where does she fit?"

"You think I haven't thought of that? You think that's not a part of what's making me crazy? Sure, I was getting annoyed with the whole wedding deal, the details that I don't give a fuck about. And still I was okay with marrying Robyn, doing the forsaking all others thing. Then, like, boom, there's this woman, messing with my head, my heart. Is this a higher power testing me?"

"You don't believe in a higher power."

"I don't not believe. I just…I don't know what to do, what to think. If I could only go back to being pissed off with Robyn about dithering over colors. Or if I hadn't fallen into those eyes. I did though, and now I'm doomed."

"You're being overly dramatic, don't you think?"

"I wish with everything in me that I was."

Tricia pulled on her bottom lip. "Okay then. What do you want to do?"

"I just told you. I want to get in the Wayback machine and not see her. My life would be so much easier if I hadn't seen her, if my heart hadn't flipped, if the damn coin hadn't glowed."

"Girl. If you've got a Wayback machine, you go all the way to before you find the coin and unfind it. Problem solved." Tricia smiled at the guy delivering their food. "Thank you."

Aaliyah poked at her chicken curry with a plastic fork, any semblance of appetite gone. "I'm screwed. Any way you look at this, I'm screwed. I ignore the sighting, go into holy matrimony with Robyn, and live happy ever after. Except for the times when I think of her, of course."

"Thinking is not cheating. I think of my old girlfriends all the time."

"But do you look at Jen and wish she was one of them?" Jen was Tricia's wife of five years. "Bet you don't. Think about it. Would it be fair to Robyn if some time in the future I look at her and wish she could make me feel like I did this morning? If I wish she was her?"

"So now you can see into the future?"

"Get serious. These are valid points. I'm fixated on a woman who isn't my fiancée, whom I don't know, and have no way of tracking down, by the way. And then what happens if I see her again after I'm married to Robyn? Do you see now? Screwed squared."

"Screwed squared," Tricia snickered. "You're such a geek."

"Hey, this geek helped you with your homework. But that's not the issue. What the hell am I supposed to do, Tricia?"

"You're going to forget about this for now, sleep on it. Then when you wake up you'll see how ridiculous it is to change your life based on a brief meeting of the eyes. Ever think this may not be about the other woman? That this may be about you not wanting to get married? Face it, girl, you've been dragging your feet all the way to the altar."

"That's not true. I've been dragging my feet about a big, overblown production. We both agreed we didn't want big. So then her mother gets involved, brings in a wedding planner, and now it's pure madness. That's what I don't want." The skepticism on Tricia's face was insulting. "I know what I know, Tricia. You may be right that I need to put this all out of my mind. I should go commune with the fish at the aquarium. Watching the fish is soothing. Then I'll take Robyn out to dinner, ask her to leave off the wedding talk for one night. That's a reasonable request, right? I mean it's not like we're getting married tomorrow."

"If nothing else, ply her with wine. Hard to talk about serious shit after three glasses of wine."

"She does love her wine."

* * *

Skye considered herself lucky when she found a parking space near the garage apartment friends of Pops were letting her use. She was pleasantly tired after a day spent with Jac, getting reacquainted with some of their old hangout spots. Now she had a couple of hours to relax before they trolled some of Jac's new haunts. If they so happened to run into the woman from this morning, that would be a bonus.

It wasn't until she was climbing the stairs leading to the apartment that she spotted a woman taping a note to the door. "Can I help you?" When the woman turned, Skye had her second out-of-body experience of the day. The elegant woman looking down at her was familiar in a distorted mirror kind of way. "Mom?"

"I was never much of a mother to you, and for that I am sorry."

Feeling like she was in Bizzaro World, where her mother wore stylish clothes, makeup, and stepped outside the house without her husband by her side, Skye finished climbing the stairs. All the things she'd wanted to say to this woman who had once been her mother flew out of her mind.

"I was leaving you a note."

"How did you know I was here?" As far as she knew, her mother had no knowledge or interest in her whereabouts.

"Jac's mother. I talked to her at church yesterday. She mentioned you were staying here."

"Jac's mother goes to the Demon's church now?" It hurt to think Jac's sensible mom would darken the door of that religious monstrosity.

"No. I go to her church now. A lot has changed in the last seven years. I've changed. As have you. You grew up."

"That happens. You uh, you want to come in?"

"Only if you want me to. I didn't mean to ambush you like this. I don't know why I assumed you'd be out until later."

She unlocked the door and gestured for her mother to enter. "I'm thinking Jac doesn't know you go to her mother's church." Jac would've mention it if she knew.

"I doubt it. I've never seen here there. I'm not sure she'd recognize me if she did."

That Skye could agree with. "Have a seat. Can I get you anything to drink? Susan and Pat were kind enough to stock the fridge for me."

"I'm good, thank you. I want you to know I'm no longer married to Damien. Haven't been for seven years. You can call me Renee. I go by Renee Newman-Manns now."

Shocked, she all but fell into the chair across from Renee. The name Renee had been a bone of contention for the Demon. He thought it was too flighty, insisted her mother go by Grace. He'd tried to change Skye's name to Faith, but she'd refused to answer to it, despite the resulting punishment.

"Don't look so surprised. As I said, I've changed. For the better. I've thought about reaching out to you before. Thought about it a lot."

"Why didn't you?"

"Too ashamed, too scared I'd mess you up more than I already had. Though I left Damien seven years ago, it's taken me longer to break free mentally. Some call it deprogramming. I had to change how I think, how I think about myself." Her smile was wistful. "I was never strong like you or like my mother. Not for lack for trying on her part. And that sounds like an excuse. It's not. Part of our problem was that I wasn't ready to be a mother when I had you."

"Who is at sixteen?"

"I was a young sixteen. Mother was outgoing…had so much presence. I wasn't, so I got pregnant by the first boy who looked my way. It wasn't mother who judged me for it, it was me. I latched on to religion to save my soul. The hell and damnation kind that promised salvation on their terms. Mother did a good job of keeping that away from you, thankfully. But after she died, when I was floundering under the responsibility of taking care of you, and me, there was Damien, ready to show me the right way. You might not remember, but he wasn't so rigid in the beginning. And I don't say that to excuse him, or me, or how you were treated."

"I understand the psychology of abuse. How it starts so slowly you might not realize what's happening." She shrugged. "Pops made sure I got counseling."

"Then I owe him more than I can say. How is James doing?"
"He has cancer."
"Oh, no. I'm so sorry to hear that."
"He's upbeat as always, determined to fight to the end. Because of the cancer, he's decided it's time to come home."
"Will you be okay with him so far away from you?"
"I'm coming back with him. He stood by me. I can't do anything else but stand by him. I'm actually here now for a job interview, to do some groundwork for the big move."
"I see. If you need any help, my church, the members could collect information you might find helpful. Housing, medical facilities, services. We're nondenominational, big on community outreach."
"No hellfire and damnation, huh?"
"Definitely not." Renee pulled on the strap of her purse. "I want to thank you for hearing me out. I know one conversation can't make up for all I've done. I'd like the opportunity to talk with you again, when it's convenient for you. How long are you planning to stay?"
"Until Sunday afternoon."
"Oh. Could...could we have dinner before you go back?"
Skye thought about Pops, about the cancer, about running out of time and nodded. "Does Thursday work for you?"
"Yes." She took a card out of her purse. "Here are my contact numbers. Wherever you want to go is fine with me."
"You're more familiar with what's good. You should pick."
"Oh, right. I've been told The Point is quite good and not far from here. I could pick you up. Seven?"
"That works for me."
She watched as Renee opened her mouth, shut it without speaking, then once again clutched her purse. "Is something wrong?"
"No. No. I was having an internal debate. I'm...no...We're having an informal ceremony at the house on Saturday. I know it's short notice, however, I want you to know you're more than welcome to come."
"Ceremony? Like an induction of some kind?"

Renee smiled. "I didn't make that clear, now did I? It's a marriage ceremony. My fiancée, Douglas, and I are having a backyard wedding. Nothing too big, nothing formal. No gifts necessary. I realize this must be awkward for you. You don't know Douglas, who is nothing like Damien. He coaches kids' soccer, does mentoring. All that to say, if you can find any way to be there, I would like that very much. There's no RSVP, so if you show you show. I should go now that I've thrown you for a loop. Thank you again for being willing to listen when you could easily have turned me away."

She stood, not sure how she felt. "Yeah, sure. Uh, see you Thursday." She watched Renee navigate the steps, then get into a newer model sedan. With a shake of her head, she closed the door and leaned back against it. Maybe she was in one of those cheesy rom-coms and didn't realize it. There was no other way to explain her day.

"Totally bizarre," she decided. First the heart-stopping sighting at the station, then a visit with a new, improved version of her mother. Something this momentous called for a drink.

* * *

Aaliyah pushed back the covers and slipped out of the bed. Her mind didn't want to shut down, despite the corrective steps she'd taken. After losing herself to the aquarium, she'd taken Robyn out for a nice dinner, where they did not discuss the wedding. And after three glasses of wine, Robyn got silly. They'd even topped off dinner with sex, all of which meant there was no reason for her to be wide awake at two thirty in the morning.

Not true, she corrected. She knew exactly why she was awake. Every time she closed her eyes, the scene from the station played in living color. It was as if the mystery woman's image was seared onto the inside of her eyelids and worse—her heart.

"Which is ridiculous," she muttered, pacing the living room. She'd had satisfying sex with Robyn, so why the hell was she thinking about another woman? A woman who wasn't even her type. She liked curvy women, ones with a big butt and a smile. The woman at the station had more of a boyish figure, nowhere near as beautiful as Robyn either.

Despite all of that, Aaliyah couldn't get her off her mind, couldn't forget the way her heart fluttered like fairy wings. How was she supposed to ignore that response when just thinking about it gave her such a rush? She couldn't. Besides the physical response, there was the coin. Sure, she'd wavered over the years, yet deep down inside her, she believed in her grandmother, believed in the coin. And hadn't it proven it was worthy of that belief?

She retrieved the coin from the bedside table and returned to the living room. If she was seriously considering taking drastic steps and not ignoring this morning, then she should have the reason for said steps in her clammy hand. Twining it through her fingers, she returned to pacing and to thinking. There was much thinking to do.

Was it crazy to change her life for a woman she didn't know, especially when change meant not getting married? Even thinking about telling Robyn the wedding was a no-go made her stomach muscles clench. But what else could she do? Despite what Tricia said, doing nothing wasn't fair to Robyn. Doing nothing was equivalent to a slap in the face, a way of saying Robyn was second best.

"This is so fucked up."

She stopped pacing to look at the coin that had been a part of her life for thirty years. It was no longer legal tender, and when it had been, it was only worth six pennies. She was going to call off a three-year relationship—break Robyn's heart—for six damn pennies.

Yeah, she knew that analogy was too simplistic. Her decision had nothing to do with money, the worth of a coin. Her decision was ultimately about right and wrong. Going through with the wedding when she felt this conflicted was wrong. Robyn deserved better from her.

"So woman up, Hamilton." Rubbing her stomach, Aaliyah dropped on the sofa and forced herself to think about the practicalities involved in a split. She drifted off before she could figure out what to do about the four months remaining on the lease.

She woke to the sound of voices. Sitting up, she looked around to orient herself and discovered she'd never gone back to bed. The voices belonged to Robyn and the wedding planner. She stretched her stiff back, wondering what wedding emergency called for an early morning conversation. Hearing Robyn's heels slapping against the hardwood floor, she figured she was about to find out. She took some solace from knowing whatever the problem, her confession was going to make it null and void. She immediately felt guilty.

"Today. I'll make it happen." Robyn stepped into the living room and came to an abrupt stop. She was wearing a form-fitting summer dress that showed off the curves Aaliyah was partial to. "I'll call you back," she said, then ended the call. "Aaliyah? You scared me for a minute. I thought you were already gone. What are you doing out here?"

"I, uh, I couldn't sleep. Came out here so I wouldn't disturb you." Aaliyah checked her fitness watch, decided she had time to yank off the bandage. "Do you have a minute? We need to talk."

"Okay." Robyn sat in a chair across from the sofa. "Is this about what I said earlier?"

"Didn't hear you." She rubbed the grit from her eyes, trying to come up with the best way to say what had to be said. "I wish…I wish I didn't need to tell you this. I wish things were different."

"Are you sick? Did the eye doctor find something wrong with you?"

She shook her head, opened her mouth, closed it, then cleared her throat. "I can't marry you, Robyn. I'm sorry as hell, but I can't do it."

Robyn reared back as if slapped. "What? What are you talking about?"

"I can't marry you. It wouldn't be right. I'm so sorry. I just…" She stopped, ran her hand over her braids, knowing there was nothing she could say to make things better.

"Really? How long have you known?" Robyn's voice was remarkable even.

"Only since early this morning. I've been thinking it over, trying to find a way where you wouldn't be hurt. I truly don't want to hurt you, Robyn. I don't. It's…there's no way I can do that. No possible way, and for that, I'm sorry."

"I have…I have things to do." Robyn hurried from the room.

"Just great." Aaliyah covered her face and let the tears come, feeling like the lowest of the low. She was responsible for that expression on Robyn's face, the tears in Robyn's eyes. She didn't bother to uncover her face when she heard Robyn's footsteps return or when she heard the front door close. There was nothing she could've said, nothing she could've done.

* * *

Skye all but danced to the train station. She knew she'd slayed the job interview. There was no way they wouldn't offer her the job, no possible way. Two days and she'd know for sure. They told her they had more interviews lined up, but she could tell she'd impressed the big boss and her future supervisor.

If there was a Goddess, she'd get the job. It was such a good fit for her IT skills, and bonus, the work vibe was more laid back than she'd expected. Bonus, bonus. She could work from home two to three days a week, depending on the need to consult with coworkers. That would give her more time to spend with Pops. Through Pat, she had the names of personal care workers who could stay with Pops when she had to go in to work, not that he thought he needed a babysitter.

They could argue about that when they argued about her moving in with him, she decided, and tapped her transit card for entrance. Her phone buzzed as she made her way down the stairs to the platform. Jac, of course. "Before you ask, it went really well. I'll be surprised if I don't get an offer. The train's here. Call you later. We should go out, celebrate." She dashed to the train and jumped on right before the doors closed.

As she moved toward a seat facing forward, she scanned the riders standing on the other side of the tracks. Chances were slim she'd be lucky enough to spot the woman from Monday, but she had to try. She continued scanning until the train cleared the station, then sighed. Despite the many things crowding her brain, that woman and the feelings she'd elicited stayed front and center, which was silly. Even if she managed to find the woman, nothing would come of it. A beautiful woman like that wouldn't want a geeky nerd like her. Thinking the woman had been fixated on her was a pipe dream. Probably had more to do with lighting in the station than anything else.

But Jac noticed it, her inner optimist pointed out. So maybe she wasn't so crazy to be searching train stations, restaurants, bars…hell, everywhere for the one who moved her heart. Maybe the other woman was out there searching for her. Maybe their meeting was fate. Wouldn't that be a kick in the butt?

She looked up when the Peachtree Center station was announced and smiled, thinking of all the times she'd gotten off here to attend Dragon Con. This station was also where she'd met her first girlfriend, Sara. Sara who dressed as an elf, with bright red hair, a million freckles and Skye's love for gaming and fantasy. They'd been madly in love as only teenagers could be. The relationship lasted six heady months until Sara's family moved to Chicago.

Sighing, she wondered how she could have forgotten Sara or the joy of attending Dragon Con. Funny how she mostly focused on the Demon when she thought of Atlanta and not all the good times. More sad than funny because she'd let him steal them. She'd given him that power. After all, she'd gone around him and his archaic rules plenty of times. And hadn't she learned to show indifference to the punishment, gotten satisfaction when that only made him madder? Getting thrown out turned out for the better. She got to live with Pops.

"Well, damn." Why was she just now internalizing this? She'd beaten him. He was nothing, and it was time to treat him as such.

After figuratively flicking the Demon into the trash, other memories returned. Atlanta belonged to her, too. Instead of transferring to the eastbound train at the next stop, she was going to take the westbound train and explore another old haunt—Centennial Olympic Park. Too bad it wasn't Christmas, as she'd enjoyed seeing the park decked out for the holiday. Instead, she'd enjoy visiting the aquarium she had yet to visit. After having an epiphany, watching the fish was good for the soul.

The park, built for the 1996 Olympics, spanned two long city blocks. It included a small amphitheater, green space as a relief from the surrounding concrete, and a water feature, ever popular with the kids. Skye took a moment to watch kids run in and out of the streams of water. She and Jac had last done that as teenagers, then stretched out on the grass to let the hot sun dry their clothes and talk about their future.

Remembering that wild and crazy summer day, she dialed Jac's number. "You'll never guess where I am."

"The insane asylum from the sound of it."

"Close. Centennial Park, the water fountain."

"Centennial Park? What are you doing there?"

"Reminiscing. Started on the train at the Peachtree Center Station. Dragon Con and Sara the Elf. Then I realized I let that crazy SOB steal my good memories. Screw the Demon, Jac. He doesn't get to define Atlanta for me. Not anymore."

"Should I sing Hallelujah?"

"No. I feel too good to hear you warble. So good, I'm going to hit the Aquarium while I'm right here."

"Just don't go to the Civil Rights Museum without me."

"I forgot it was around here. This must be a tourist attraction center now." An extra loud shriek drew her attention back to the kids. "Oops. Some kid just— Oh my god, it's her! Jac, it's her! I'll call you back." She took off running in the direction where she'd caught a glimpse of the mystery woman. It had been like it was at the station, where everything seemed to stop, where her heart leapt in her chest. Pumping her legs, she headed for the crossing, hoping to catch the green light. Of course the light turned seconds before she could reach it. All she could do was watch as the blue shirt got farther away.

"Damn!" She was tempted to shake her fist at the cars keeping her from her goal.

The blue shirt had been absorbed into the crowd by the time the light changed. Despite that, Skye sprinted to the spot where she'd lost visual contact. Slowing to a walk, she realized she was at the World Congress Center with its many entrances and exits. Several conventions and meetings were going on, judging by the signs. She'd never find her in this maze of meeting rooms and exhibition spaces.

With a sigh, she rang Jac. "I lost her, damn it. If only I'd noticed her sooner."

"Are you sure it was her?"

"Trust me, it was her. I was so close."

"Third time will be…something or another, right?"

"Charm. Third time is the charm. And I certainly hope so. If for nothing else, to see why I have such an intense reaction to her. Which is kind of crazy seeing as I don't even know her."

"You will. It's fate, Skye, so you'll see her again."

She clung to that sentiment on her way to the aquarium.

* * *

"This is getting to be a habit." Tricia dropped down on the bench next to Aaliyah. "Lucky for you, I had a cancellation."

"Hey, I have food." She handed Tricia the bag containing a meatball sub, barbecue chips and a pickle.

"Well, what is it this time? An actual alien abduction?"

"Don't I wish." Aaliyah carefully unwrapped her Italian sub. "I called off the wedding," she admitted reluctantly and wasn't surprised by the look of horror on Tricia's face.

"No, you didn't! What the hell, Aaliyah? I thought we said you were going to sleep on it, get your head straight."

"I sort of slept on it. Meaning I didn't sleep until I reasoned out the right thing to do. I didn't make this decision lightly, Tricia. I can't marry Robyn, knowing what I know. It's not right.

I know you think it's crazy, but it's what I feel." She patted her chest. "Here."

"I can't believe this. You're giving up Robyn for a fantasy. You realize that, right? You don't know this woman. You don't know if you'll even like her if, and that's a big if, you do manage to find her."

"And so what? I should take the bird in the hand? Play it safe?" She bent her head back, blew out a breath. "Think of how that sounds. How would you feel if Jen saw you as her bird in the hand, someone she was making do with?"

Tricia frowned, pulled at her bottom lip. "Well, damn. That would be fucked up. I won't ask how she took it. So, what happens next?"

"I'm going to move in with Mom for a few months while I help Robyn with the rent. Figure I owe her that much."

"Why not move into the other bedroom?"

"You didn't see her face after I dropped the bomb. There's no way she wants to see my mug for the next four months. I sure wouldn't if the situation were reversed." She looked out over Centennial Park, at all the other lunchgoers. "I know I did the right thing, and still I feel like such a shit. She literally reared back like I slapped her, Tricia. They never show that side in those Hallmark movies Jen makes us watch."

"So, will living with your mother make you a scrub? You know, like in that song TLC sings."

"Damn you, Tricia. Now that song's going to be stuck in my head."

* * *

Skye halfway listened to Pops once again go on and on about how he didn't want her to rearrange her life for him. "Listen old man," she finally said. "Save your breath. I got the job, sent off my letter of resignation. Done deal."

"You're as hardheaded as your grandmother. I never could tell Luna a damn thing either."

"That's why you loved her, Pops. And me. It's like I told you Tuesday. I'm seriously enjoying being back. You won't believe how much this part of Intown has changed. I can't wait to show you."

"Are you sure you can do this, Skye? Be honest with me. Last I heard, that poor excuse for a man was still around."

"I really can, Pops. He doesn't matter. I won't let him matter. On the plus side, my dinner with Renee went well. I think we can forge a good relationship. Not mother-daughter because we never were, but friends. We can be friends. I think you'll like who she's become."

"We'll see. What'd you find out about that church of hers?" The suspicion in his voice came through loud and clear.

"I talked to Jac's mom, did my own research and it's nothing like her old excuse for a church. For starters, it's all are welcome, even the gays. They feed the poor, provide all sorts of resources for members and nonmembers. They do stuff I guess churches should do. She's changed, Pops, believe me."

"Okay, then. You always were good at reading people, girl. But do this old man a favor and make sure your eyes and ears stay open. I don't want you hurt again."

"My eyes and ears are wide open."

"That's my girl. Now how soon does that new job of yours start?"

She smiled, knowing she'd won the battle. "I've got some leeway. They know I need to get an old man settled. Thanks to your network of friends, we have a house we can rent until yours becomes available. They really want you back, Pops."

"That's good 'cause I'm really ready to be back. And having you there with me? That's just gravy. You've brought so much joy to my life. Don't ever forget that, Skye. I love you."

"I wouldn't want to be anywhere else. Love you back, Pops."

Skye set her phone on the table and gave a happy sigh. Everything was working out. She had a new job, a new place, and the beginnings of a relationship with Renee. She could add the possibilities of connecting with the mystery woman, but that might be asking for too much.

***

Aaliyah experienced a brain fart as she approached Renee and Doug's house. Obviously, her brain had been on simmer earlier when she helped set up for the wedding. Otherwise it would've occurred to her that since she'd recently torpedoed her own wedding, she should not be attending anyone else's wedding. Talk about your bad mojo.

"Shit!" She took out her talisman, twined it through her fingers and paced. There was little doubt she was, at best, carrying dubious wedding vibes. Would her presence at the wedding cause them to be released and doom Doug and Renee's marriage before it started?

"Aaliyah? What are you doing out here?"

She jumped, not having heard the door open. "Renee. Hey. I was thinking of…stuff."

"I want to thank you again for the wonderful job you, Jen, and Tricia did in the backyard. I was just telling Doug we couldn't have done better using pros."

"It was fun." The kind of thing she could see doing for her own wedding. "You look great, by the way. That dress is perfect for a backyard wedding."

Renee smoothed a hand down her full-length, tie-dye dress in all the colors of the rainbow. "Thanks. It reminded me of my mother. Makes me feel like she's here."

"Wait. You didn't let Doug see you like, in it, did you? Isn't it supposed to be bad luck for the groom to see the wedding dress before the wedding?"

Renee laughed. "Doug and I make our own luck. And frankly, I've had enough bad luck already to last me a lifetime." She put a hand on Aaliyah's arm. "I meant to ask earlier if you're okay coming to the ceremony. I imagine this might be hard for you so soon after your wedding got called off."

"That's funny. I was just thinking my attendance at your wedding so soon after I called off my own would mess you guys up. Leftover bad vibes, you know?"

"Not one bit," Renee assured her. "I'm not that superstitious. Although I confess, I am wearing something old, new, borrowed, and blue to cover all bases."

"I wonder..." She looked down at Renee's ballerina flats, thought about the coin in her hand. It had helped her, why not someone else? "Would you like to wear my sixpence in your shoe? Supposedly it brings brides good health, wealth, and prosperity. Another base covered, so to speak."

"You wouldn't mind? I hear that coin is special to you."

"Positive. Might even cancel out any bad vibes I'm carrying. You put it in your left shoe."

Renee stood on her tiptoes and kissed Aaliyah's cheek. "I'd be honored." She toed off her left shoe.

"Let me." She knelt, slipped the coin into Renee's shoe and felt all her nerves settle. "Now what else can I help with?"

* * *

Skye stepped onto the walkway leading to the bright yellow door of the house Renee shared with Douglas, and mentally called up her party persona. Being around Pops and his thousands of friends and acquaintances, she'd learned to do it seamlessly. She and Renee had agreed Skye would skip the actual ceremony, to be attended by only a few family members, and attend the bigger after party. She wouldn't stand out as much.

She looked down at her colorful, tie-dye shirt, her best pair of jeans, hoping Renee would see the shirt as a tribute to Luna Skye Newman-Manns before she rang the bell. She was taken aback when a white woman about her age opened the door. Did she have the wrong address? Surely not, given the voices and music coming from the back.

"I uh, I'm here for the party?" Skye held up the bouquet of flowers she'd picked up on impulse. "Renee invited me," she added at the blank look.

The blonde smiled. "Right. I thought I knew everyone who was coming. Come in, come in. I'm Jennifer Burks. Doug's daughter."

She hoped her surprise wasn't written on her face. Her mother had married a white guy. Remembering the Demon's reaction to her consorting with white people, she bit back a laugh. How the times have changed. She almost wished he was around. His head would surely explode. "I'm Skye. I'm, uh, I knew Renee when I was younger."

"I'm glad you were able to come today. We're mostly out back." Jen led the way past the staircase, through a bright kitchen and out a set of patio doors. "Renee's going to love those flowers."

In the backyard, Skye came to a stop when she spotted Renee slow dancing with a man she assumed was Doug. The song playing took her back in time. Her grandmother had written it and helped rocket a new R&B group up the charts.

The newlyweds shared a kiss when the song ended. Skye joined in the enthusiastic applause. The song and the dress that her grandmother would've loved warmed her heart. One look at the dress and Pops would realize she was right about Renee. She pulled out her phone and took a picture.

"They're so good together." Jennifer wiped at tears.

She nodded, then waited for the crowd to dissipate before approaching the happy couple. Skye couldn't help but notice the way Renee's face lit up when she got within eyesight.

"You came." Renee said it like it was an answer to a prayer. "And look at your shirt."

Skye grabbed onto the hand Renee held out, squeezed. "I, uh, I brought flowers. It's not really a gift."

Renee held them to her nose. "Wildflowers. Mother's favorite. They go with the dress, your shirt. It means a lot. Thank you so much."

"You're welcome."

"Hi. Douglas Burks." He held out his hand, shook hers vigorously. "I'd like to second that thank-you."

"Skye. I'm Skye." She thought he shared a strong resemblance with Richard Gere. Very cute. "Thank you for inviting me."

"Why don't Skye and I go put these in water?" She gave Doug a quick kiss. "Be right back."

In the kitchen, Renee found a vase and filled it with water. "It really does mean a lot that you came."

"The song you danced to? That meant a lot. Nana would've approved. The dress she would've loved, although knowing her, she would've been barefoot."

Renee laughed, stroked a hand down Skye's arm as if she couldn't help herself. "She would've. But if she'd been barefoot, she couldn't have had a sixpence for luck."

"Sixpence? Like British money?"

"It goes with the something old, something new, something borrowed, something blue bridal tradition." Renee removed the coin, held it up.

"That's a weird place to store money. But I guess wedding dresses don't have pockets. You know if it was a black tradition, you'd stuff it in your bra. Good as a bank."

"I never thought of that. You always were smart. Even when you were little." Renee's eyes filled. "I'm sorry we missed—"

Now Skye did the stroking. "No sorries. Not today. Today is for celebrating. That's a handsome man you got out there waiting for you."

Renee's smile was watery. "He is. More important to me, that's a good man I have out there."

"I bet. I was surprised he's white."

"Please tell me that doesn't bother you."

"Of course not. I'm gay. You love who you love."

"I should've—Do you see that?"

"See what?"

"The coin. It looks like its glowing."

"Renee, where's— You! It's you, it's you, it's you."

The wonder in the voice pulled Skye's attention away from the coin. It's her, she thought as her heart did what felt like a slow roll. Her skin suffused with heat, and the air stilled. It was the woman from the train station, tall and gorgeous and in the same room with her.

Without thought, she moved until she was standing in front of her mystery woman, her smile as big as the moon. "It's me and it's you. I'm Skye. I've been looking for you."

"I'm Aaliyah. I can't believe it. You're actually here."

Skye took the outstretched hand, felt the click of connection run up her arm to her heart. "Believe it. I'm here." Jac had it right. The third time was the charm.

INN TROUBLE

Cade Haddock Strong

The floorboards of the Telemark Inn creaked as the waitstaff darted around, clearing dessert plates and pouring coffee. The rehearsal dinner had gone off without a hitch, and although the family was among the strangest Casey had ever hosted at her inn, everyone seemed to be enjoying themselves, and for that she was grateful. This weekend marked the end of the fall wedding season and she was exhausted. Her threshold for drama stood at a negative ten.

The groom stood at the center of a group of men near the bar. It was difficult to hear the jazz band over their boisterous laughter. Throughout the evening, the bride and groom had barely uttered a word to each other, although in truth, that wasn't unusual. Like most weddings held at the Telemark, family and friends had traveled to Vermont from all over the country, and the happy couple was no doubt excited to see some of them and felt obligated to talk to others.

The bartender held up a nearly empty bottle of vodka and signaled to Casey; he needed more. She cut through the inn's library to reach the small storeroom off the kitchen.

The bride, Elise, and her mother were seated on the spare dining chairs lining the wall outside the storeroom.

"Oh, I'm so sorry," Casey said. "I didn't mean to interrupt."

Elise dabbed her eyes with a tissue. "Oh, it's okay," she said. "We'd best rejoin the party anyway." She stood and helped her mother to her feet.

Casey grabbed two bottles of vodka from the storeroom and followed them back to the dining room. Of all the brides who'd married at her inn, Elise was by far the most beautiful. Her lavender silk dress hung perfectly on her lean frame, and although she was petite, she had strong arms and perfect posture, like a long-distance runner or a ballerina. Her dark hair was pulled back in a high bun, exposing the smooth olive skin of her neck and shoulders.

A gray-haired woman stopped Elise and her mother just as they stepped into the dining room and gushed over the enormous yellow flower centerpieces adorning each table. Elise gave the woman a faint smile.

Casey slipped past them, anxious to replenish the vodka before it ran out, but as she neared the bar, the lights flickered and the music faded. Gasps echoed through the crowd when the room went dark. Casey glanced out the windows lining the back wall of the inn. Even the lights in the garden had gone out. There was no moon to speak of and she could barely see the person next to her.

"What the hell is going on?" the groom's gruff voice demanded. "Is this some kind of joke?"

"It appears the power has gone out," Casey said evenly.

"No shit," someone grumbled.

Casey gritted her teeth and jumped into action. Within minutes, she and her staff had lit candles and scrounged up a handful of flashlights. A neighbor called to inform them that the entire valley was without power. According to the police scanner, someone had taken out a utility pole with their car.

Casey waved a flashlight over her head and made an unpopular announcement; the power wouldn't be back on anytime soon.

More grumbling ensued.

Charles, the groom, came up beside her and snatched the flashlight from her hand. He swung it back and forth over the crowd. "Elise," he shouted. There was no response. "Where's Elise?"

"The last time I saw her," Casey pointed toward the library, "she and her mother were standing there." A quick roll call indicated Elise wasn't the only one missing. Her mother was gone too.

Using flashlights and candles, they scoured the Telemark and its vast grounds for the two women. Elise's purse and phone were on her bedside table, but there was no sign of her. She and her mother had just vanished. Charles became hysterical and insisted they call the police.

Casey stared out across the back deck of the inn and kneaded the base of her neck. *So much for a drama-free wedding.*

A few hours later when the electricity was restored, the Telemark lit up like a Christmas tree. There was still no trace of Elise or her mother. Casey did all she could to cater to the distraught groom and the rest of the guests. The day of the wedding came and went. The bride and her mother never reappeared. Two days later, the groom stormed out of the inn, climbed in his BMW and drove away.

* * *

Casey waved at her neighbor. "Morning, Aretha. I'm here to get Benita," she said, referring to the small RV she kept parked in Aretha's barn.

"Time to head south?" Aretha asked.

"Yeppers."

Aretha walked Casey down to the barn and together they drew open its heavy wooden doors.

"When was the last time you started Benita up?"

"Two weeks ago," Casey said. "Had her tuned up. She's in tip-top shape. Even all stocked with provisions." She unlatched the side door of the RV and peered inside. Two sets of eyes stared back at her. Casey shrieked and jumped back, nearly knocking Aretha to the straw-covered floor.

"Jeez, what's wrong?" Aretha asked.

Before Casey could respond, a head poked out the RV's door. It was Elise.

Casey's hand flew to her heart. "What the—"

"I can explain." Elise stepped out of the RV and ran a hand through her long, dark hair.

Just the sight of the beautiful woman sent a quiver through Casey. She cleared her throat and reached into the back pocket of her workpants for her phone, to call who she didn't know. The police? The groom?

"Please, hear me out," Elise pleaded. Her mother climbed out of the RV and stood beside her.

Casey's hand hovered over her phone. She was all packed and ready to go to Florida for the winter. This was the last thing she needed right now. She huffed out a sigh and stuffed the phone back in her pocket. It couldn't hurt to hear what the woman had to say.

* * *

Elise sat at the tall butcher-block table in the Telemark's kitchen. She was fresh from a shower and clad in the flannel shirt and sweatpants the innkeeper had given her. The clothes hung on her slight frame, but the warm, soft fabric felt wonderful against her skin. She watched the innkeeper make them both a mug of peppermint tea. Her strong, broad shoulders strained the seams of her blue work shirt and her tightly-clipped, blond hair was slicked back with hair gel.

Mugs in hand, the innkeeper lowered herself onto the stool opposite Elise and glanced up. Her beautiful blue eyes held no malice. She pushed a steaming mug in Elise's direction. "Why were you and your mother hiding out in Aretha's barn?"

Elise racked her brain for the woman's name. Corey? Cassie? Casey… That was it. "Um, Casey, I don't want to be a burden. If you'll please just let us get our belongings, we'll be on our way."

"Your fiancé took everything with him when he left."

"Oh." Elise slumped against the butcher-block.

"I have no idea what your story is, but—"

"I didn't want to get married. Or rather, I didn't want to marry Charles." She pointed toward the room above where her mother napped. "When you found me crying back by the storeroom, that's what my mother and I were discussing."

Casey's shoulders stiffened but she didn't say anything.

"I was in kind of a bad place when I met Charles," Elise continued. "My girlfriend had just dumped me and I was pretty low. This probably sounds callous, but Charles showered me with attention and it felt good. It was exactly what I needed at the time. I'd just moved to New Jersey to be closer to my mom and I didn't know many people. He and I hung out and we had a good time. It wasn't until I tried to break things off that I saw his true colors. He got crazy upset." A tear trickled down Elise's cheek. "I'm sorry, you probably don't want to hear all of this."

Casey nodded. "Yes, I do."

"Okay. Well, anyway, somehow Charles discovered…" Elise swallowed hard and lowered her voice. "My mother is here in the US illegally. He hinted he might try to get her deported if I left him."

Casey gasped. "Oh my God!"

"I had no choice but to stay. My mother has been deported before and she's got a criminal record. She's not a bad person. It's complicated."

"So you agreed to marry Charles to protect your mother?" Casey asked.

"Yes, and to be honest, part of me felt bad for wanting to leave him. He'd been there when I needed someone to prop me up." Elise reached for her mug and it shook as she lifted it to her lips. She took a few small sips before continuing. "When the lights went out during the rehearsal dinner, my mother took my hand and we ran."

"Wow."

"At first, I resisted, but my mother was determined. She saw it as my chance to get away from Charles once and for all."

"How'd you know to go to Aretha's barn?"

"Apparently, my mother had peered into the barn during her morning walk and spotted the RV."

"Well, that was fortunate."

"Crazy fortunate. My mother is very curious and resourceful. This time it really paid off."

"You mentioned she was here illegally?"

There was no judgment in Casey's gentle voice and Elise began to tell her the whole sordid tale. "She fled El Salvador when she was very young—seventeen or eighteen—and snuck into the United States. She and my father fell in love. He was an American and my mother had me when she was barely twenty. My parents never married but they had a good life until my father died in a construction accident."

Casey's eyes crinkled as if she were in pain. "That's horrible. How old were you when he died?"

"I was thirteen. After he was killed, my mom did her best to provide for us. She's whip smart, and she's always been good with numbers. One day the owner of the hotel where she worked offered her a higher paying job in accounting. He was a godsend, or so we thought. Turns out, he ran a major money laundering operation. My mother knew nothing about it. He kept a separate set of books but it didn't matter. When he got busted, she went down with him. When she was released from jail, they deported her back to El Salvador."

"But then, how'd she get back here?"

"She paid a smuggler to bring her back over the border. All Charles had to do was pick up the phone. ICE would have pounced." Elise hung her head and covered her face with her hands.

Casey set her mug down hard on the table. "Charles had no right…"

Elise lifted her head and peered at her. "I know, but I couldn't risk defying him."

"We could report him to the police."

Elise's lips trembled. "And tell them what? I played along. Everyone, including my mother, thought I was in love with him."

heart rattled the chains she'd bound it with. *Get a fucking grip, Casey.* After her one and only serious relationship had crashed and burned in spectacular fashion, she'd put her heart in solitary confinement and thrown away the key. She stood tall and hurried across the lobby's blue tile floor, trying desperately to remember where she'd been headed.

Later that afternoon, Casey whistled, "You Are My Sunshine" as she stacked chaise lounges alongside the inn's pool. When Elise emerged from a nearby shed wheeling a bike, Casey stumbled backward and fell into the flower bed.

Elise propped her bike up against the wall and ran to help Casey. "Are you okay? I'm so sorry. I didn't mean to startle you."

Casey cleared her throat. "No worries. I was in my own little world."

Elise pointed to the spot where Casey had fallen. "Well done. You crushed the yellow flowers."

Casey was confused. "I thought yellow was your favorite color."

"What gave you that idea?"

"Your rehearsal dinner, the centerpieces, they were all yellow."

"I detest the color yellow. If it had been up to me, the centerpieces would have been blue. That's my favorite color."

"Sorry I brought it up."

Elise shrugged. "It's okay." She nodded toward the bike against the wall. "I was going to take a ride along the beach. Want to join me?"

Casey's first instinct was to say no. She had so much to do around the inn, and she was still unsettled by the reaction she'd had that morning when she'd seen Elise laughing with Bernice. "Oh, gosh, I haven't ridden a bike in years. I'm not sure I remember how."

"Come on. It'll be fun, and everyone knows, you never forget how to ride a bike." Elise snatched a frisbee from a bin near the shed. "And maybe we can stop along the way and toss this."

Casey caved. She pulled a bike from the shed and followed Elise to the path along the beach. They pedaled side by side, occasionally exchanging a glance but saying very little. The tension in Casey's neck and shoulders gradually eased. It was late fall and a cool breeze came off the ocean. The sun hung low on the horizon and the beach was vacant except for a lone jogger. Elise slowed, propped her bike up against a streetlamp and twirled the frisbee on her finger.

Their feet sunk into the sand as they made their way toward the water. Elise sent the purple disk flying in Casey's direction. She jumped up, caught it expertly with one hand, and in one fluid movement, flung it back to Elise.

"Let me guess," Elise said. "You used to play Ultimate?"

Casey laughed. "Yeah. For many years. It's sort of a prerequisite for lesbians in Vermont."

As the sun inched lower and lower in the sky, it became difficult to see the frisbee. "Want to sit and watch the sunset?" Elise asked. She didn't wait for Casey to answer and plunked herself down on the sand.

Casey sat beside her and stared at the ocean. The last rays of orange and yellow streaked across the water. "This is nice. I can't remember the last time I stopped to watch the sunset."

"That's a crime." Elise nudged Casey with her shoulder. "You mean to tell me you don't woo all the ladies with romantic sunset walks?"

"Oh, there's no wooing going on. I keep to myself. It's better that way."

"Uh-oh. Sounds like there's a story there."

"It's not something I like to talk about."

"Suit yourself," Elise said, "but I'm a good listener."

Seemingly without her consent, the words began to spill from Casey's mouth. "Many years ago, I was deeply in love with a woman named Sophia. I decided to ask her to marry me and I spent weeks orchestrating the perfect proposal." Casey bit her lip but the tears came anyway. Elise reached over for her hand and gave Casey the courage to go on. "Right before I got down on one knee, Sophia came out with a bombshell of her own. She announced she'd joined the Peace Corps to 'find herself.' She'd just signed on for a two-year stint in Rwanda."

Elise squeezed her hand. "Oh, wow. And you had no idea?"

"Not a clue. I thought we'd spend our lives together, when in reality, she'd been planning to leave me for months. I was totally devastated."

Elise wrapped an arm over Casey's broad shoulder. "Geez. Understandably so. Talk about a serious kick in the stomach."

"So now you know. There hasn't been anyone since. Like I said, I'm better off alone."

"Sophia was an idiot. To give up an amazing woman like you."

Casey sucked in a breath of sea air to calm the flutter in her heart.

* * *

"Where are you running off too?" Elise asked when she spotted Casey hurrying across the lobby of the inn with a duffel bag slung over her shoulders.

"Just an overnight trip to Lake Okeechobee. My friend Jam lives there. They're a sculptor and I commissioned a piece for the Swizzle. I'm going to pick it up."

"Wow, really." Elise glanced at the floor and then back up at Casey. "I've always wanted to see Lake Okeechobee. Mind if I, um, tag along?"

Casey hooked her thumbs in the belt loops of her faded jeans. "No, not at all. That'd be great."

Elise bounced on her toes. "Super, give me a sec to toss some stuff in a bag."

The drive to the lake took them back up through the Keys, the way they'd come when they'd driven down from Vermont. "Can you believe it's only been a month since we got here?" Casey asked.

"No. It seems like a lifetime ago."

"I feel the same way."

"When will you go back there? To the inn in Vermont?"

"Not until after Easter," Casey said. "I'll make the drive north right before the spring wedding season shifts into high gear. Beginning in May, I'm booked solid through the summer."

"You're lucky to split your time between two beautiful places. Vermont and Key West, the best of both worlds."

"I am lucky. Sometimes I forget that. Every year, I say I'm going to carve out time to go hiking or get out on my boat, but I never do it."

"You have a boat? Here in Florida?"

"Sure do. I'll take you out on it sometime."

"Sweet, I'd like that."

It was nearly dark by the time they got to Jam's bungalow. Before dinner, they loaded the sculpture into the back of Casey's truck and parked it in the garage.

"Hadn't counted on you coming with a companion," Jam said when it came time to go to bed. "Don't recall you ever bringing a lady friend with you before."

Casey cracked her knuckles. "Elise isn't, um, a lady…"

Elise put her hands on her hips and gave Casey a look of mock disbelief.

"I didn't mean—"

"I know what you meant." Elise laughed and slung an arm over Casey's shoulders. "You're adorable when you get flustered."

Jam's studio consumed most of the house, and they hastily set up an air mattress next to the bed in the guestroom. Casey insisted Elise take the bed.

After the lights were out, Elise stared at the ceiling and listened to Casey's slow and steady breathing. "You still awake?"

"Yeah," Casey said. "I can't seem to fall asleep."

"Me either." Elise faced Casey and propped her head on her elbow. "Do you want to come up here? There's plenty of room for both of us and I hate the thought of you sleeping on the floor."

The air mattress creaked as Casey rolled to its edge. She stood, pulled back the covers and slipped beneath them. Without saying a word, she wound a strong arm around Elise and spooned against her.

"I feel safe when I'm with you," Elise whispered.

Casey pulled them tighter. "I feel happy when I'm with you."

A warmth swelled in Elise's chest and flowed toward her belly. Every muscle in her body relaxed when Casey slipped a hand into her hair and gently stroked her head until she fell asleep.

When they got back to the Swizzle, Elise helped Casey find the perfect spot for the small sculpture Jam had made. Once it was in place in front of the inn, they stood back to admire it. Elise took Casey's hand and squeezed it. "It's perfect."

"It is, isn't it? I may have Jam make another one just like it. I could put it back by the pool."

"What a great idea." Elise nudged Casey with her hip. "I'd happily take another road trip with you to Lake Okeechobee."

"It's settled then. Remind me to call Jam tomorrow."

That evening, Elise cut a handful of delicate purple and white flowers from the garden behind the inn, bound them together with a piece of string and carried them next door to the small cottage where Casey lived. The scent of crab meat—a smell Elise had discovered was quite common in Key West—floated from Casey's screen door.

With the bundle of flowers hidden behind her back, Elise knocked softly.

Casey greeted her with a broad grin. "Hey, hi. It's good to see you. Come on in."

Elise stepped over the threshold and presented the flowers. "For you."

"How sweet of you."

Elise smirked. "Well, they're technically from your garden, so…"

"It's the gesture that counts." Casey waved toward her small kitchen. "Can I get you something to drink? Wine, beer, a margarita?"

"Um, I don't want to interrupt. It smells like you're cooking dinner."

"I just steamed some stone crabs." Casey fiddled with the button on her shirt. "Why don't you stay? I've got plenty and I'd love your company."

"Okay, twist my arm."

Casey poured them each a glass of sauvignon blanc and reached for the bowl of freshly cooked crab claws. Elise smiled as she watched Casey's able hands snap the claws and arrange them on a platter with big rainbow-colored crabs etched into it. In the month she'd been in Key West, she'd only seen Casey whip up meals in the inn's industrial kitchen. Here in her cottage, Casey's movements were more deliberate. She drifted between the fridge, sink, and stove and whistled as she divided a bowl of dark yellow sauce into two ramekins. It was a simple task, but here, away from the hustle and bustle of the inn, it felt intimate.

"Did your mom make it to New Jersey safe and sound?" Casey asked when they sat to eat. Elise's mother and her friend Dora from Key West had gone up north to help their friend Julia, who'd broken both her arms in a car accident and needed help caring for her three preschool-age granddaughters.

"Yep. She called about an hour ago. She and Dora had commandeered the kitchen and were already busy cooking."

"It was really nice of them to drive all the way up there."

"Friends and family are paramount to my mother, and as much as she loves it here in Florida, I know she misses her friends in New Jersey."

"Me too," Casey said, "although I'm pretty sure your mom already knows half of Key West. You better watch out. They might make her honorary mayor."

After they finished eating, Elise helped with the dishes and gathered her purse and jacket. "Thank you for dinner."

Elise shuffled her feet as they stood awkwardly by the door. She closed the distance between them and brushed her lips over Casey's. They were soft and warm. Casey jumped back, her eyes wide with surprise.

Elise's stomach sunk. Maybe she'd crossed a line. She pushed open the screen door and said, "See you tomorrow," hurrying out into the night.

"Any idea when you and Dora will head back to Key West?" Elise asked her mother. She pinned the phone to her ear with her shoulder while she dug around the shed for a bike pump.

"I'm not sure. The casts won't come off Julia's arms for at least another two weeks, and she still needs a lot of help with the little ones."

"Okay. Be careful up there. Talk to you tomorrow."

After she ended the call, Elise wheeled two bikes out of the shed and pumped their tires full of air.

Casey strode up beside her. "I'll have to add bike mechanic to your long list of skills."

A few strands of hair had come loose from Elise's ponytail and she swept them from her face. "Bike mechanic might be a bit of a stretch." She stood and gave Casey a big grin. "Although I do know how to change a flat tire."

Casey laughed and rubbed her thumb over Elise's cheek. "You've got bike grease on your face."

Elise shrugged and set the bike pump aside. "Ready?"

"As I'll ever be." Casey reached for one of the bikes, swiped the kickstand with her foot and slid onto the seat.

Elise followed her out of the inn's parking lot and zoomed ahead when they reached the wide bike path along Smathers Beach. She raised her hands in the air. "Look, no hands."

A woman on roller blades careened toward Elise. "Watch out!" she yelled. "I don't know how to stooop!"

Elise grasped for her handlebars and jerked them to the right. Her front tire sunk into the sand alongside the path and her bike came to an abrupt halt, sending her sailing over the handlebars. Her helmet ricocheted off a lamp post and she went facefirst into a bright red fire hydrant. She landed on the ground in a heap and a metallic taste accompanied the stabbing pain in her mouth.

Casey was at her side in an instant, her eyes wild with concern. She brushed Elise's hair from her face. "I'm calling an ambulance, baby."

Elise wanted to smile but her mouth wouldn't cooperate. *Casey called me baby.* The thought did wonders to ease her pain. She wiggled her arms and legs. "Not nethessawy. I fink I'm owkay." After Casey helped her sit up, Elise roamed her mouth with her tongue. She whimpered. Her two front teeth were razor sharp and one wiggled when she touched it. She didn't need a doctor; she needed a dentist.

Casey called the inn. Moments later, Ricky arrived in the Swizzle's maintenance truck and whisked them off to the offices of Dr. Roberta France, the best dentist in all the Keys, according to Casey.

Aside from her damaged teeth, Elise had a few nasty cuts and bruises. When they got back to the inn that evening, Casey helped Elise into her cottage and drew a bath. With great care she pulled Elise's bloodstained T-shirt over her head and unlatched her jog bra. When Elise's breasts spilled out, Casey blinked a few times and cast her gaze toward the tub. "Um, maybe I should add a little more bubble bath."

Elise eased out of her gym shorts.

Casey put the cap back on the bubble bath and stood to face her. Her cheeks flushed as her eyes roamed Elise's body. "Just checking your injuries."

"Uh-huh. Whatever you say." It was the first time Casey had seen her naked, but Elise wasn't shy standing bare in front of her. With a hand around Elise's waist, Casey helped her into the tub. Her gentle touch made Elise's skin tingle and if she hadn't been in so much pain, she would have kissed her then.

The warm water stung at first, but gradually eased Elise's aching muscles. She closed her eyes as Casey dabbed her skinned elbows and knees with a soft, soapy sponge. She opened one eye and smiled up at Casey. "You're an excellent nurse. I've never felt so cared for in my life."

Casey's laugh echoed off the tiled bathroom walls. "Shhh, don't tell anyone. It'll ruin my image as a big, tough butch." She pulled a towel off a nearby rack and wrapped it around Elise when she emerged from the bath. "Hungry?"

"Starving."

"How about some soup?" Casey brushed Elise's cheek with her finger. "Don't imagine you'll be able to eat anything solid for a while."

After Elise ate, Casey tucked her into bed and crawled in next to her. It was ironic, Elise's whole body throbbed, yet she was happier than she had been in her whole life. She drifted off to sleep in Casey's arms with a smile on her face.

The next morning, Elise was stiff but the pain was a lot better. Thankfully, it was Saturday and she didn't have to work. Casey made her a cup of strong, black coffee and scrambled eggs and when Elise finished her breakfast, she said, "Well, I should probably get back to my room."

Casey looked down at her plate before peering up at Elise with her bright blue eyes. "Please, stay. It's nice having you here." She gestured toward the windows. "It's supposed to rain all day. I've got to check on a few things at the inn, but when I get back, maybe we could watch a movie or something."

Elise couldn't think of a better way to spend the afternoon. "Okay, I'd like that."

Casey returned to the cottage with a bag full of bandages, pain reliever, more soup and bubble bath. She and Elise snuggled under a blanket on the couch and listened to the rain batter the windows. They'd known each other for two short months and had only shared one chaste kiss, but without a shadow of a doubt, Elise was falling in love with the strong, confident innkeeper.

* * *

It took multiple visits, but Dr. Roberta France worked her magic and got Elise patched up.

"I told you she was amazing," Casey said when Elise got home from her final visit to the dentist. Aside from a tiny scar on her knee, Elise had made a full recovery and she'd been a trooper through the whole ordeal. "You're as good as new."

"Actually," Elise said, "I'm better than new." She ran a finger over her newly-fortified front teeth. "As you probably noticed, before the crash my front teeth were crooked. Now, they're perfectly straight."

"You had a beautiful smile before and you have a beautiful smile now."

Elise beamed. "You always make me feel special."

"You are special." Casey trailed a finger over Elise's cheek. "Don't ever let anyone tell you otherwise."

"It's ironic," Elise said. "Charles hated my crooked teeth, always said they were the only blemish on my otherwise beautiful face. He begged me to get them fixed but I refused."

The mention of his name made Casey's blood boil. "What an asshole."

Elise let out a long sigh. "You can say that again. Thanks to you, I'm free of him." She waved a hand around the cottage and her glorious brown eyes bore into Casey. "Life here with you… it's, I don't know, idyllic. Sometimes I have to pinch myself to make sure it's not all a dream."

A lump formed in Casey's throat. The last of the thick ice around her heart melted away. For the first time in a very long time, it thumped freely. She rested one hand on Elise's waist and slipped the other into her hair.

Their kisses were tender at first, but Elise opened her mouth and welcomed Casey inside. Pure joy shot through Casey. It was as if she'd been pumped full of helium. She pulled Elise tightly against her, afraid that if she didn't, Elise might float away. They fell onto the couch and she kissed her passionately. Elise pulled back slightly and stared into Casey's eyes with such intensity, it took her breath away. Gentle fingertips ran over her collarbone and up the nape of her neck. Warm lips found hers again. Elise hummed when Casey slipped a hand under the back of her shirt and roamed the soft warm skin beneath it.

"Knock, knock," a tentative female voice called.

Casey jerked back and squinted toward the front door. It was Bernice from the front desk.

"I'm so sorry to, uh, interrupt," Bernice said, "but there's a guy at the front desk who's throwing a hissy fit and insisting to talk to you."

"I'll be right there," Casey said. She gave Elise one last kiss. "I'd like to finish this later."

"Hurry back," Elise said.

Casey trotted over to the inn with a spring in her step but froze when she stepped inside. Charles paced back and forth in the lobby. Casey's mind went to Elise. She had to warn her. She spun on her heel and made for the side door of the inn, but it was too late. Charles had spotted her.

He stormed across the lobby. "Where is she? Where's Elise?"

"I don't know what—"

"Save me the theatrics." Charles jabbed a finger in her face. "I saw a photo of Elise on the Swizzle-Telemark Facebook page."

Casey had no idea what he was talking about. Bernice handled all the social media for her two inns. Had she unwittingly posted a photo of Elise? She cringed at the possibility. "You must be mistaken. Elise isn't here."

As if on cue, Elise strode through the front door of the inn.

"There you are!" Charles lurched toward her and grabbed her arm.

"Get your hands off me!" Elise jerked away from him. "I don't know who you are."

"Bullshit!"

"I've never seen you in my life."

Charles snarled at her. "Smile," he barked.

"What?" Elise asked.

"I said smile."

She obliged, brandishing her two perfectly straight front teeth.

Charles seemed thrown off guard. Casey held her breath as she waited to see if it was enough to convince him it was a case of mistaken identity. Elise's hair was a lot shorter than the last time he'd seen her, and the Florida sunshine had lightened it considerably.

"So, you got your teeth fixed. I'm not fooled. I know it's you." Charles reached for her arm again.

Casey'd had enough. She pulled Charles away from Elise and pressed him against the wall. "This is private property. If you don't leave right now, I'll call the police."

Ricky and Bernice came up beside her and Charles threw his arms in the air. "Fine, I'll leave, but you haven't seen the last of me."

Casey released her grip and he shoved the door open.

Before he stepped outside, he spun back to face her. His nostrils flared and saliva bubbled from his lips. "You stole my wife!"

Casey planted both hands on her waist. "I did no such thing. And newsflash, she's not your wife."

Charles grunted and let the door of the inn slam behind him.

* * *

Elise pushed through the door after Charles.

Casey followed behind her but Elise waved her off. "Please, stay here. Give me a minute alone with him."

"The hell I will." Casey's eyes glowed with fury. "I don't trust that asshole as far as I can throw him. I'll let you do the talking but I'm standing guard."

Elise stepped on the porch and called after him. "Hold on!"

As he marched back toward her, she thanked her lucky stars that her mother was still up in New Jersey. She held her head high and looked him straight in the eye. "I'm begging you, please walk away and leave us alone."

When he opened his mouth to argue, Elise held up her hand. "Do I have to spell it out for you? I don't love you and I don't want to be your wife."

He stared back at her, like he couldn't believe the words had come from her mouth. He jammed his hand in the pockets of his perfectly pressed khakis and hung his head. For a second, she almost felt sorry for him.

When he finally spoke, his voice was barely above a whisper. "I'm sorry."

She wasn't sure what she'd been expecting him to say, but it wasn't that.

"I wanted to be with you so badly…I hope someday you can forgive me."

Before she could respond, he turned and trudged down the front steps of the inn. She watched him slink down the sidewalk.

He never looked back. When he was out of sight, she collapsed against the railing and sunk to the ground.

Casey picked her up and carried her back to the cottage.

As soon as they got inside, Elise burrowed her head into Casey's shoulder and cried until she had no more tears. When her sobs abated, she lifted her head and sought out Casey's kind blue eyes. "Thank you."

"For what?"

"For being my rock. For protecting me."

"You're welcome, baby, but based on what I just witnessed, you don't need protecting. You were so strong. The way you stood up to him. It was epic."

Pride shot through Elise. "I don't know what came over me. I got this burst of courage. And God, it felt so good to tell him off."

"I'm sure it did, but his showing up obviously opened the emotional floodgates. I need you to talk to me, tell me how you're feeling. We can't brush this aside and move on."

Elise took a few deep breaths as she thought about her answer. "Right now, I think I'm in a state of shock, but I'm also relieved. Life here with you…It's like living in a cocoon. Safe and warm. It's been easy to pretend the outside world doesn't exist but deep down I knew this day would come." Elise took both Casey's hands in her own. "Because of you, I had the strength to face it."

"Together we can get through anything."

"I know we can."

* * *

"Morning," Casey said when Elise's eyes blinked open the next morning. "You sleep okay?"

"Like a rock. I don't think I've slept that soundly, well, probably ever."

"How about we have breakfast and then go out on the boat. It would probably do us both good to spend the day outside. Just you, me and the sea."

Elise propped her head up on her hand. "That sounds perfect. But what about work?"

"I'm the boss. Let's play hooky."

Elise gave her a quick kiss on the lips. "Who am I to argue with that?"

After they ate, they drove to the marina and climbed onto Casey's twenty-three-foot Grady White. There wasn't a cloud in the sky and the water was like glass. With Elise nestled next to her on the captain's bench, Casey piloted out to her favorite shoal. They tied up to a buoy and jumped into the warm shallow water. Given it was a weekday morning, there wasn't another soul around.

Casey didn't think she'd ever been happier than she was at that moment. She sought out the sandy bottom with her feet and bounced into the air, splashing down into the water like a dolphin. She found the ground again and backflipped into a handstand. When she surfaced, Elise giggled and swam toward her. "If I didn't know better, I'd guess you were born in the sea. It's wonderful to see you so playful."

Casey plunged her head back into the water and circled Elise with just the point of her elbow sticking above the surface.

"Oooh, I'm so scared." Elise let out a mock squeal. "A big bad shark."

Casey popped out of the water and pulled Elise into her arms. "Don't worry, I'll save you."

"You already have."

Casey bent down and kissed her saltwater-slicked lips. An ache burned between her legs when their tongues met. She ran her hands up Elise's bare torso and slipped a hand beneath the cup of her bikini top. Elise's nipple hardened at her touch. Casey yanked the string of Elise's colorful top loose. It fell to the water, and her full breasts floated just below the surface.

Casey brushed her lips over Elise's ear and waved in the general direction of the nearby spit of sand. "I want nothing more than to drag you to the beach so I can have my way with you." She pulled back and twisted her lips into a pout. "But with my luck, the second I get your sexy naked body beneath me, a pleasure craft full of tourists will appear on the horizon."

A wicked grin crossed Elise's face. "Boat!" she hollered, and took off swimming toward the Grady White. "Last one in is a rotten egg."

Laughing hysterically, they both hoisted themselves over the stern of the boat and landed on the floor next to the outboard motor in a heap.

Casey peered over at Elise. Her chest was still bare and although a broad smile adorned her face, her eyes were hooded. Casey crawled on top of her and pinned her to the floor with a searing kiss. The throbbing between her legs became almost unbearable as Elise tugged at her faded tank top and yanked it over her head. Her jog bra went sailing after it and the cool breeze tickled her bare chest.

Elise rolled on top of her and guided Casey's hand to her breast. Casey caressed one and then the other before taking a hardened nipple into her mouth. When Elise moaned, Casey sucked harder. She trailed a hand down Elise's side and slipped a finger under the waistband of her skimpy bikini bottom. Elise rocked against her thigh and Casey got an idea. She rolled to a sitting position.

"What are you—"

Casey held a finger to her lips. "Shhhh." She pulled Elise to her feet, picked her up in her arms and carried her to the captain's bench in the middle of the boat. She gently set Elise on the white leather cushion and knelt before her. She spread Elise's legs and ran her hand along the inside of her thighs. Elise squirmed when Casey skimmed her fingers over the cloth of her bikini bottom. Casey pulled the fabric back and teased Elise with her tongue before stripping the garment down her legs and tossing it toward the hulking engine.

With both feet planted on the dashboard, Elise guided Casey between her legs. When Elise's middle began to tremble, Casey grabbed her ass and intensified the swipes with her tongue. Elise's whole body shook. "Oh, yes! I'm so close."

Seconds later, Elise's knees squeezed Casey's head before she crumbled across the bench. Casey gazed into her eyes. "That was the sexiest thing I've ever experienced."

Elise tugged her up on to the bench and circled Casey's bare nipples with the tips of her fingers. "Start the engine."

"What?"

"I said, start the engine. I want to do you while you drive the boat."

Casey obliged. She released the boat from the buoy and shifted it into gear. As she navigated away from the shoal, Elise untied her swim shorts and let them fall to the floor. "Drive faster," she whispered into Casey's ear.

Using one hand to massage Casey's breast, Elise scratched the other down her back. She pressed Casey against the steering wheel and entered her from behind, first with one finger and then with two. She wound her other arm around Casey's waist and worked her clit as she drove into her matching the rhythm of the boat bouncing over the waves. When Casey clenched around her fingers, she doubled down, moving with the thrusts of Casey's hips.

Casey stilled. Her head fell back, and she let out a long low moan. "Jesus Christ. I've never come that hard in my life." She collapsed against Elise. "Remind me to take you boating more often."

Elise came up beside her and took her hand. "This has been the best day of my life."

"You mean it?"

Elise nodded and reached up to run a hand through Casey's hair. "Yeah, I do."

Casey slowed the boat and snaked her hands behind Elise's head. Much to her surprise, she didn't even hesitate to say the words. Perhaps because they had been so much on her mind. "I love you, Elise. With all my heart."

After the glorious day out on the Grady White, Elise officially moved into Casey's cottage. The two women became inseparable and the dwindling weeks of winter in Key West sailed by. Before Casey knew it, Easter was upon them and it was time to head north, to her inn in Vermont, to prepare for the impending wedding season.

Elise's mother opted to stay in Key West. She'd moved in with Dora and volunteered three days a week at the animal shelter. Spending the next five months in Vermont was out the question, but she promised to visit. Elise and Casey loaded up the RV and meandered up the east coast together.

"Are you sure you're okay?" Casey asked as they crossed into Vermont. She'd been anxious about bringing Elise back there after the events of the previous fall.

"Yep." She rested a hand on Casey's thigh. "I'm excited to build new memories with you in Vermont."

Casey smiled. "That we can."

"No need to dwell on the past anymore. Charles has consumed enough of my life. I don't intend to let him gobble up any more of it."

Two hours later, when Casey pulled her RV up next to the barn behind the Telemark Inn, Elise jumped out and ran through the grass waving her hands in the air. "I'd forgotten how beautiful it is here."

The first wedding of the season was only two weeks away, and even though the Telemark stayed open through the winter to cater to the skiers, there was so much to do to get it in tip-top shape. But Casey was sure, no matter how hard they worked, the bride would find fault in something. She'd been a serious bridezilla every step of the way.

For that reason, Casey wasn't surprised when the groom called two days before he and bridezilla were due in Vermont. The wedding was off. She shared the news with her friend Freida as they caught up over coffee at the bakery in town. As the only Episcopal priest for nearly thirty miles, Freida presided over most weddings at the Telemark. "Well," Freida said, "better to get cold feet *before* the wedding rather than after."

Casey raised her coffee mug to that.

"I once had a bride who asked me to 'undo' her marriage an hour after she'd said, 'I do.'" Freida leaned back in her chair. "You happen to know anyone who wants to get married this Saturday? I suddenly find myself free."

Casey bolted upright. "Actually...don't go making any plans quite yet. There might be a wedding at the Telemark this weekend after all."

Frieda gave her a blank stare. "What do you—"

"Elise!" Casey sprung to her feet. "I'm going to ask her to marry me."

Frieda jumped up and pulled Casey into her arms. "I'd be honored to marry you two."

"Hold your horses, I've got to ask her first. She might say no." The anxiety hit Casey like a freight train. She gasped for a breath of air as she thought back to the last time she'd been about to propose. *This time is different. This time is very different.*

Frieda rubbed Casey's back and slipped a finger under her chin. "Look at me."

Casey complied.

"I see the way you and Elise look at each other, it's like nobody else exists."

Casey knew she was right. What she and Elise had was something Casey hadn't known was imaginable. She grabbed her phone off the table. "If you'll excuse me, I've got a wedding to plan." She kissed Frieda on the cheek and ran out of the café. First she called the owner of the local ski area. He was an old friend and he agreed to fire up the chairlift. Next, she called the florist. Assuming Elise said yes, Casey needed blue flowers and lots of them.

The next afternoon when Casey watched Elise walk up from the barn, her heart threatened to leap out of her chest. She grabbed the picnic basket and blanket off the counter, pulled the champagne from the fridge and dashed out to greet her.

"Where are we going?" Elise asked.

"You'll see."

The chairlift swayed as it glided up the mountain. Tall oak and maple trees flanked its path, their branches dotted with small green buds. The leaves on the ground rustled in the breeze.

The safety bar was lowered and Casey curled her hands tight around it as the chair crept further and further up the mountain. In her head, she recited the words she would soon utter to Elise.

"What a beautiful evening," Elise said.

"Yes, yes, it is." Casey sought out Elise's dark eyes with her own. She'd intended to pop the question when they reached the top of the mountain, but she couldn't hold the words back. "Will you marry me?"

Elise blinked a few times and tears welled up in her eyes. "Oh, my God. Yes. Yes! Nothing in the world would make me happier."

Casey took both her hands and kissed her softly on the lips. Her heart thumped. She felt certain that if she tried, she could fly. Thankfully, the safety bar held her firmly on the seat.

When they reached the top, Casey whipped out her phone.

"Who are you calling?"

"Your mom. She and Dora are all packed. They're just waiting for the thumbs-up."

When they wandered into the Telemark's dining room the night before the wedding, Elise burst into tears. Beautiful bouquets of blue flowers adorned every surface. Hanging baskets overflowing with delicate forget-me-nots circled the front porch of the inn.

"What's wrong, sweetheart?" Casey asked.

"Nothing's wrong. Everything's right. The flowers are beautiful. I can't believe you remembered."

Casey's heart swelled. She wrapped an arm around Elise's waist and placed a tender kiss on her lips. "Consider it your 'something blue'."

That evening, the inn's staff made an elaborate meal for Casey and Elise and a handful of their friends and family.

After dinner, Elise excused herself to go to the bathroom.

As the staff prepared to serve dessert, Casey grew concerned. Elise still hadn't returned to the table. She scanned the room. "Has anyone seen Elise?"

She sprung to her feet and darted through every room of the inn calling out, "Elise." Her voice grew more and more frantic. *This can't be happening again. There had to be an explanation.* She and Elise were soulmates. Elise would never run off. A terrifying thought sent a shiver up her spine. *What if it was Charles? What if Elise was in danger?*

Casey ran back through the kitchen but came to a halt when her eyes landed on the small door that led to the cellar. Maybe Elise was down there. It was the one place Casey hadn't checked.

The door creaked when she opened it. The cellar lights were on. That was odd. Casey scrambled down the stairs and scurried across the dirt floor toward the wine cellar. That's when she saw her. Elise's beautiful face looking back at her from the other side of the wine cellar's glass door.

Casey reached for the knob, yanked open the door and Elise fell into her arms. "Baby, are you okay?"

"I'm fine," Elise said. She held up a magnum of Dom Perignon. "I came to get this and I got locked inside."

Tears ran down Casey's cheeks. "I was so worried. I love you so much. I don't know what I'd do if I lost you."

Elise set down the champagne, slipped her hands into Casey's hair and kissed her. "I'll forever be by your side. You're the love of my life." She linked an arm through Casey's. "Now let's get back upstairs. We've got some celebrating to do. This time tomorrow, you'll be my wife."

LIBERTY

Kate Gavin

Laurie Jackson closed her bedroom door and stripped off her clothes. She gathered them into a ball and tossed them into the laundry basket on the floor of her walk-in closet.

She headed into the en suite bathroom and turned on the bathtub faucet, wanting the water to be as hot as she could stand it. Her muscles were sore from a long and tiring day and she looked forward to the relief a steaming bath could provide.

She pulled out her hair tie and let out a slow, contented moan, or maybe it was more of a groan. After the day she'd had, she was looking forward to some alone time. She had spent the day running last-minute errands with Sarah, her best friend and sister-in-law. Tomorrow was Sarah's big day—her wedding day. After the errands, the wedding rehearsal and dinner had followed. They spent their night drinking wine and writing out puns on popsicle sticks, which would be set out at each table in mason jars as an icebreaker for guests at the reception.

The shared bottles of wine led to Sarah passing out in the guest room down the hall. Of course, Laurie made sure Sarah was in a proper position in case she got sick. Letting the bride die before her wedding day would eliminate any future bridesmaid prospects.

She dipped a foot into the tub, resisting the urge to pull it out of the hot water. She'd adjust to it soon enough. Slipping in until the water hit just below her shoulders, she shut off the faucet with her foot and leaned back. She closed her eyes and enjoyed the stillness. Tomorrow was going to be as much of a whirlwind as today, and she sent a silent plea to the universe for Sarah to have the wedding of her dreams.

Sarah had been Laurie's best friend since seventh grade and had joined her family when Sarah and her older sister, Rowan, had moved in with Laurie and her dad after their parents had died in a car accident. They legally became family after Laurie married Rowan three years ago. Now it was time for Sarah to marry Joel, and Laurie wanted everything to be perfect for her best friend. As matron of honor and the only bridesmaid, she'd had her hands full over the last several months and she thought she was more nervous about the day than Sarah.

Her thoughts drifted to her own wedding. She and Rowan had married in a small ceremony outside of Denver. The months of planning had passed easily and quickly. They had always been on the same page when it came to every decision that needed to be made. Once the wedding week had arrived, though, Laurie had been a bundle of nerves, not because she was nervous about marrying Rowan, but because she wanted everyone to have a good time.

When their photographer had taken them to a secluded area inside a small forest of fir trees for their first look, Laurie's anxiety melted away when Rowan tapped her on the shoulder. A calm washed over her when she faced her soon-to-be wife and she was certain Rowan was the right person for her. No matter the situation, one word, touch, or look from Rowan brought her a peace she'd never known.

Too bad that source of calm would be absent tomorrow. Rowan was currently deployed to Germany with the United States Air Force. It was her second deployment and Laurie didn't find it any easier than the first. Periodically she still reached for the empty side of the bed, but each time her hand came up empty. It was like a punch to the stomach. At least Rowan was stationed in Germany this time instead of Afghanistan and communication occurred more frequently. She was able to text at random times during the day and have regular phone calls. But she still counted how long Rowan had been gone—eight months, three weeks, two days, and seven hours. She was scheduled to come home in three months and Laurie begged the universe to keep that timeline intact.

The drumbeat of her ringtone jerked her upright, splashing water onto the floor in the process. She snatched her phone off the counter and smiled as she read the caller ID. "Hey, you."

"Hey, yourself. How's my beautiful wife?"

"Good, especially now that I'm talking to you. But I'd be even better if I could see your face. No video?"

Rowan cleared her throat. "Ah, no. Sorry. Internet connection has been spotty since last night."

Laurie dropped the tone of her voice and purred, "Oh, that's too bad. You would've gotten a nice view."

"Really? What are you wearing? Maybe that skimpy red number I got you for your birthday?"

"I'm not wearing anything at all."

She groaned. "Fuck. That's even better."

"You know, we could have…" Laurie heard a distant voice and then silence. She pulled the phone away to see if the call was still connected. "Ro? You there?"

"Y-yeah. Sorry. It was just, um, a base announcement. Little too loud." She sighed. "Look, I know what you're going to ask and I would love to, but I actually need to go."

"What do you mean? You just called me."

She closed her eyes and held back a sigh. She understood that interruptions happened, and Rowan usually called at the right times to mitigate shortened calls. Laurie's chest tightened as the disappointment took over. The heartache of knowing Rowan wouldn't be here tomorrow had already put her in a shitty mood and cutting the call short threatened to push her over the edge.

"I'm sorry. I know. I gotta go. I'll try to call you later, okay?"

"Oh. Okay." She needed to be strong and she hoped Rowan couldn't sense how upset she truly felt. "You do what you need to do, babe."

"I love you so much," Rowan said.

"I love you too. Until next time."

"Until next time."

The call disconnected and Laurie stared at the phone in her hands. The background picture was Rowan holding up a cup of coffee with a wide smile, showing off the engagement ring Laurie had given her the night before. She relaxed against the tub as she thought back to that night.

Laurie had planned for the proposal for months, but when the time came, nothing went right. She had booked a weekend away for them, but in the week leading up to it, there was one disaster followed by another. First, their water heater leaked and they needed to replace it. Two days later, their golden retriever, Scout, had cut her paw on some glass during a walk and needed stitches. Then on the morning they were set to leave, Laurie was called in to work since the coworker she'd ask to cover for her was out with food poisoning.

Once she'd gotten home from work, Laurie's stress bubbled over and she picked a fight with Rowan about something stupid like laundry. Right in the middle of it, she had yelled at Rowan, "Marry me!" She'd stunned them both into silence. What followed had been tears, Rowan saying yes, and incredible sex that had lasted well after midnight. Despite the rocky start, their relationship had been smooth sailing ever since.

She blew out a breath and emptied the tub. After drying off, she slipped into bed and held the phone in her hand, willing it to ring again. She gave up after a few minutes and turned on her side, still clinging to the phone as she slid her hands under her pillow. She pictured Rowan's bright blue eyes and drifted off to sleep.

The shrill alarm pulled Laurie from sleep. She refused to open her eyes as she blindly tapped the screen on her phone until the god-awful sound stopped. She yawned so wide that both sides of her jaw popped. Letting her eyelids flutter open, she gasped and sat up, making sure to cover her chest with a sheet.

Once her brain registered Sarah staring back at her with a grin, she took a deep breath and settled against her pillow. "What the hell? How long have you been there?"

Sarah chuckled, pushed herself onto her elbow and propped her head in her hand. "Since four."

Laurie grabbed her free hand and intertwined their fingers in the empty space between them. "Oh, sweetie. That was three hours ago. Why didn't you wake me?"

"You looked so peaceful so I figured I'd curl up with you and try to sleep. But when I slipped my arm around you, I realized you were naked. So I slipped it right back to my side and fell asleep for like an hour. Didn't want you waking up to that kind of awkwardness," Sarah replied as she scrunched her nose.

Laurie snorted and rolled her eyes. "I appreciate that. But you still could have woken me before now."

"I tried. When I woke up again, I poked at your nose until you smacked my hand away, and you haven't moved since. I'm just thankful you didn't smack me with your phone hand." She pointed down to Laurie's other hand, clutching her phone. "Late night talking to Rowan?"

"No. After I put your drunk ass to bed, she called while I was taking a bath but she had to cut our call short. I was hoping she'd call again, but no dice." Laurie shrugged.

"I wasn't that bad. It was only a couple…okay, several drinks," she replied before rolling onto her back and staring up at the ceiling. "I'm sorry she couldn't make it back."

"No, I'm the one who should be sorry. It's your day. I hate that she's going to miss it." She frowned thinking how unfair it was that Rowan was missing her sister's wedding. Over the past few weeks, Laurie had tried to get Sarah to talk about it, but every time she brought it up, Sarah brushed it off like it was no big deal and changed the subject.

Sarah turned away from Laurie, her chest rising and falling with a few deep breaths. When she met Laurie's gaze again, she gave her a thin smile and shrugged. "We'll just have to celebrate again when she's home."

"Deal." Laurie looked down at her phone. "Okay, time for breakfast and packing everything up. We need to be at the venue in two hours."

"So bossy," Sarah grumbled. She stuck out her tongue and retreated from the room. Laurie needed to put aside any sadness when it came to missing Rowan. Sarah was also missing her and it was unfair for Laurie to bring it up again. Sarah deserved to have her dream wedding, and it was Laurie's goal to make today as perfect as possible.

After a quick breakfast, Sarah relaxed while Laurie packed her car with their dresses and some last-minute items for Emily, the wedding planner. They drove to the venue singing along to a playlist Sarah had created the day after Joel proposed. They had been adding love and wedding-themed songs to it ever since. Several songs reminded her of Rowan so it was a little bittersweet whenever those songs played.

Laurie pulled into a parking space at the front of the venue, an old barn at the center of an actual working vegetable farm. Emily directed vendors as flowers, tables, and chairs were carried inside. A lot was going on, but it seemed controlled chaos rather than hectic and stress-inducing pandemonium. She gathered their bags as Emily's assistant took the dresses and led them inside.

Laurie glanced at the soft yellow lights strung from the ceiling, the white drapes perfectly hung in the front room, and the dark wooden chairs workers set up in neat rows. It was beautiful and exactly how she imagined it would look for her best friend's wedding.

They were escorted into the bridal room and instructed to get ready immediately. Laurie sat in the makeup chair while Sarah sat with the hair stylist and eventually they swapped. The time passed quickly with easy conversation, singing to the wedding playlist, and enjoying mimosas and snacks that Emily brought them throughout the late morning and into the early afternoon.

Around three the photographer and videographer arrived to take pictures of them getting ready. Laurie did her best to look as natural as possible with each shutter click she heard. She wasn't the biggest fan of photos because she always felt photographers caught her when she was giving them the weirdest looks. Whenever she felt herself tensing up, she focused on Sarah's brilliant smile and contagious giddiness. Seeing her best friend at her happiest could always soothe any discomfort.

When the makeup artist and hair stylist deemed her ready, Laurie quickly changed out of her sweats and flannel button-up shirt and into her bridesmaid dress. It was a one-shoulder, floor-length chiffon dress in periwinkle with a flowy bottom half that had a slit up one side. She slipped into her ballet flats, giving herself a quick check in the tall mirror. Satisfied, she turned to Sarah, who was getting a touch-up on her lipstick. "Ready to get in your dress?"

Sarah hopped off her chair and clasped her hands in front of her chest. "Beyond ready."

The photographer and videographer stepped out of the room to give Sarah privacy. Laurie took the dress off the hanger and held it open by her feet. It wasn't a very elaborate dress so she didn't need much help getting into it, but once it was on, that was another story entirely. The dress had over a dozen buttons that went up the back, and it was Laurie's job to secure them.

When Sarah tugged the dress up her hips and slipped her hands through the sleeves, Laurie called out into the hallway, "You can come back in."

The photographer and videographer re-entered the room, snapping pictures and calling out cues. As Laurie slowly buttoned up the back of the dress, she admired the beauty of the lacy dress with long illusion sleeves and a sweetheart neckline. Even though she'd seen Sarah in the dress several times before, she couldn't ignore the sting of tears in her eyes as she gazed at her.

The photographer instructed them to hug and give each other sweet, adoring looks which they didn't need to be told to do. She dabbed at her eyes with a tissue as she stood back so they could get individual shots of Sarah standing by the large windows at the end of the room.

Within a few minutes, the photographer had the shots she wanted and it was time to head outside. Sarah wore an odd look on her face, not necessarily nervous. Maybe anxious excitement.

Laurie stood in front of Sarah, holding on to her shoulders. "Ready to see your hubby-to-be?"

"Yeah, of course," she replied with a watery smile.

"Just take a few deep breaths." Sarah obeyed and Laurie took those breaths along with her. "There you go. This is the day you've been waiting for ever since you barged into our dorm room senior year and told me you'd met the hottest, dorkiest guy and you were going to marry him someday. Well, sweetie, that day is here. Let's go see him."

"Are you sure I look okay?" Sarah looked down at her dress as she wrung her hands together.

Laurie lifted Sarah's chin to meet her gaze. "You look absolutely beautiful. And I bet you will take Joel's breath away when he sees you."

"Thanks."

"That's what I'm here for. I'm your hype woman."

Sarah chuckled. "You're also a big goofball."

On the way out of the room, Laurie picked up each of their bouquets while Sarah hitched her dress off the ground. Laurie slowed as Sarah and the photographer walked ahead.

Sarah and Joel had their own semiprivate first look for a few minutes while Laurie stood off to the side with Adam, Joel's older brother and best man.

"You look beautiful, Laurie," Adam said as he bent down to kiss her cheek.

"Thanks. You're looking quite dapper yourself."

He adjusted his black bowtie with mock arrogance. "What can I say? I clean up quite well."

"That you do."

"They look so happy, don't they?" he said as Joel held Sarah's face and gently kissed her.

"Yeah, they really do."

He cleared his throat. "I'm sorry Rowan couldn't make it. I know they still feel bad that they couldn't wait until she was home."

"It's okay. I totally get it and so does Rowan."

Joel and Adam's mom had been diagnosed with terminal cancer six months ago and her doctor figured she only had about a year left. As soon as she had learned of the diagnosis, Sarah was adamant they get married as soon as possible. She called Rowan and explained the situation, and without hesitation, Rowan agreed that moving up the wedding was the right thing to do.

With a bump to his hip, Laurie said, "She just asks that we celebrate when she gets home. She even threw around the idea of a reenactment, so you might have to get all fancy again."

"I don't know. That'll be one hell of a hardship." He winked and then nodded to the photographer who was waving at them. "Looks like they're ready for us."

For the next hour, they took pictures around the farm. It could have felt monotonous but the photographer kept them laughing, indulging them whenever they goofed off or made silly faces at each other.

Once they finished, everyone headed inside the barn and Sarah and Joel separated with a quick kiss. Laurie set the bouquets on a table inside the room and said, "Be right back. Just need to use the bathroom. You should do that too before everything gets started."

"Yes, ma'am," Sarah said with a small salute.

When she returned to the bridal suite, Sarah was hunched over on the other side of the room, talking quietly into her phone. "Love you too. See you soon."

Laurie snorted and Sarah turned, wide-eyed, gripping her phone to her chest. Laurie teased, "Wow. You just finished pictures with the guy and you'll be walking down the aisle in…" She looked at the clock on the wall. "Ten minutes. Couldn't wait that long to talk to him again?"

Sarah let out a long breath but didn't reply. She cleared her throat and set her phone on the table before adjusting her hair in the mirror.

Laurie noticed the thin line of Sarah's lips and hurried over to stand behind her. She rested her hands on her shoulders and gave them a light squeeze. "Hey, what's wrong? Are you nervous?"

"I'm okay. I promise," she replied, smiling back at her in the mirror. "Big day, ya know?"

"It is. But everything is fine. You and Joel are perfect for each other. And I'm so happy for you," she said, swallowing back a fresh hit of tears.

Sarah stood and pointed a finger at her. "No. No tears."

She wrapped her in a hug. "You know I'm the emotional one," she said, sniffling into Sarah's neck.

"I know. One of the many reasons I love you. We balance each other out."

Laurie chuckled. "Yes, we do."

A knock at the door pulled them apart and she carefully drew a finger under her eyes to stop the tears. Emily poked her head inside. "I'll be lining you up in two minutes. Fix whatever needs to be fixed and meet me in the back."

"We'll be there," Laurie replied before turning to Sarah. "Okay, last-minute checks. Hair, good. Makeup, good. Got everything? Old, new, borrowed, blue," she muttered as she noted Sarah's mom's ruby earrings, the diamond bracelet Joel gave her earlier, and the hair clip Laurie had worn on her wedding day. With wide eyes, she asked, "Wait, where's the blue? Where's your dad's handkerchief?" A year after their parents died, Sarah and Rowan went through their belongings and Sarah had kept her dad's handkerchief that had been embroidered with his initials ever since. "Do you have it?"

Sarah snapped her fingers and looked away. "No. I must have forgotten it."

"Forgotten it? I thought we double-checked everything before we left the house. Are you sure?"

She was about to reach into the pockets of Sarah's dress, because yes it was amazing and had pockets, when Sarah stopped her with a light grasp. "It's on its way." She opened her mouth to ask where it was but Sarah said, "I left it at my house. That, um, wasn't Joel on the phone. It was actually your dad. He was telling me he found it and was almost here."

"But he's walking you down the aisle," Laurie replied, throwing her hands in the air.

"And that means we can't get this party started until he gets here. He'll be here soon. I promise."

"Wait. When did you realize it was missing?"

Her gaze darted around the room for a moment. "Um, earlier."

"Earlier when? Why didn't you say anything? Sarah, it's almost time for the wedding to start."

"Okay, now it's your turn to take a deep breath." Sarah squeezed her hand as Laurie took a slow breath. "Don't worry, he'll be back in plenty of time. Everything will be okay."

"I know. I just didn't want you to be stressed today. Everything needs to be perfect for you."

"It already has been. And that's because of you and all your hard work. I owe you big time."

Laurie waved her off. "Nah. You did the same for me. I think we're even." She took another deep breath and extended her elbow to Sarah. "Shall we?"

"We shall."

Sarah looped her arm through Laurie's as they proceeded through the back hallway and into the lobby. A heavy, dark gray curtain shielded the guests from this area. Adam stood with his hands in his pockets as he stared out the back doors that led to the parking lot.

He turned to face them, his eyes lighting up as he spotted Sarah. "Ready to join the family officially? You know you've been a part of our family since the first day Joel brought you home."

"I am. Are you ready for it?"

"Of course. I know my little brother is in great hands."

Laurie smiled at him and asked, "Have you seen my dad?"

He opened his mouth to reply but stopped when Emily slipped through the curtain, holding it closed behind her back.

"Guests are seated. Joel and the officiant are standing at the front. Everyone ready?"

Laurie frowned. "Not quite. My dad isn't here. He had to run back to Sarah's place for her something blue."

Emily's mouth quirked up, but she didn't seem concerned as she quickly glanced at her watch. "Right. Almost forgot about that. He's on his way, correct?" She raised her eyebrows at Sarah.

"Yep," she said, biting at the corner of her lip.

"No problem then. We can wait a—" She looked over Sarah's shoulder and into the parking lot. "Is that him?"

Laurie turned and saw her dad's navy SUV pull into a parking space. "That's him."

"See. I told you he'd be back in time," Sarah said, giving her a knowing look.

Laurie held up her hands. "Okay, okay. Time to get you hitched."

Emily whispered into her headset and peeked through the curtain. "Adam, Laurie. You're up."

Adam extended his arm and Laurie slid her hand through and held on to his elbow. "I promise not to let you fall."

Laurie grinned. "I appreciate that."

She looked back and gave Sarah a wink before taking a deep breath and focusing on the aisle in front of her as Emily opened the curtain. Everyone turned in their seats and gave them their full attention. Adam rested his hand on top of hers and Laurie reminded herself to smile so she wouldn't look nervous for the photographer. She didn't particularly enjoy being the center of attention so events like this always felt odd to her. As they continued to their designated spots, she nodded at friends and family.

When they reached the front, Adam squeezed her hand, kissed her cheek, and let her go so they could step to their respective sides. She smiled at Joel and tears pricked her eyes as she saw his lips quiver as he smiled back, joy and excitement glimmering in his eyes.

The music changed to a new instrumental and Laurie watched as everyone turned in their seats, just waiting for the curtain to open so they could see Sarah walk down the aisle.

Today wasn't Laurie's first time being a bridesmaid, but it was definitely the time that meant the most to her. She had done a good job keeping her emotions in check for most of the day but looking around the room threatened to undo it all. Each person had a wide smile and anticipatory glint in their eyes. Everyone who loved Sarah and Joel was present.

Well, almost everyone. Rowan's absence was magnified when Laurie looked toward the front row where her dad would sit after he walked Sarah down the aisle. She frowned for a moment at the empty seat where Rowan should be sitting. Instead, someone had taped a picture to the back of the chair of Rowan with her arm slung around Sarah's shoulder as they looked at each other with wide smiles. It had been taken by a friend at a party a couple weeks before Rowan deployed.

Laurie pulled her gaze away from the chair and took a deep breath and let it out slowly, willing herself to stay calm and focus on the moment. Within seconds she'd see Sarah in a new light. It didn't matter that she had spent the whole day with her. Seeing her now as she walked toward the new chapter in her life was a momentous occasion and Laurie was grateful to be a part of it.

Emily's hand gripped the curtain as she pulled it back. Laurie's gaze focused on the bright smile on Sarah's face, but when she turned to look at the person escorting her, she sucked in a breath.

Standing next to Sarah was Rowan.

"Holy fuck," Laurie whispered as she covered her mouth to stifle a cry.

Joel chuckled, "Good thing we're not in a church."

What was going on? How was she here? Laurie stood glued to her spot. She wanted to run down the aisle and wrap her arms around her wife, but she didn't yet fully understand what was happening. Rowan was supposed to be in Germany. She was supposed to be missing this. She wasn't supposed to be fifty feet away looking as handsome as ever in her dress blues.

Laurie's hand still covered her mouth and she started to cry. Her heartbeat quickened as they approached. She glanced at Sarah, who gave her a wink, as if to say, "Gotcha."

Rowan mouthed, "It's okay," and Laurie nodded, removing her hand and taking a few shuddering breaths. She shuffled her feet and bounced up on her toes as Sarah and Rowan closed the final distance.

Sarah let go of Rowan's arm and nudged her forward. "Now go on and kiss her. We both know she's who you're here for."

Rowan quickly hugged Sarah and stepped in front of Laurie, reaching for her free hand that wasn't holding a bouquet. "Hey there, beautiful."

Laurie threw her arms around Rowan and clung to her, burying her face in her neck. She whispered, "How is this possible? You weren't supposed to be here."

"Surprise," Rowan chuckled.

She pulled away and stared into the watery, blue eyes of her wife before leaning in for a kiss. As soon as their lips met, she let out a sigh. Rowan was home. She was with her, here and now. Rowan held onto her face as they kissed, brushing her thumb along her cheek.

"Okay, okay. Can I get married now?"

Sarah's voice pulled them out of their little bubble and the crowd laughed. Rowan rolled her eyes. "Sure thing, sis." She gave Laurie a quick peck on the lips and took her seat next to Laurie's dad.

Laurie pointed at Sarah. "I'm gonna have a talk with you later."

"Okay, but for now, how about you take my flowers and let me get married?"

She took several breaths to calm her still racing heart as the officiant started the ceremony. She knew she should pay attention to everything he was saying, but she couldn't stop her gaze from landing on Rowan every now and then. She hadn't seen her wife in person in almost nine months, and to have her here today felt surreal, and she still wondered if it was all a dream.

As Joel and Sarah turned to each other for their vows, Laurie didn't even try to stop the tears that had started to fall again. Warmth filled her and her cheeks hurt from constant smiling.

Sarah and Joel were pronounced husband and wife, and as they kissed, everyone stood and applauded. Laurie held Rowan's gaze until Sarah reached out to take her bouquet. She handed it over, looped her arm through Adam's, and they made their way up the aisle.

As soon as he released her, she gently gripped Sarah's wrist and spun her around. "You are such a sneaky little shit." She wrapped Sarah in a tight hug. "And I love you for it."

"I love you too." They held each other for a moment. "So, good surprise?"

Laurie pulled back and held her by the shoulders. "Are you fucking kidding me? It was the best." She crossed her arms. "To be honest, I can't believe you pulled it off."

"I know, right? It was so hard, especially when you got all mopey whenever you mentioned her not being able to come."

"I didn't get mopey," she muttered.

"Keep telling yourself that." Sarah pointed behind her. "Speaking of, here she comes now."

Laurie turned and found Rowan, her dad, and other guests walking through the doorway previously closed by the curtain. The area where they were milling about would be transformed into the space for cocktail hour. She dropped her bouquet onto a nearby table and pulled Rowan to a quieter corner of the room, cupping her face in her hands. "I still can't believe you're here."

"Me neither," she replied, her gaze dropping to Laurie's lips.

"Well, now that you are, I really think you should kiss me."

"Sounds tough, but orders are orders." Rowan grinned.

Laurie closed the distance quickly and planted a firm kiss on her lips. The people and noise around her faded away and she got lost in Rowan's taste and the natural way their lips always seemed to move.

Too soon, she felt a tap on her shoulder. "I hate to break this up, but we need to take some family photos," Sarah said.

Laurie pulled away with a groan. "Can't I have a little time with my wife?"

"Later. Now, photos."

Trying not to pout, Laurie grabbed Rowan's hand and walked to the front of the room where the photographer gave them instructions.

During each photo where Laurie and Rowan stood together, Rowan took the opportunity to let her hands wander. The first time they faced each other and Rowan trailed her finger through the slit in Laurie's dress and along the back of her thigh. She fought against the shudder that spread through her and she stopped Rowan with a discreet hand on her wrist and a glare.

After about twenty minutes of various photo combinations, Laurie was standing next to Sarah with Rowan and Joel on the outside. Sarah leaned over and whispered, "They're taking us out to a bridge on the other side of the property for some sunset photos so the bridal room will be empty." She caught her gaze with raised eyebrows.

"Really?"

"Yes, really. Just be ready to be announced at six thirty."

"Oh, thank you."

Once they had been dismissed and Joel and Sarah headed outside, Laurie gripped Rowan's hand and practically dragged her away from everyone and into the bridal room. She closed the door behind them and pushed Rowan against it, clutching the lapels of her uniform coat. She crushed their lips together, enjoying the hint of pain when Rowan bit down on her bottom lip.

She groaned as she pulled away and peppered kisses down the side of her neck. "God, I've missed you so much." She unbuttoned Rowan's coat and reached for her shirttail, but Rowan stopped her with a hand on her wrist.

"Wait. Hold on. We don't have a lot of time and I really need to touch you." Rowan grabbed her waist and pushed her backward until she hit a table. "Sit."

Laurie pulled her dress above her thighs. She watched as Rowan slowly took her coat off and hung it on a chair.

"It's so nice that dresses give me easy access." Rowan licked her lips. "Spread your legs." Laurie complied and Rowan stepped between them, lightly trailing her fingers up the side of her leg.

When she reached her center, she groaned. "My, my. Someone doesn't need any warming up. You're so wet," she whispered against her ear.

"Well, someone was doing some rather blatant teasing just a few minutes ago. Can you blame me?"

Rowan chuckled, "Not at all."

Laurie shivered as Rowan pushed her underwear aside and slid a finger through her slit. She gasped and clamped her hand around Rowan's bicep. "Fuck, baby. Inside. I need you inside."

Rowan complied and Laurie clenched around it. She gripped the back of Laurie's neck and roughly brought their lips together, increasing her pace as she slid her tongue along Laurie's bottom lip and then inside her mouth. They groaned in unison when she added a second finger.

Laurie tried to pay attention to the straining muscles underneath her hand as she held Rowan's arm, anything to distract her from her impending climax. It had been months since Rowan had touched her and she didn't want to come too soon. She wanted to revel in the feel of her. The smell. The taste. She wanted this to last forever. But with every stroke, Rowan curled her fingers forward and she needed more. When she swept her thumb over her clit, Laurie's head fell back and she let out a low moan.

Rowan gently nipped at the length of her neck until she reached her ear. "Shh. You need to be quiet."

Laurie let her head come forward and rest against Rowan's forehead as she nodded. Her breathing quickened and she knew she was close. "Faster. Please. Almost. There."

Rowan pumped faster and Laurie shut her eyes as the climax hit her and she felt it from her head to her toes. She buried her face in Rowan's neck to stifle her moans. Her breathing slowed along with Rowan's strokes and she held her close with her fingers still inside.

All of a sudden, tears pricked her eyes, and instead of muffling a moan against Rowan's neck, she had to hold back a sob.

Rowan pulled away to meet her gaze. "What's wrong? Did I hurt you?"

She started to pull out but Laurie grasped her wrist. "No. Stay. It's just…I really missed you."

"I missed you too." She wiped away a tear on her cheek before pulling her close. This time Rowan brought their lips together in an achingly slow kiss, as if she could only convey her feelings with this one moment.

They broke apart with a gasp when someone knocked on the door.

"Time's up, lovebirds. Make yourselves presentable and meet us in the bar area in two minutes. It's time to be announced," Sarah yelled.

"Shit," Laurie hissed. She hopped off the table and straightened her dress. As she checked herself in the mirror, she heard Rowan murmur in pleasure and looked up to see her licking her fingers with a wicked grin.

"Guess this taste will have to tide me over until later."

She whimpered, "You can't say things like that when we have to wait so long for round two. That's so not fair."

Rowan chuckled and washed her hands in the small sink at the other end of the room. "Sorry."

Laurie stepped behind her and wrapped her arms around her waist. "Don't worry. You'll get yours when we get home tonight."

Rowan turned in her embrace. "Counting on it," she replied with a quick kiss.

As Rowan straightened her sleeves and put on her jacket, Laurie took one last look at herself in the mirror and reapplied her lipstick. She glanced over at Rowan and chuckled, pointing to her lips. "You might want to fix that."

Rowan turned and looked in the mirror. "Huh?" Her eyes widened as she took in her reflection. "Shit," she muttered as she grabbed some paper towels and wet them under the faucet. She roughly rubbed all the spots where Laurie's lips had left their mark—her lips, her cheek, her neck, even her ear.

"Sorry, not sorry," Laurie said with a shrug.

As she tossed the paper towels in the trash, she rolled her eyes. "What am I going to do with you?"

Laurie twisted the door handle but didn't open the door. "I don't know. Maybe you should punish me later."

Rowan opened her mouth to reply but closed it when Laurie opened the door. "Now you can't say things to me like that."

Laurie winked. "Payback's a bitch, ain't it?" Rowan huffed and Laurie grabbed her hand and led her down the hallway.

Out in the bar, she could clearly hear and feel the bass from the DJ's speakers. As they walked farther into the room, Sarah noticed them and grinned. "Have fun?"

"Not nearly enough," Rowan grumbled.

Laurie smacked her stomach and changed the subject. "So, is it time?"

"Yep. Sorry, Rowan, you'll have to head in and take your seat."

"No problem." She kissed Laurie and smiled. "See you out there."

Laurie bit her lip and watched Rowan walk away. Sarah snapped her fingers in front of her face. "Sorry. What were you saying?"

Sarah rolled her eyes. "I was *saying*…You'll walk out with Adam down the center of the room and up to the head table. Once we're in there and as soon as people sit down, you'll be up to start your speech."

Oh boy…the speech. She hadn't thought about it at all, too distracted by the hustle and bustle of the day. And then, of course, by Rowan, which was her favorite distraction by far. She'd had her speech written weeks ago, which had kept her nerves at bay. She shook her head and blew out a breath, shifting her focus to the upcoming task. "Let's do this."

She held out her hand to Adam just as the song changed. Emily signaled for them to start. They hadn't planned any kind of dance for their walk across the room so they just smiled and waved to folks they knew until they reached their table where they separated. Laurie stayed standing and Rowan stood alongside her as the DJ started his introduction of Sarah and Joel. They made their way toward the table, showered in applause, whistles, and cheers.

The rest of the evening went by in a blur. There were speeches and dances. Great food and an open bar. Everyone who knew Rowan was excited to see her home and they spent a fair amount of time stopping by each table to say hi and ask how she pulled off her surprise. By the time they had finished with the last table, Laurie was ready for some seat time at the head table, cooling off with a glass of wine.

But Rowan had other ideas. She reached out her hand and gave a slight bow. "May I have this dance?"

Laurie frowned at the up-tempo pop song. She really didn't want to dance to something so fast. She was about to decline and suggest they sit for a bit instead, when the song changed to something much slower, something familiar. She instantly recognized her and Rowan's first dance song at their wedding, an acoustic version of, "I Choose You" by Sara Bareilles.

"Did you ask him to play this?" Rowan simply shrugged. Laurie took her hand and intertwined their fingers. "You are such a softy."

As they made their way to the dance floor and Laurie wrapped her arms around Rowan's shoulders, Rowan said, "Only when it comes to you."

She gave her a smile and a gentle kiss. "And cheesy too. Must be why I love you."

Rowan chuckled and pulled her close. They swayed to the music and Laurie was unaware of anything else. She felt Rowan's heartbeat as their chests pressed together and she rested her hand at the base of her neck, toying with a few small strands of hair that had come out of her bun.

She felt Rowan take a deep breath before she said, "You know, I was thinking…"

Laurie pulled back, narrowing her eyes. "Good thinking or bad thinking?"

"Good thinking. At least, I think so. You will too. I hope."

"Okay. Go on."

"I don't want to extend and I'm ready to switch to inactive reserve."

"But I thought—"

"I'm ready to be home."

Laurie was thrilled at the prospect. She had always been supportive of Rowan's career but selfishly she missed her wife. "Are you sure? You know I will support you if you want to get your years in and retire. I thought that was your initial plan."

"It was but things change. And maybe it's time to start thinking about expanding our family?"

Her eyes widened and she felt the sting of tears. "Really?" she whispered.

"Yes, really. I want everything with you, Laurie. Kids, memories, maybe a new house for all of those kids."

"Uh-oh. How many kids do we need for a new house?"

Rowan laughed quietly. "Two? Three? I just know that I'm ready for our next chapter to start." She licked her lips as her eyes got misty. "I promise to love you each and every day…"

Tears fell and Laurie's bottom lip quivered as she finished the last line of their vows in unison with Rowan. "…through whatever life may bring."

GROUNDS FOR PANIC

M.B. Guel

Marnie sighed, looking at the sad animals in the lobby. Her overnight shift at the vet clinic was exhausting and the stream of injured animals broke her heart. Being a vet tech was supposed to be her dream, but she was starting to wonder if she was too soft.

A message from Jenna blinked onto her phone.

Hey, mind stopping by The Filling Station today about catering?

She had almost forgotten Jenna wanted to see if she could get the coffee shop to do a coffee bar at dessert hour of her wedding. It was a bit of an ask since the wedding was two months away, but Jenna saw the idea on Pinterest and had to have it.

Marnie *should* say she'd deal with it tomorrow. Getting off at six in the morning was enough of an excuse, but the strong people pleaser part of her told her to say yes. It was the hardest part of her personality to break.

Two seconds later she was typing. *Send me the address. :)*

Bonus, the owner is cute and queer. If I wasn't in love with Kate…

Marnie snorted. If they were cute, they were taken. She scanned the lobby where a little dog was limping around. She frowned in pity and pushed curly, dark hair behind her ear.

She just needed her shift to end without any more sad patients to make her rethink her career.

Finally it was time. She quickly changed out of her scrubs before heading out, tight jeans on her thick, curvy frame and an old tie-dyed T-shirt tied up near her waist, pausing to pet a dog out front for a quick serotonin boost.

Working graveyards was weird. She always got a burst of energy for the first couple of hours, and even after eight hours in the harsh fluorescence of the vet hospital, she would do some errands before crashing at home, until it was time to start her day around five at night.

Being Jenna's Maid of Honor was expected. She'd been looking forward to it since Jenna met Kate almost three years ago, and to be honest, she was *killing* it. Uncomplicated emotional support was her jam.

She suppressed a yawn as she pulled into the parking lot of the coffee shop. It looked like an old gas station with the tiny overhang out front painted a light yellow with white trim and windows all around. The old cherry-red gas pumps were out front, the shop's logo in the top bubble: a coffee cup that looked like a gas can that said Filling Station.

She admired the cute shop. She was surprised she hadn't at least driven past it before, but she rarely ventured to the west side of town.

She raised an eyebrow at the number of people in line, slipping past them to go inside. She was hit in the face with the aroma of brewing coffee. The sound of the steam from the espresso machine rang over the loud chatter of the patrons inside.

The shop was about as long as two cars and half as deep. The counter looked original to the place and was maybe ten feet away from the entrance with an old diner menu with plastic lettering stuck to the surface. There was a vintage register on the counter and a beautiful espresso machine beside it. The decor was decidedly eclectic but somehow worked. Little round tables smashed against bookshelves littered with plants, books, and gas station memorabilia. Someone bumped into the back of her as they tried to come in, and Marnie apologized, quickly moving away from the door and toward the end of the counter where people were waiting for their drinks. She saw one worker behind the counter, furiously adding steamed milk to a row of drinks.

She fidgeted nervously for a moment, pulling her plump, pink lip between her teeth. She wanted just to get the catering info and get out, but there was no visible flier or card to take. After driving all the way here she figured the logical thing to do was ask the employee.

She settled in to wait against the wall near the end of the counter, watching as the employee worked. They had on a worn, blue flannel and a baseball hat for some hockey team, sleeves rolled messily up to their forearms to reveal lean muscle working under tan tattooed skin. Dexterous hands poured foam and…

Marnie blushed and cleared her throat, louder than she intended. She couldn't just be horny on main like this, openly staring at people's forearms like a freak. Sure, it'd been a while, but she had to have some decorum.

Her throat clearing got the employee's attention and they turned around. It looked like everything was in slow motion, but maybe it was because Marnie had stopped breathing.

The person was stunning. Their cap was squashed down over brown curls, nearly blocking dark, almond-shaped eyes. Their shirt hung loosely around their built frame, jeans hugging them in *all* the right places and tucked into heavy, black work boots. She saw that on their knuckles was a tattoo that read, Fuck Off. Somehow it made them more attractive.

Marnie's heart pounded and her face got redder with each second this person looked at her. She felt like she was trapped in their gaze. Their thick eyebrows furrowed as they set the coffees on the counter without looking away from Marnie.

"Are you here about the job?" they asked, voice like a rumble in Marnie's chest.

"Uh—"

The person looked down at the silver watch on their wrist. "Just in time."

They reached under the counter to pull out an apron, tossing it at Marnie. She caught it, wide-eyed and staring as the gay panic dragged her under.

"You can run register while I make drinks," they said.

She finally blinked herself out of her queer-induced paralysis and shook her head. She had to tell them that's not why she was there. She had a job.

"Um," was all she could manage. She kicked herself. She was a smart, capable woman! And yet, put her in the presence of an attractive person and she was useless.

The person blinked. "You're cute, but you're going to need to work on those conversation skills." Their face scrunched up a little. "Not with me. The customers. I'm Quinn, by the way."

They turned back to making drinks.

She stood there, internally debating whether Quinn was the sexiest name she'd ever heard, or if it was just because the name was attached to a dreamboat.

"Hey, new girl," Quinn called from behind the counter. They sighed and pushed up the front of their cap a little. "Sorry, I assumed. Pronouns? Name?"

"Marnie. 'She' is right," she said, clutching the apron tighter. She opened her mouth to tell Quinn that she wasn't actually here for the job, but instead what came out was: "A-and your pronouns?"

"They," Quinn said with a dismissive wave of their hand. "Now come on, the line is getting out of control."

Quinn turned back to the espresso machine and Marnie looked at the apron in her hands. She should just fess up that she wasn't here for the job. She *had* a job, a good, full-time job that she just came from and kinda just wanted to take a shower and sleep. She gritted her teeth, trying to shake her impulsive people pleasing behavior. She took a deep breath and looked up at Quinn.

Without another thought, she slipped the apron over her head and shuffled behind the register. She smiled widely at the first customer.

"Hello! How can I help you?"

The time flew by. Surprising, since it took Marnie a second to get used to the digital pad set up in front of the vintage register.

The first time she looked up and there was no line, she smiled and let out a long sigh of relief. She looked at the clock on the wall, surprised that two hours had passed already. Once she got in a rhythm, the line dwindled quickly but not fast enough with the continuing onslaught.

"Good job, new girl," Quinn said. They were still at the espresso machine, wiping down the steaming wand with a rag and not bothering to look at Marnie. "Can I make you a coffee?"

"I don't really like coffee," she said casually, eyes on Quinn's long fingers as they scratched at a stubborn stain on the wand. They froze and looked at Marnie.

"You don't like coffee?" they asked incredulously.

"No," she said, drawing out the 'o' with an awkward smile.

"So, you're the owner?"

"Yeah, this is my shop. Why would you apply for a job here if you don't like coffee?"

Here it was. Marnie's chance to tell Quinn that she wasn't here for the job. She was just a big gay mess who apparently couldn't function properly around an attractive person.

Wow, Quinn had really pretty eyes.

"I just prefer tea," she shrugged. She mentally kicked herself for not correcting the situation but Quinn was just *looking* at her. It made her palms slick, which she subtly tried to wipe off on her apron.

"You're weird."

The bluntness of the statement didn't bother her. It actually felt like a compliment, the way Quinn said it. Even if she hadn't seen them smile, she was sure there was one just under their scowl.

"Thank you," she said genuinely.

Quinn stared at her for another moment and Marnie was starting to feel a tingling low in her belly. She blushed and brought a hand up to her face in an awkward gesture that ended with her cupping the back of her neck just out of sheer *not* knowing what to do with her hands. Quinn seemed unaffected by her flailing and tilted their head.

"Come meet Cheech," they said gruffly.

She blinked, a thousand questions on her tongue. Cheech? A partner? One half of the famous stoner duo Cheech and Chong?

Quinn turned on their heels, carabiner of keys jingling on their hip, and pulled back a curtain, disappearing behind it. Marnie followed Quinn cautiously. It was a backroom area, shelves of supplies lining the walls. There was a back door leading outside and a tiny desk that had various colored papers piled all over it.

Quinn let out a sharp whistle and a little chocolate brown head perked up from what looked like a pile of laundry. A chihuahua with long fur, big ears with dramatic fur coming off the sides, and tan paws. Its nails clicked on the floor as it trotted over. Marnie cooed, already in love.

"This is Cheech," Quinn said. The dog put its paw on Quinn's knee and they patted its baseball-size head. "He stays hidden down here because, you know, stupid health shit," Quinn scoffed. "You know, Cheech is pretty clean, besides all the fur. Babies are way dirtier than dogs, if you think about it. They shit in their pants and just sit in it. It's disgusting. But you can't tell someone their *baby* violates the health code." Quinn rolled their eyes. "Anyway, I didn't want him to scare you if you came back here to get things. He scared the shit out of someone once. They thought he was a rat."

Marnie crouched down and Cheech wiggled up to her, putting two paws on her knee so she could scratch his back.

"I love dogs. He's so *cute!*" She growled the last bit a little aggressively but Cheech didn't seem to mind, squirming with his tiny tongue, trying to get at her face.

"Yeah, well, that's all." Quinn snapped their fingers and Cheech dropped back on his haunches with a huff. "Go back to bed."

Quinn turned and squeezed past Marnie to return to the main part of the shop. As they passed, the scent of soap and pine needles mingled among the general overtone of coffee and hit Marnie's tongue, nearly making her gasp. She almost followed Quinn with her nose but managed to keep herself in one spot, taking one last look at Cheech before following Quinn into the shop.

Quinn glanced at their watch. Now, Marnie thought, would be a good time to mention that she was not in the market for a job. She could already feel the itchy signs of exhaustion behind her eyes. All she wanted was to go home. Suddenly she realized she smelled like a vet office and BO.

"That morning shift kills me," Quinn groaned. "I've been handling it fine but it's like there are more of them every day. I swear, ever since I got Instagram they've been relentless."

"Customers?" she asked.

Quinn looked up like they forgot she was there.

"How long do I have you on shift?" Quinn took off their baseball cap, running a hand through unruly curls and smashing the hat back on their head. The curls looked so soft.

"Um—"

"Four hours, right?" Quinn mumbled to themself. "I know it's not much."

"No, it's perfect." Marnie practically sighed. Oh shit.

"Great," Quinn said. "I'm desperate for help during rush hour. You know how to make drinks?"

She grinned. "I'm a fast learner!"

Quinn shrugged and went back to cleaning. She had so many opportunities to tell Quinn she wasn't interested in the job. Instead she went over to the trash can behind the counter and tied it up.

"Dumpster is out back." Quinn threw their thumb over their shoulder and Marnie nodded as she walked outside. Her phone buzzed in her pocket and she took it out with one hand, bag of garbage in her other, wet coffee grounds surprisingly heavy.

What'd they say?

Marnie could hear Jenna's enthusiasm over text. She grunted as she tossed the trash bag into the dumpster, hearing it land among the other bags. Wiping her hands on her apron, she looked down at her phone. Her tired brain generated a chirpy, noncommittal response.

Don't worry!

She still didn't know if Quinn did catering. "Shit."

She made her way back inside where Quinn was handling the register, two girls in skirts smiling shyly as they ordered. Quinn didn't even smile when they handed the customer their card and mumbled, "Have a nice day."

The two girls shuffled off to the side, heads bent together and giggling as they glanced up at an oblivious Quinn. Marnie felt her own insecurity bubbling up but tapped it down. How silly. *She* was the one who—no, she could *not* be an employee here. She needed to get it together. She slipped back behind the counter and smiled brightly at Quinn, who barely looked up from where they were making the drinks.

"Good job, um, taking out the trash," Quinn said stiffly.

She frowned at the sheer adorable weirdness of the being in front of her and felt her heart *thump* hard against her chest— just once—but almost enough to jerk her toward Quinn. This gay panic situation wasn't a good look.

With a heavy blink, she came back to Quinn squinting at her suspiciously.

"You all right?"

"Hm? Oh, yes."

"You're not, like, narcoleptic."

"No! Just thinking about coffee," she said. Was it getting hotter? Maybe she was standing too close to the espresso machine. The longer Quinn stared at her, the hotter her neck became.

"Tomorrow? Same time?" Quinn asked, jogging her out of her gay lust fugue.

"Yes," she blurted.
Shit.
Quinn gruffed what seemed like approval. "You can keep the apron but bring it every day. I only have so many."
"Okay." Marnie willed her legs to move.
"All right, later," Quinn said, going back to cleaning.
Thankfully Marnie managed to get herself back around the counter, sidling just close enough to treat herself to another deep scent of Quinn's distinctive smell. The small proximity between their bodies felt like it was crackling with electricity as she squeezed past without brushing Quinn's back. They remained bent over and fiddling with something. Marnie still couldn't help but look over her shoulder as she slipped out of the shop and caught just a glimpse of dark eyes peeking over the counter before they ducked out of view.

* * *

Marnie noticed the container of espresso beans was getting low and excused herself to get a refill. She wandered to the backroom, bending down to get them.
Suddenly she felt two strong hands on her hips, pulling her back and against something or…some*one*.
She looked over her shoulder and saw Quinn behind her, dark eyes staring intently. A thrill started low in her belly as she stood.
"Need help with those beans?" Quinn rumbled.
She cupped the back of Quinn's neck, pulling their lips to her neck and shivered when Quinn pulled her tighter. A hitched moan pushed its way from Marnie's throat and her nails cut into Quinn's neck. Her heart beat in her clit and she turned around, moving to kiss Quinn's lips and…
She jerked up in the bed with a snort. She felt spit drying on her cheek and groaned. Another Quinn dream.
She'd been going dutifully to the coffee shop for a week now. Every day she walked through those doors, telling herself that was her last day. She'd tell Quinn the truth and *finally* find

out if they did catering and get Quinn's number. For flirting reasons. But every day she would look into Quinn's eyes, usually under some sort of frown, and her brain became rainbow glittery oatmeal in her skull, seeping out of her ears and revealing the gay mess she was.

Her new routine became leaving The Filling Station, go home, take a shower, change into her jammies, then flop into bed. Then she'd startle awake, always right before Dream Quinn kissed her. She couldn't even get laid in her dreams!

She'd wake up throbbing between her legs and have no choice but to bring herself a bit of relief.

No surprise. She was exhausted working two jobs when she only needed one, but Quinn was addicting, and she couldn't imagine giving up their four-ish hours together just because she didn't *need* the job. She could just put it off until they were friends.

She huffed as she fell back into her pillows. *Friends*. The pounding between her thighs just reminded her that *friends* wouldn't cut it. She couldn't look at Quinn without thinking of them bringing her to a toe-curling orgasm. She pulled the blanket over her face. Her hand darted out from under the covers to grab her phone, pulling it back into her blanket cave.

She brought up the Instagram for The Filling Station, even though it hadn't been updated in weeks. Quinn complained about the influx of customers like it was a mystery, but she saw *exactly* what the draw was. Even though there were only six pictures on the IG, two of them featured Quinn, and those got exponentially more likes than the ones of the shop and drinks. One showed Quinn making a latte, T-shirt tight over their muscular back. The name of the shop across the taut fabric was clearly not what people were interested in.

The latest picture posted was of Quinn on the bike they rode to work every day, Cheech bundled up in a backpack strapped to their back wearing little goggles.

Of course business was blowing up, now that the entire queer world was aware of how hot the owner was. Maybe Marnie was a little biased because she was definitely going above and beyond in the "what would you do to be close to your crush" category. Visiting a queer-owned coffee shop to check out the cute owner seemed less wild then pretending you needed a job there.

Her phone pinged with a message from Jenna. She groaned. Jenna was the only one Marnie talked to about relationship stuff and she felt helpless not having her now because she was trying to hide the fact that she hadn't asked about catering yet.

Bridesmaid dress fitting today!!! <3

Right. The fitting before work. She hated trying on clothes and this was the last thing she wanted to do, but it came with the territory.

I'll be there!

Throwing off the covers, she started the day.

Marnie smoothed her hands over her hips, admiring how the deep blue silky material of the dress seemed to accentuate them. Her bosoms were pushed up over the top but that was just a bonus of having awesome boobs, she guessed.

"How does it look?" Jenna said, opening the curtain.

Jenna leaned against the cubicle, arms folded. She was tall and slender with beautiful dark skin and long eyelashes fanning around deep brown eyes. Basically, a smokeshow.

She took in Marnie in the dress and gave an approving nod. "You look hot. I knew blue was your color."

"Jenna," Marnie said, truth bubbling up in her throat like a burp. "I want to tell you something."

Jenna frowned. "Is this going to ruin my day?"

"No, I don't think so."

"All right. I'm ready."

"I didn't ask about catering from The Filling Station."

"Wha—"

"But! It's because I panicked when I saw how hot the owner was and accidentally accepted a job there."

"You—"

"Yes!"

"*And* your other job?"

"Yes."

Jenna tipped her head back in a loud, almost guttural guffaw, one hand slapping Marnie's arm while the other clutched at her own stomach. "You adorable gay idiot!"

"I know!" she moaned. "I'm so dumb but I haven't gotten the guts to tell Quinn."

"You have to! You're going to work to death," Jenna said. "And I need to know about the catering. I can—"

"No, I'll do it," Marnie said, not needing any more embarrassment in her life. "I'll ask them after my shift."

Jenna looked at her for a moment before a smile crawled over her features. "Super hot, right?"

She let out a long groan. "*God*, Jenna, they're just my type. It makes me so mad."

"Ask them out!"

"No, what if they're not interested? My ego couldn't take it."

"False," Jenna said with a smirk. "You're super hot and could totally bag tons of people. You just refuse to acknowledge how powerful of a pansexual you are."

"This mystical pansexual power you seem to believe in is fake," she said, looking back at herself in the mirror.

"Fuck, your ass looks great in this dress." Jenna smoothed out a wrinkle at Marnie's waist. "It's not a pansexual power; it's just a *Marnie* power."

"Seems fake." Marnie tilted her head and cupped her boobs. "My boobs look amazing."

"I bet your new crush would like how they look. Can we go back to that?"

"Must we?"

"It's directly affecting me."

Blushing, Marnie turned her back to Jenna. "Unzip me." Jenna complied as Marnie sighed. "Their name is Quinn."

"Covered that."

"They're *so* hot."

"I'm aware."

"And grumpy. But it's cute." Marnie hoped she was able to keep the stars out of her eyes. "Like, I've never seen them smile but I can still tell when they're amused. Their eyebrows will kinda scrunch together. It's either amusement or gas but I'm choosing to believe it's amusement. Even their dog is cute."

"Damn, do we need to make this a double wedding?"

"It's probably a lost cause."

Jenna gave her a look. "Listen. Just tell Quinn this was all one big misunderstanding because you want in their pants. Then they can be your date to the wedding *and* do the coffee."

Marnie just wished she had the same amount of confidence in herself that Jenna seemed to have in her. It would make this whole thing a hell of a lot easier.

When Marnie pulled up to The Filling Station, the first thing she noticed was the customers milling around outside, the shop dark. She pulled into her usual spot just as she saw Quinn sprinting up on their bike. They streaked across the parking lot, disappearing behind the building.

She got out of the car, ran a quick hand through her thick locks and followed them.

Quinn was just getting off their bike, Cheech cocooned in the backpack.

"Sorry, running late," Quinn mumbled as they reached for the keys on their carabiner. She noticed for the first time that Quinn wasn't in their usual outfit of some nondescript T-shirt, but today they had on a crisp, black-collared shirt, sleeves buttoned neatly to their wrists and a thin black tie.

"You look nice," she said, eyes drifting down to Quinn's ass as they unlocked the door.

Quinn looked down at themself. "Right. Lawyers."

With that, Quinn opened the back door of the shop and walked their bike into the backroom, setting it against the wall. They stripped off their backpack, loosening the top so that Cheech could hop out. They took his goggles off and he shook out his little body. Quinn held the keys out to Marnie as they loosened their tie with one hand. Her eyes lingered on the "Fuck" tattooed across their knuckles.

She wondered if that was the hand they —y'know—fucked with.

She smiled, taking the keys from Quinn and feeling a spark under her fingers as their skin touched. She blushed and scurried away, heading up front to open. The crowd of customers outside had swelled in just a few moments and she quickly started taking orders.

Quinn emerged from the backroom with their sleeves rolled up to their elbows and tie loosened. It really was distracting. As the line dwindled, Marnie allowed herself a calming breath and turned to look at Quinn, who was finishing up a line of drinks.

She leaned against the counter and decided today was the day she'd ask about catering. She picked up a rag and wiped down the area where Quinn set the drinks when they were done. It always became a mess and *plus* it gave her the perfect vantage point to look at Quinn's face.

They were especially cute when they concentrated. Usually Marnie's staring would go unnoticed, but today seemed like her unlucky day. Just as Quinn finished off a foam heart, they looked up and caught her staring. She blushed and blurted out the first thing that came to mind.

"So, a lawyer, huh?" She wished she could pull the words back into her mouth.

"Divorce," Quinn said flatly, putting a coffee on the bar with a perfect foam heart at the top. They disappeared behind the espresso machine.

She didn't have much time to ponder because the second morning surge of customers was starting. The rest of her shift, Quinn only grunted when she asked them questions or said something. She wished she could have kept her giant mouth shut. But she had questions.

How long had Quinn been married? Was she emotionally unavailable? On the rebound? She wasn't against some rough dirty rebound sex. Maybe against a wall…

"Do you do catering?" she blurted, trying to distract herself

"Catering?" Quinn said as they put the bag of espresso beans away.

"For a wedding?" she asked hopefully. "My best friend is getting married and she loves your coffee. She wants to do a fancy coffee bar at the end of the night."

"My coffee isn't fancy," Quinn said dismissively.

"Sure it is. I mean, you're in an *old gas station*."

"That doesn't make it fancy."

"So you don't cater?"

Quinn leaned back against the counter. "When is this?"

"September nineteenth," she said, already excited.

"I don't cater," Quinn said. She felt her hope wilting. "For you, maybe." They squinted for a moment, a hint of a smirk. "But still no."

Quinn pushed off the counter and disappeared behind the curtain. She blinked at the spot where they once stood.

Did Quinn just flirt with her? Her heart fluttered. She felt the heat of a blush on the back of her neck and was too paralyzed to move. Her brain tried to process the situation. If Quinn was flirting then…

No.

But maybe…

She stood at the register, tapping her fingers against the counter as she gathered up the courage to follow Quinn and ask for clarification. With a deep breath, she stepped beyond the curtain and let her eyes adjust to the dark room. She felt tiny paws on her leg and looked down to see Cheech standing on his back legs, tail wagging as he looked at her.

"Hey," she said, scooping him into her arms. Cheech licked her cheek in excitement as she wandered further into the backroom.

There was a bang and a curse and she noticed Quinn near the overflowing work desk, rubbing their head like they'd hit it. The pile of laundry had grown since the last time she had been down here. Empty food containers spilled from the trash, and a thick blanket lay over the beanbag in the corner. She gasped in realization.

"Have you been sleeping here?"

Quinn shrugged. "It's just the time of the year that paperwork gets crazy. Easier to just sleep here."

"You sleep here to do paperwork?"

"Yeah, what's the big deal?" Quinn shuffled through some papers.

"How much more do you have?"

"I don't know. I should be done in a couple of weeks—"

"Do you need help?"

"Nah. It's mostly organization."

She snorted and shook her head. "This will not do. I'm going to go home and take a shower, change and I'll be back with some beer. We'll finish tonight."

"I don't—"

"No arguing! Just accept it." She smiled, excited at the potential of a project with Quinn.

Quinn looked up from the mess. "It's a lot, though."

"This kinda thing is my jam," she said, delighted that Quinn accepted her proposal. "I'll be back!"

She set Cheech down on the ground and headed to her car.

Marnie pulled back up to the shop, wondering what she was doing. She hadn't told Quinn that she couldn't keep this job. Mistake number one. And she thought she was going to be able to spend a whole night with Quinn and not make a fool of herself? Mistake number two.

It was too late, though, and she was committed.

And yes, maybe she put on the tight jeans that made her ass look great and a crop top that made her feel good and flaunty. Her date outfit. Even though this was definitely not a date.

She grabbed the beer from the back of the car and got out, noticing Quinn stacking chairs. She walked in, little bell overhead announcing her presence.

"We're closed," Quinn said flatly, not looking up.

"Even for your favorite customer?" She couldn't help but flirt with a small smile. Quinn's head jerked up and the corner of their mouth twitched in an almost smile.

"It's you."

"I said I was coming back." She held up the bag. "I brought beer."

"I thought you weren't…I don't know. I thought maybe you wouldn't…" Quinn shook their head and slid their hands into their back pockets, lifting themself up on the balls of their feet nervously. "I ordered Chinese food. I wasn't sure what you liked so I just got a little of everything."

Marnie smiled, heart fluttering. Quinn seemed to exude charm without trying. "Delicious."

"Great," Quinn said, a smile threatening to crack across their features. "Let's get started."

Things began a little awkwardly. Marnie was so distracted hanging out with Quinn one on one, that she didn't know what to do. She felt destined to be weird and awkward. They sat on the stools in the basement as they ate the Chinese food, conversation a bit slow.

Quinn seemed just as nervous as Marnie, thankfully, even if she wondered what they had to be nervous about.

"So you always sleep here to do your paperwork?" she inquired, casting about for a light topic.

"Nah, but my ex was getting her stuff out of my apartment this week, finally." Quinn looked like they were shocked at themself for offering up that information.

"Sorry, that sounds not fun," she said as she picked at her food.

"It wasn't that bad. It's been over for a while. But she traveled a lot so she hasn't had a chance to just do it."

Quinn nodded toward a box that had their name on it. "She brought that back. Mostly trash."

Marnie popped a piece of broccoli into her mouth, watching Quinn pick at the label on their beer, staring at it like it would reveal something to them.

"Still, I'm sorry," she said.

"Nothing to be sorry about." Quinn sighed and looked back at her. "It was my own damn fault. I trusted her too much."

"You were married. Aren't you supposed to trust your spouse?"

"Sure, but then I found out all she did was lie to me the entire time we were together. Kinda fucked."

"Yeah." She looked down as the guilt crept up her spine. Maybe now was the time to come clean, to say she was sorry she'd lied to them, but in her defense it was because she thought they were very, very hot. "Sometimes a lie can be justified," she reasoned. "But not when it's the whole time you were together."

Quinn chuckled, a foreign sound that made her flesh hot and the apex between her thighs pound with need. "You don't look like you've lied a day in your life, Marnie."

Well, now she really had to say something. She opened her mouth to respond but Quinn was already standing up from the stool with a grunt.

"All right. Let's get this paperwork over with."

"Yeah, paperwork," she muttered as she set her food aside. She couldn't eat anymore if she wanted to. So instead, she drank. They were down to the last two bottles by the time they finished the paperwork. She could feel the alcohol floating in her veins and making her relax a little more. Quinn had seemed to dissolve onto the beanbag chair in the corner, Cheech dozing on the laundry.

They were both tipsy. Marnie could feel herself just on the edge of drunk, about to topple over. The alcohol told her to keep going, so she did, taking a long chug of her beer as she wandered over to the box with Quinn's name on it.

Something bright caught her eye and she gasped as she reached in, pulling out rainbow striped bikini bottoms. She held them up with a smug smirk.

Quinn groaned. "What?"

"*What?* Don't act like this is a totally normal thing to have in your box of divorced people stuff." She twirled the bikini bottoms on her finger. She could feel the alcohol in her system making her brave. Quinn just looked up from their beanbag chair with an amused tilt of their lips. It wasn't a full-blown smile, but Marnie was addicted to it all the same.

"I wore it to pride," Quinn mumbled as they took another long sip of their beer.

"*Just* this?"

"No, of course not, with pasties."

Marnie guffawed. "I cannot imagine that at all."

But she wanted to. Oh, did she want to.

"There are pictures somewhere," Quinn said with a dismissive wave. "Maybe if you're lucky, I'll show you."

Quinn's eyes focused on her, dark pools that she felt herself falling into helplessly. She dropped the bottoms back in the box, eyes not leaving Quinn's as she slowly stalked toward them. The alcohol told her this was a great idea.

All of the little quips and remarks were too much. She had to know if Quinn was flirting with her and preferably get the chance to kiss them. Their eyes never parting, she stopped when her feet hit the edge of the beanbag. Quinn still hadn't moved, legs spread wide and one hand resting on their thigh. Now, with the moment so close, she felt doubt creeping in.

"Do you like me?" she said softly.

Quinn looked up at her and she felt all the confidence she had just a moment ago drain away. Oh god, she was wrong. Quinn totally didn't have a thing for her at all.

All of her thoughts stopped in her head when she watched Quinn set the beer down.

"Why don't you get down here and find out," Quinn said lowly.

She was instantly wet. Her knees buckled and she fell helplessly down, her legs bracketing Quinn's as she sank into the beanbag. She felt Quinn's hands on her thighs, pulling her down so that they were chest to chest. She hovered over Quinn until they gripped the back of her thighs, jerking her forward so she pressed them into the beanbag.

She was ready to push herself off Quinn, nerves setting in, but as she turned her head, Quinn leaned forward and pressed their lips together. Her stomach flooded with warmth as Quinn squeezed her hips.

She moaned as the seam of her jeans pressed against Quinn's stomach and up against her heated sex. Quinn gripped her ass as they deepened the kiss, tongue tracing the seam of her lips. She gripped the front of Quinn's shirt, feeling the soft fabric under her hands.

Quinn let out a long sigh, one hand cupping her face as they held her close. Quinn tugged at her bottom lip with their teeth and Marnie let out an obscene groan. She could feel the cold air of the room along the exposed skin of her lower back and it brought her back to her senses for a moment. She had to tell Quinn the truth before this went any further.

"Wait," she breathed as she pulled back a little. Quinn's lips chased her before they sank back down against the chair. Their lips were swollen and red, all the more enticing, and their baseball hat was askew.

"Are you okay?" Quinn asked quickly, hands moving to more neutral territory as their concerned eyes darted over her. "I'm sorry."

"Don't apologize." She shook her head, her heart filling with affection. "You didn't do anything."

Quinn looked concerned. "Did you change your mind?"

Her heart shattered at the vulnerability in Quinn's voice. She shook her head and kissed Quinn softly. "Not at all. I really, *really* like you, Quinn."

Quinn blinked, thumbs brushing the skin above her jeans. It was as if they were processing and Marnie watched as the first smile she'd seen on Quinn stretched their cheeks to reveal two deep dimples. Fuck. *She* had been the cause of that.

"I really, really like you too," Quinn said as they brushed their noses together. "I've been trying to flirt but I'm not very good."

"I'd say you're doing fine." She kissed Quinn again as all thoughts of revealing the truth fled from her mind.

The next morning Marnie woke up under a soft heavy blanket with Quinn spooning her from behind, one hand on her breast. She hummed and snuggled back into Quinn. She went to stretch her legs but her naked feet touched cold concrete and she jerked them back under the covers. They were somehow still on the beanbag. Marnie snorted and Quinn groaned into the back of her neck.

"Wha' time?" Quinn's voice, thick from sleep, tickled the back of her neck.

She turned in their arms and they leaned forward to peck her face, eyes still closed.

"Sleep time," Quinn mumbled as they threw their leg over Marnie's hip and pulled her close so her face folded into their neck.

She breathed Quinn in and thought about how she could definitely be happy just staying like this the rest of the day. They smelled like pine and sex and she wanted to have Quinn any way she could.

She kissed the hollow of Quinn's throat just as Cheech jumped on top of them. Quinn grunted in annoyance and Cheech stomped all over their tender bits in a tiny, happy dance.

"All righ', jeez." Quinn sat up, setting Cheech back down on the floor.

Marnie pouted as Quinn got up and started pulling their boxers back on. They picked up their binder, paused, and threw it back on the ground, searching in their laundry pile for a sweatshirt and threw it on, hair out of control as their head popped out of the neck.

"Time to open?" Marnie yawned.

"Yep." Quinn popped the 'p'. "Oh, I'll um, do the catering."

Marnie beamed and jumped up from the beanbag, blanket falling from her. "Yeah?"

"Yeah. But no tux," Quinn said, smile barely visible as their eyes roamed her body.

"Tux? What kind of wedding do you think this is?" she teased, arms around Quinn's neck.

Quinn kissed her, whispering against her lips. "Give me your phone."

Marnie pulled away reluctantly and got her phone. Quinn took it in one hand and entered their number.

"I can't tonight, but tomorrow after closing we can get a drink and talk about it?"

She almost blurted, "fuck, yeah," but remembered. Work. Her real job.

"I can't," she stumbled, watching as Quinn's eyebrow twitched just a little. "I want—"

"No, it's fine—" Quinn slowly pulled away from her, and she reeled for something to say.

"I want to but not…Ask me again. Next week," she said, anything to put off the inevitable awkward conversation. Hopefully when she wasn't naked in a backroom.

Quinn smiled with a bit of hope. "Okay weirdo," they said before disappearing into the front of the shop.

She could hardly concentrate at her vet job on Sunday. She never thought having sex in the backroom of a coffee shop on a beanbag would be the most romantic moment of her life, but here she was.

She sighed dreamily just thinking about it, even as she checked in a bird that had flown into a wall and now had a broken wing.

Squeezing her thighs together, she reveled in the soreness that still lingered after their tryst on Friday.

It was great until the guilt set in. She felt terrible for not telling Quinn she didn't need the job. It was hard being in the same space as them without blurting it.

Quinn texted her while she was at work.

Wanna come over tomorrow? Movie?

She sighed, looking around the waiting room. She should just tell Quinn now. But not over text.

I can't tomorrow. Wedding stuff.

Mentally, she face-palmed herself.

It's cool. I get it. Casual. We can stay casual.

She wanted to scream that she wanted the opposite of casual but Quinn sent another message that distracted her.

Hey. I miss you.

She felt happiness expand in her chest.

I miss you too.

She wanted to text Quinn all day but quickly shut off notifications for their messages. The more she talked to them, the more she risked telling the truth over text as the guilt ate away at her.

They'd had such a good time together! She was head over heels, and she was too worried about Quinn's response, especially after they told her all about the ex. No, the time for this had to be perfect.

The next day at work was awkward to say the least. Quinn would smile at Marnie and then visibly pull it back. They ignored her most of the day even if she wanted to kiss them and ask about their weekend.

When the crowd died down, she went into the backroom to say hi to Cheech and as she was patting his head, Quinn came in. They walked toward her, hands in their back pockets.

"I know you said casual," Quinn said. She stood, intent on correcting Quinn when they pressed against her, backing her against the newly cleared desk. Their lips were dangerously close and she was dying to close the gap. "Is this casual?"

Entranced by Quinn's lips and the pounding between her thighs, she nodded before closing the distance.

"Hey, look at this," Quinn came up behind her and set a coffee cup in front of her, latte art of a bow tie on top. "I call it The Tux."

She hummed, distracted by the scent of pine and the beating of her heart. "Cute."

"For the wedding. It's sweet. You might like it."

"You're sweet," she sighed, leaning a little into Quinn. The whole week they'd basically gone through shifts before fucking in the backroom. The guilt of keeping the full truth from Quinn was starting to outweigh the amazing orgasms.

Quinn dropped a quick kiss on her shoulder before going back to the espresso machine, leaving her with her guilt.

The next day as she was leaving work, Marnie was so preoccupied that she could have sworn she watched Quinn turning the corner from the parking lot to the front of the vet. She blinked, expecting the illusion to be gone, but Quinn was still there and staring at her.

Holding Cheech.

Shit.

"Marnie?" Quinn frowned as Cheech squirmed in their arms.

"What's wrong with Cheech?" she asked, brain shorting out. She was panicking about being caught, but worried, and *shit*.

"Cheech ate a bunch of mocha powder," Quinn mumbled, dark eyes darting to her scrubs. "Do you work here?"

She adjusted the purse on her shoulder and looked back at the vet. She let out a long sigh. "Yes."

Quinn nodded, looking at her like they were still trying to figure things out. "So you work here then go to the shop to work?"

"I work the overnight shift."

"Why did you get the job at the shop?"

She could see the hurt and confusion on their face and she wanted to kiss it away. She wanted to tell them she was sorry and that it was all a big stupid mistake and she was an idiot, but shame kept her stuck.

"I never meant to take it," she admitted quietly. Each word fought its way out of her mouth, begging to be swallowed again. "I—"

"It's fine. You don't have to explain," Quinn said firmly. "I have to get Cheech in. He isn't feeling well."

Quinn kept walking past her and even as her heart broke she just stood there. "Quinn!"

Quinn stopped in their tracks, back to Marnie, and hope fluttered in her chest for a moment as Quinn turned around and walked up to her. "You always made it clear that whatever was going on between us was casual. I shouldn't be upset, I just didn't think…well, that you'd sleep with me to get catering for your friend's wedding." Marnie was too shocked to answer. She stared at Quinn as it looked like tears gathered in the corners of their eyes. "Don't bother coming back to the shop."

With that, Quinn walked into the vet.

Marnie took the next day off work. She had someone at the office call her to make sure Cheech was okay and he was. It was too soon to return to the scene of the crime and thankfully she was very good at faking sick.

She watched reality TV and cried all day, replaying the moment. It morphed every time. Mostly Quinn got angrier than they had actually appeared and called Marnie all types of names. It stung just like Quinn had said those things, even if it was just in her mind.

She texted Quinn, asking if they could talk, but they went ignored. This was her own fault, but she still wallowed. The remaining few weeks until the wedding flew by, weeks of Marnie driving past the coffee shop every chance she got, hoping for a glimpse of Quinn.

Thankfully, the closer it got to the wedding, the more distractions she had. Jenna was sympathetic to her heartbreak but also had her own things to be worried about, meaning she dragged Marnie to any remaining planning meetings she had left. Jenna had given up on her coffee hour, which was more than fine with Marnie.

As the day of the wedding finally arrived, Marnie couldn't help but feel down. She had been hoping Quinn would be her date to the wedding and she could flirt with them all night.

The wedding venue was lovely, a family's small farm with a large field for the ceremony and a grass area with trees next to a barn for the reception. The whole place smelled like hay and horses, but charming.

Marnie cried like a baby during the ceremony, the whole *love* thing being a little too much for her right now, but also happy for her friend. From there she went immediately to the bar to drown her sorrows in alcohol. She looked at the two custom drinks printed out and framed on the bar. One called a Love Eternal and one named the U-haul. Marnie read over their ingredients for a moment until she heard a voice over her shoulder.

"The Love Eternal is gross."

She felt a chill run up her spine at the familiar sounding voice but swallowed thickly instead of turning around like she wanted to. Her mind was just playing tricks on her.

"What about the U-haul?" she asked.

"Nah."

Marnie licked her lips and slowly turned toward the voice, gasping when she saw Quinn standing there, hands awkwardly tapping on the side of a glass with violently green liquid in it. Their hair looked brushed for once and they wore a button-up shirt with a dark blue vest and matching bow tie. Black slacks hugged them perfectly and their shoes were shiny oxfords.

"What makes you think I wouldn't like it?" she asked, stepping out of the line. She still couldn't drag her eyes away from Quinn and her heart felt like a frightened bird trying to escape the cage of her ribs.

"It's spicy." Quinn tilted their head, dimples popping. "You don't like spicy."

They stood there staring at each other. Finally she blurted, "What are you doing here?"

"I said I would cater."

"I thought you hated me." She cursed how vulnerable her voice sounded. Yes, she was vulnerable, but she didn't want Quinn to know that.

"I like your dress," Quinn said, taking a sip of their drink and making a face.

She couldn't help but chuckle, even as the compliment made the back of her neck heat. "I thought you didn't like that."

"I don't," Quinn said, wiping their mouth with the back of their hand. They stepped closer and set the glass on the bar. She flushed from the closeness. Quinn was gone just as quickly as they were there. "Can we talk?"

Her hand shook in anxiousness. "*Yes*, I mean…yes. Follow me."

Turning quickly, Marnie led Quinn around the barn to a large oak tree. Quinn's hands were deep in their pockets and they looked a little nervous but not as nervous as Marnie felt.

The awkward silence filled the space between them and she blurted, "I'm sorry."

Quinn's head fell, chin to their chest and kicking the dirt under their feet. She kept rambling. "I'm really sorry! I got to the shop and you were so hot…"

Quinn's head jerked up.

"...and, and I wasn't thinking and took the job because I'm a fucking idiot—"

"Hey, hey," Quinn chuckled and stepped into her bubble, fingers brushing along her forearm. She calmed, mouth clamping shut to keep any more words from falling out. "Jenna actually told me everything."

"What?"

"Yeah, she came by a few days ago, asking if I would still do the catering. I told her only if she kept it a secret," Quinn said.

She blinked until she noticed a small smile on their lips. She breathed a sigh of relief. "I'm sorry."

"I'm sorry too," Quinn said. Their hands went back to their pockets and they rocked on their heels. "I reacted poorly. I should have let you tell me your side."

She shook her head. "I didn't deserve it."

Quinn let out a small laugh. "Can we agree we both fucked up a little bit?"

"Fine," she chuckled.

"Thank you."

The silence settled over them again but this time it wasn't awkward. It was like there was something mending between them that Marnie had thought was broken forever. She didn't know how to describe it, but she knew in her heart that Quinn was meant to be a lot to her. She knew that if Quinn would still have her in their life, she would make sure they wouldn't regret it.

"I like your vest," she said, desperate to break the silence. Her hands itched to reach out for Quinn but she was worried she'd chase them away.

Quinn looked down at their vest briefly as they backed her up against the oak tree. Her heart beat loudly in her ears as Quinn leaned closer, hands on her hips.

"I borrowed it," Quinn said, eyes looking down at her lips. "I wanted to look good for you."

"You look *really* good," she breathed, hands cautiously landing on Quinn's shoulders. Her thumb stroked the side of

Quinn's neck and they brushed the end of their nose against hers, stealing her breath.

"And you look absolutely beautiful," Quinn said, leaning forward and kissing Marnie so deeply that she forgot where she was for a moment.

SEND OUT THE CLOWNS

Jessie Chandler

"Come on, come on, come on, let's go people."

I thumped the steering wheel. For a brief moment I considered trying to bust a move past a lollygagging taxi, but the effort was pointless since traffic was moving about as fast as a root canal without Novocain. Interstate 494 at rush hour was not conducive to arriving at a destination in a timely manner.

My car's digital clock read five thirty-six. If everything else was running on time, my girlfriend's plane was due to land at the Minneapolis/St. Paul airport in ten minutes. I glanced back at the road in time to slam on the brakes a half second before my front bumper kissed that damn taxi's ass.

How the hell did I sweat the never-ending months, weeks, days, and now the hours for this moment to arrive and still manage to be late to pick up the woman of my dreams? If only the star witness in a domestic terrorism case we were working had been available an hour earlier…

I was employed by a Federal alphabet agency as a special agent and my work partner, Cailin McKenna, and I had to make that interview a priority. That made me late in picking up a special item I'd commissioned Cailin's artist girlfriend to make. If only Kate's plane wasn't arriving during rush hour. If only, if only... I knew all about the If Only Syndrome. There's even a website covering the subject. But, still. If only all of that hadn't happened, I wouldn't be creeping past the Mall of America and a blocks-long row of jumbo jet airplane hangars at ten miles an hour.

Luckily, Kate Goldsmith was nothing if not understanding. My love for her was boundless, but I also had an all-consuming notion she deserved someone better. She came from money, and I came from the wrong side of Manhattan's East River. Kate could care less about the almighty buck and often told me I thought too much about the wrong things, which I probably did. I simply felt like she could do so much better. She loved to tell me she already had the best. Recently, I'd concluded it was time to get out of my own way.

Seven excruciating minutes later I peeled off the freeway and entered the funnel of vehicles heading into the airport. So close and still way too far away. Even after all these years, my stomach still did its patented "Kate Flip," and giddiness sluiced through my veins at the very thought of seeing her beautiful, crooked grin in person. Even after almost a decade, Kate melted me into a happy pile of goo.

My cell phone rang as I passed the parking ramp, headed for the Arrivals level. I cut the chorus of David Guetta's, "Without You" short with a breathless, "Babe, I'm sorry—"

"Sorry for nothing." I could hear that adorable smile in her voice. "I'm coming down the escalator now, and I'll be at Three in just a couple minutes." Door Three was "our" door. She'd made the trip to Minnesota from New York a dozen times, and Door Three was where I always grabbed her.

"See you soon as I can."

I disconnected and slid the phone into the cup holder, then took stock of the cars around me. Picking up someone at the airport was always an exercise in patience, and right now mine was pushed to the limit. I crept around the curve and into the tunnel-like, drab, gray concrete racetrack that was the lower-level Arrivals area. MSP was a Delta hub, and being the hub meant lots of Delta arrivals. Luckily, most of their baggage claims were at the far end, and the majority of cars passed Door Three and continued on.

I spotted an opening and slid over to the curb, glanced around to make sure the airport parking patrol wasn't close by, and bolted from the car. The odor of jet fuel and automotive exhaust hit hard, heady and somewhat dizzying. I wanted to leap in the air and maybe even yelp in ecstatic happiness.

The glass doors opened. I sucked air and held it. Oh, baby, here she—ah, shit. Nope, just a furry-faced dude who walked into the arms of another furry-faced dude. I pressed my lips together and exhaled hard through my nose. Calm down, Flynn. You're an adult. You carry a weapon and try to stop bad people from doing bad things. But, damn, every time we reunited, I felt like a nervous fourteen-year-old all over again.

The dude-who-was-not-Kate was followed by a wizened woman with a somewhat snooty-looking, silver-blue bob. She swept past me, hopped into an idling Honda with an UBER logo in the window, and waited for the driver to sling her luggage in his trunk. Okay, not somewhat. Definitely snooty.

More world-weary passengers emerged and shuffled past me. The door opened once again and—there she was! My Kate. Her skin was more golden than the last time I'd seen her, and her honey-butter hair was just-woke-up askew. She wore a green and purple, tie-dye T-shirt I'd sent for her birthday and familiar faded jeans that I knew hugged her well-toned ass.

As soon as she crossed the threshold, she caught sight of me. Her entire face lit up. "Flynn!"

Then she was in my arms, her laughter a balm for my lonely heart. A warm, eager mouth found mine, and the tip of her tongue teased my lower lip before she pulled away. The heated glint in her ice-gray eyes warmed me in a most delicious way.

We both laughed and I could truly breathe once more. She was solid and real and warm. I buried my face in her neck and nuzzled the smooth skin covering her hammering carotid.

She always smelled so good, so familiar, like a gentle Key West breeze at sunset.

Reluctantly she let me go. I grabbed her battered blue carry-on and headed for the rear of the car. "How was the flight?"

She followed and stopped at the curb. "Smooth, except for some turbulence when we went through a rain squall somewhere over Ohio. Got homework done before I conked out. You'll be happy to hear I'm all caught up for the next few days."

Kate had recently gone back to school for an all-consuming advanced architectural degree. Allowing herself a few days off was nothing short of a minor miracle.

My entire body suffused with heat at the implication. "Those words are even better than warm brownies with chocolate chips and maraschino cherries." I deposited the bag in the trunk and slammed the lid shut.

"Hard to beat those brownies. Come here, my love machine." The tone of her voice did nothing to cool the now ignited blood speeding through my veins. She still stood at the edge of the curb, its three-inch height boosting her almost even with me.

I complied and kissed the tip of her nose.

She wound her arms around my neck and pulled me tight. Hot breath caressed my cheek, and then her lips found the lobe of my ear. She knew exactly what that did to me. I could feel her lips curve against me in a lazy grin. "I have a few ideas for all our spare time."

A shudder of lust ripped through me and I repressed a groan. "You're gonna kill me, baby."

"The French call an orgasm *la petite mort*, and for as many little deaths as I'm going to give you, Mikala Flynn, I just might."

I couldn't stifle my moan this time and almost had a little death right then and there.

"Hey, ladies." A deep voice broke our embrace as easily as if we'd been physically pulled apart. A neon-yellow vested traffic cop made a circular motion with one hand. "Sorry to break up the reunion, but you gotta get the car out of here."

Three minutes later the airport was in my rearview mirror, and we headed for Northeast Minneapolis, where I rented a room from my partner Cailin's best friend, Eleanor Pickford, better known as Pick. We lived in a big, drafty, old house that'd been turned into a duplex, and Cailin and her girlfriend lived in the other half. It was a good thing we all got along okay, or the proximity might've been a bit much.

Kate reached over the console and laced our fingers together. "I can't believe I'm finally here."

"Me neither. I really am sorry I was late. This case…It's a doozy."

"You guys have been hammering away on it for months. Are you going to be able to sneak away?"

I peeled off Crosstown, headed north on Hiawatha. "I made a deal for Thursday through Sunday off."

"No way."

"Yes, way."

Kate bounced in her seat. "Best news ever." Then she side-eyed me. "What'd you have to do to make a four-day weekend happen?"

"Well…"

"Oh, boy. What?"

"We're going to a wedding tomorrow."

"A wedding? Tomorrow?"

"Tomorrow. Four p.m. Wedding bells, Batman smells, Robin gets laid."

Kate shifted and faced me. "Are you serious? Who's getting married? Why haven't I heard about this before now? I didn't bring a thing to wear to a wedding."

"I'm totally serious. It's a bit spur of the moment." Her panicked expression made me laugh. "Besides, I'm sure you didn't plan on wearing many clothes while you were here, anyway."

"That may be true, but seriously, Flynn, if you would've told me before I left home, I could've packed something appropriate. Holy crap, we gotta go shopping."

"No, we don't."

"The Mall of America's close—"

"Honey, you don't need to buy anything." I stifled the bellow of laughter that threatened. "It's a clown wedding."

"But…What did you say?"

"The wedding. It's clown-themed. Remember JT, one of Cailin's Minneapolis cop friends?"

"Of course."

"Did you meet their friend, Rocky? He's a little different." I braked for a red light. "The short, round, aviator-hat-wearing savant with a photographic memory and a head full of more facts than an encyclopedia?"

She scowled at the windshield. "I don't think so. Last time I was here Cailin and Alex had us over to their annual Christmas party, much of which you probably don't remember. JT and her girlfriend were there along with about half the Minneapolis police force. We played Drinking Jenga. I do remember JT recounting a story involving Rocky and Tulip and an abandoned go-cart track, but I never met either one."

"You're right. That memory's maybe more than a little foggy."

I did have a fuzzy recollection of stacking Jenga pieces, each marked with a direction like MAKE A RULE, or WHISTLE HAPPY BIRTHDAY, or TAKE TWO SHOTS. I had absolutely no idea how I wound up half-naked on the small balcony off a second-story bedroom belting out "Santa Baby" in the middle of a blizzard. If Cailin didn't have video evidence on her phone, I never would've believed my own actions. I disliked the song before that little escapade, and now I had to turn off the radio every time it played during the Christmas season because just hearing the opening melody, made me feel queasy.

Kate rubbed my knee. "One of the most entertaining nights ever, Santa Baby."

I made a sour face. "For some of us. Anyway, Cailin agreed to help me get off work for a four-day weekend if we came to the wedding." That much was true. "They want to make sure there's a good turnout for Rocky and Tulip."

"Bribery. I see. What does this have to do with not needing appropriate wedding attire?"

"Tulip used to busk for tips in New Orleans making balloon animals. Apparently, the buskers have some kind of a clown wardrobe procurement channel, and Tulip's NOLA friends sent up a van full of clown gear."

"Are you kidding?"

"Nope. No two outfits are the same and all come with matching clown shoes."

"Like Ronald McDonald's?"

"Dunno. Haven't seen them yet, but reports are the shoes would make great rafts."

"Never a dull second with you, baby."

I pulled her hand to my lips and kissed it. When I was in the sunny presence of this woman, all of my concerns and hesitations disappeared like magic. "It's going to be a real extravaganza."

Once we got home, we caught up with Pick and her squeeze of the week, a cute redhead whose name, for the life of me, I couldn't seem to keep in my memory bank. It began with an R. I'd eventually given up and thought of her as Red.

Kate and I made polite excuses and bailed after five minutes. For the rest of the night, we didn't leave my bedroom except to sneak down to raid the refrigerator, borrow two—or it could have been three—bottles of wine, and use the bathroom. Time trickled like a slow-moving wine river through some of the sweetest love we'd ever made.

Morning arrived entirely too fast. A knock-knock-knocking bled into my dreams. The knock-knock-knocking became a pound-pound-pounding, eventually dragging me into the land of groggy half-consciousness. Half of me was sprawled atop a very warm Kate and none of me wanted to budge.

The sad fact was that all good things had to come to a screeching halt. "Coming," I mumbled.

Kate muttered something incoherent and pushed me upright. I staggered to the door, realizing in the nick of time I was clad in nothing but the skin I was born in.

The pounding recommenced.

"Hang *on*." My tone was sharper than I'd intended. I grabbed a piece of clothing that'd been carelessly flung onto a chair by the dresser and held it in front of me like a shield. Then I cracked the door wide enough to see Pick's spiky blond hair and one of her eyes.

She surveyed me through the crack, her eyebrow jacking higher as her gaze hit my chest and quickly returned to my face. "Didn't know if you realized it's a quarter to three. We gotta be at the Rabbit Hole at three thirty. Wedding bells at four."

Holy crap. "It's two forty-five? In the PM?" I expected maybe ten, or even noon. But three?

"Yes, ma'am."

What happened to my alarm? My sex-soaked brain apparently really had *une petite mort* of its own.

"Jesus, Pick. Thanks. We'll be right down." I did my best not to slam the door. When I dropped my security blanket to the floor, I realized my shield had been a pair of jeans. I'd been holding them upside down by one leg, which had probably done little to hide my level of undress. No wonder Pick had given me that look. Good thing there wasn't much I could do to surprise my landlord these days.

Twenty frantic minutes later, Kate and I followed Cailin's SUV as she led the crazy train bound for the Rabbit Hole. I piloted my NPIU-issued, unmarked Dodge, which would've been cool if it didn't already have over a hundred-fifty thousand miles and way too many undercover surveillance hours on it. I'd managed to clear out empty fast-food bags and disposable cups before I picked Kate up, so all that was left was the stale aroma of coffee, old fries, and greasy grub. Despite the invitation to ride crammed into Cailin's SUV, having my own vehicle at the Hole was a necessity for a quick getaway once the "I dos" were done.

Cailin parked behind the Victorian housing the coffee shop, and I pulled in beside her.

Kate glanced over at me. "Ready?"

"So long as we don't have to deal with Pennywise, I am."

"I thought you hated Stephen King."

I scrunched up my face. "I won't touch his books with a ten-foot reading lamp. He gives me nightmares. But I love the movies."

Kate gave me the side-eye.

"What?" I asked.

"And the movies don't give you nightmares?"

"Doesn't matter. I can wake you up to comfort me." I bared my teeth in a leering grin.

"Oh, Flynn. I love you. Come on."

In Eddy Quartermaine's place, which occupied the rear half of the enormous house, the sharp scent of freshly ground coffee beans wafted into the kitchen, probably from the Rabbit Hole. The familiar smell helped calm my now zinging nerves.

"Okay, everyone!" Eddy yelled. "Get the lead out." From the sound of it, she was choregraphing things from the living room.

Cailin and I cautiously peered through the archway, and sure enough, the master of ceremonies stood in the center of the carpeted floor, waving her hands like a choir director.

Shay and JT, in matching red and black clown clothes, were just disappearing through the French doors, presumably headed toward the café. Coop looked up at our entrance as he struggled into too-short coveralls. "You guys better hur—"

"Shush," said Eddy, "and finish zipping yourself into that thing, Nicholas. There you are, Cailin. Was afraid you might miss the festivities. Everyone's outfits are separated on the kitchen counters. Names on Post-its. Hop to it." She clapped her hands together twice. "Flynn. Get your patootie over here and introduce your girl to me."

Eddy was a force, and it was better not to mess around when she wanted something. She was the mother hen to JT and her girl Shay, their ragtag crew of friends, and any stragglers, like me, who showed up on their stoop. Equal parts caring, bossy, adventure-loving and stubborn, she'd do anything for those she considered under her care. A couple of weeks ago Rocky floated the idea of hitching himself to Tulip, and Eddy went online to get herself ordained. Now she could officiate weddings, and as

Rocky liked to say, "join people in ultimate holy matrimony and bliss." After introductions and a whispered word in my ear, she sent us off to change.

Our duds consisted of a red foam nose, striped jumpsuit, pillows for padding, face paint, a wig, and appropriately-themed footwear. My color scheme was red and yellow. Kate's was green and pink. Add in everyone else's vibrant getups and this wedding was going to look like a drunken double rainbow. Maybe even a triple rainbow.

Kate slapped red paint on my cheeks and painted blue triangles around my eyes. Then she slathered her entire face with creamy white goo and turned one eyebrow neon green and the other pink to match her overalls.

Once I pulled my assigned curly yellow wig on top of my head, my transformation was complete. As I peered over my pillow-enhanced belly, I realized how dangerous clowning might be. I could only see the tips of my boat-sized shoes because of the two pillows extending my belly way past my beltline. If I tripped, I'd go down like a neon-striped beluga.

"You good?" Kate asked.

"Yeah, I think so."

"Don't forget this." The smirk in her voice was clear as she picked up the red foam ball from the counter and shoved it on my nose.

"Thaks, I thick." If only Tubs, my grandmother, could see us now. She'd be laughing her butt off. Instead, she was back in Manhattan working on a new installation at the Museum of Jewish Heritage.

Kate gave me a playful shove. "We better get moving, you daydreamer. Let's go."

"Wait a sec. Let's take a quick selfie. For Tubs."

"Brilliant." Kate extracted her phone, and we gave a whole new meaning to clowning around. She sent the pictures off. "Done. Let's go. We're gonna be late."

I hadn't realized Cailin and her cadre had already finished and vanished into the Church of the Rabbit Hole. I followed Kate's greenish pink glory through the living room into the café. Tables had been pushed aside. Rows of chairs were lined up in front of the hearth and occupied by Rocky's and Tulip's favorite Rabbit Hole customers. Half wore some semblance of clown gear while the rest got by with only the nostril-squashing red schnozzes. More guests than outfits, after all. Damn it. If only we'd been late to the party.

Dawg, Shay's boxer, and Bogey, JT's bloodhound, sprawled on either side of the unlit fireplace, eyeing the proceedings from ankle level.

Eddy, the high-styling ringmaster of this nutty fête, stood in front of a mantel covered with homemade paper hearts. A black top hat sat on her head at a jaunty angle above a tomato-red tuxedo jacket with epaulets of gold braid. Beneath the jacket, she wore a white, ruffled shirt and a bright, neon-green bow tie. Her short legs were encased in black pants, and bow tie-matching green high-tops completed her outfit. She pointed us to chairs that'd been left open, a perfect ringside view.

Rocky, wearing a blue- and purple-striped clown suit and a glee-filled grin, faced the gathered guests on Eddy's right.

Coop stood a step behind the groom. He towered over Rocky, looking like an escaped convict in orange and black. JT and Shay were Rocky's "groom's-girls," and took their places beside Coop to await Tulip's grand entrance.

On Eddy's left was a gap for Tulip, and then came another Kate, this one the Rabbit Hole's co-owner, and her sister Anna. They wore matching bright red and green, and looked like a couple of overjoyed but deranged Christmas elves.

One of the coffee shop customers I recognized as a regular was seated in the front row along with us. "Now?" he asked.

"You betcha." Eddy gave him two thumbs-up.

He whipped out a kazoo and tooted a rousing rendition of "Here Comes the Bride."

A few seconds later, Tulip marched through the front door. She was clad in a baggy white T-shirt with narrow black horizontal stripes. Fuchsia polka dot suspenders held up raggedy jeans. Maroon shoes and a straw hat took care of the rest.

Rocky squeaked when he saw her. I thought for a moment he was going to swoon in giddy delight. Tulip lurched to a stop beside him, a fifteen-mile-wide smile on her white grease-painted face. She reached over and honked a clown horn hooked to Rocky's belt. He beamed and they both turned to Eddy.

Kate held my hand and leaned forward in her chair, captivated by the goings-on.

With a few words from Her Pseudo-Honor, Rocky and Tulip exchanged very short vows consisting of dual "yesses" to Eddy's question of who took whom. They exchanged tie-dyed neck kerchiefs, and it was all over in about three minutes.

Eddy turned them to face the audience. "May I present to you Rocky and Tulip, bound together forever in ultimate holy matrimony and bliss. Rocky, you may kiss the bride."

Cheers and applause erupted. Rainbow confetti sailed through the air.

As the colorful pieces fluttered toward the floor, Rocky said, "Millions of marriages are performed in these United States. The divorce rate varies between forty-two and forty-five percent. That means there's almost a fifty percent chance my Tulip and I will make it to forever, and almost a fifty percent chance we won't. But I'm not worried. I love her one hundred percent!"

He plastered a big smacker on his wife, and they strolled down the aisle hand in hand, to the Hole's front door, where they stopped and turned around. Whispers of confusion rippled through the room, and my breath caught in my chest. The newlyweds were supposed to stroll out of the Hole and into the brightly festooned horse-drawn carriage that waited curbside to whisk them off to their circus reception at the Hands-On Toy Company and Game Room.

My palms began to sweat as I redirected my attention to the mistress of ceremonies.

"We just have one more thing to attend to," Eddy said in an appropriately dramatic fashion. "Mikala Flynn, will you please come up here?"

Kate peered at me in confusion.

I squeezed her fingers, rocked back and forth a couple of times to build up enough momentum to gain my feet, and wobbled up to Eddy. The rest of the wedding party had faded from the altar and parked themselves along the walls of the coffee shop. They had no more of an idea of what was about to transpire than my girl did.

"There you are, child." Eddy took my elbow and turned me to face the audience.

My pulse beat so hard I could feel it thump in my neck.

"Ladies and gentlemen, Flynn has something she'd like to say."

Kate's wide eyes caught mine. I attempted to keep my face neutral, but man, it was difficult, almost as difficult as breathing. Was I about to make the mistake of a lifetime? Was I pushing things too far too fast? The back of my head ached and I felt sick. This was the stupidest idea I'd ever had.

Eddy dramatically brought her hand to her mouth and stage-whispered, "Come on, Flynn. You can do it."

She was right. This wasn't the time to overthink myself. Feeling like I was in the midst of an out-of-body experience, I gazed at the variety of colorful outfits, all those clowns and red-nosed goofballs watching my every move like a parliament of owls. Or a cauldron of bats. Is there a choir of clowns? Whatever, they were all looking at me with gleaming expectation. Focus, Flynn!

From my pocket I pulled a sheet of paper and unfolded it with trembling hands. The words blurred as I peered at it. I squeezed my eyes shut and took a deep breath. The words came back into focus.

"One day, so very long ago, I ran into you, Kate Goldsmith. Literally. At a fundraiser in a museum. From that point on, my life was never the same. You put up with a pizza-dough-covered teen terrified of caring, and you stayed." Quiet laughter gave me courage to continue. "You survived incredible, unimaginable loss, yet you stayed. On those nights when we go out and I have a few too many cocktails, to keep me safe you drag me home, and you stay. We've gone our separate ways in the circus of our lives—more than a few times—but your heart has always stayed. Stayed with mine even when I thought you'd be better off without me."

Her eyes, glued to mine, glistened with tears unshed.

I swallowed at the lump that'd formed in my own throat.

"Kate, I love you more than chocolate."

Real laughter broke some of the tension.

I took three shuffling steps toward her, being extra careful not to trip over my shoes. "I love you more than any lovesick cliché I can think of." Another step brought me in range. My hand shook as I withdrew a black jewelry box from one of the coverall's pockets.

Kate peered up at me, tears now flowing unchecked down her cheeks.

Okay, Flynn, I lectured myself, you've imagined this moment a trillion times. Don't fuck it up. I awkwardly dropped to one knee. Because I was going to need both hands, I tossed over my shoulder the creased paper upon which I'd so painstakingly written Kate's proposal and let it flutter to the ground.

My hands steadied. I pried the jewelry box open and turned it to face Kate. Nestled inside the gray velvet interior was a handmade, white-gold ring Cailin's Alex had designed. The ring might have been created in a hurry but it was created with exacting detail. "Starry Night" by Vincent van Gogh was Kate's favorite piece of artwork, and Alex had somehow managed to capture its essence in one of the most beautiful rings I'd ever seen.

Kate's hands flew to her face and her fingers covered her mouth.

My gaze drilled into those mesmerizing ice-gray eyes. "Kate Goldsmith, would you do me the honor of becoming my wife?"

"Are—you...Jesus, Flynn. Are you serious?"

"Serious enough to make a fool of myself in front Rocky and Tulip's guests."

The entire space went completely silent. I actually felt the room's occupants straining to hear her answer.

"Oh, Flynn. My Flynn. Of course. Yes. Yes, a trillion times yes."

Relief made me so weak I almost fell onto my very padded belly. But I rallied and pulled the ring out of the box. Kate held out her left hand and I slid it home.

I leaped up, tried not to stomp on Kate's shoes, and crushed her in a hug. I twirled her in a circle and set her back on her feet. "She said yes!" I shouted. "She said yes!"

"And I'm not clowning around!" Kate hollered.

The roomful of people erupted into cheers. Back-slapping, fist pumping merriment ensued. I thought my heart might shatter in happiness.

"Hey baby," Kate leaned toward me, a smile teasing the corners of her mouth, "will there be a clown car?"

"Every day. At your beck and call."

Kate laughed then, a little hysterically, and wrapped her arms around me again. With her head tucked under my chin, I felt like I could do anything, be anybody—even in these crazy clown shoes.

"All right, harlequin girls and jester boys, send out the clowns!" Eddy produced her own clown horn and gave it a few toots. "Follow Rocky and Tulip right out the door. It's time to celebrate."

And that is exactly what we did.

SOMETHING (REALLY) OLD

E. J. Noyes

I raised my voice so everyone in the room would hear me. "I do."

Morgan strolled out of the kitchen with a platter of food balanced on a palm and a fresh bottle of champagne in the other hand. The bulge in her cheek made it obvious that she'd been sampling some of the food while preparing the snack for us. She swallowed and her voice took on the school-teacher-ish tone it always did when she was mildly exasperated with me. The problem with my fiancée using that tone was that in her British accent, she sounded less disciplinarian and more melt-my-knees sexy.

"Jane, don't think I haven't noticed the increased usage of the words *I* and *do* together in your vocabulary these past few weeks. Don't you think you should save them for tomorrow?"

I raised my face and offered a smile. "Just practicing. Plus, it's quicker than answering the question of who wants a top-up with, 'Yes I would like my champagne refilled, thank you.'"

"You could have just said, 'me please,'" Morgan pointed out dryly.

"True, but—"

Damn it, she'd caught me. Okay, she was right. For the past few weeks I had been obsessively working on my vows and everything I'd say tomorrow like it was a speech for a Nobel Peace Prize. The last thing I wanted was to screw up one of the most important moments of my life, so what was wrong with a little practice?

While Morgan and I had been discussing language logistics, one of my Maids of Honor, Emma, had dealt with the champagne bottle Morgan set on the coffee table. "I'm on it." Once Emma filled my glass, she waved the bottle around. "Anyone else?"

My other Maid of Honor, Georgina, held out the champagne flute. "Me, please."

Morgan moved even closer to me, her voice low and intimate. "I cannot wait to hear the real thing tomorrow." She kissed me, lingering to suck my lower lip. "And every other word you're going to say to do me the honor of becoming my wife."

Emma threw a cushion, which bounced off Morgan's shoulder. "Get a room, you two."

I pretended to stand. "Okay, we're just going upstairs for a while, back soon."

Georgina made a champagne-soaked gesture that seemed part *good for you* and part *make it quick*. "Don't be too long, you'll miss the stripper."

"Georgina!" I scrambled over the couch, holding my glass aloft to protect my champagne, and slapped her arm. I'd almost just blinked myself to her side but thankfully caught myself at the last moment. I hadn't told most of my friends about my recent transformation from Jane Smith, Regular Human to Jane Smith, Death's Minion Who Won't Die And Who Can Do Things Like Teleport Around The Universe. "I thought we'd discussed this. No strippers!"

Morgan's eyebrows hit her hairline. "Strippers?" The word sounded hilarious coming from her mouth—a mesh of lewd interest and old-world manners.

I tried to sound forceful but ended up with a squeaky, "There are no strippers. I mean, this isn't even a real bachelorette night. Just a post-rehearsal gathering." I gestured emphatically at my friends. "They're just trying to wind me up."

"And succeeding," Morgan observed. "But this is also my bachelorette, uh…gathering, so shouldn't it be my choice if we have strippers?"

"Technically it's a shared bachelorette gathering," I pointed out. "So we're at an impasse regarding strippers."

"Yes," Morgan mused. "It seems we are." She sat on the couch, slung an arm over the back and crossed her legs. Morgan patted the couch seat to entice me back, and once I'd settled beside her, she asked, "So when we say strippers, are we talking about all the way, or—"

"Morgan!" Apparently my friends weren't the only ones trying to wind me up.

"What? I thought strippers were part of the bachelorette tradition, even if we're not strictly adhering to that particular one." She smiled sweetly at me and did a very good job of not sounding sarcastic when she said, "Given we're not big on tradition. Are we, Jane?"

Both Emma and Georgina did an admirable job of not dissolving into fits of laughter on the floor. My friends and family were all too aware of my admittedly odd and newfound obsession with wedding traditions. To be fair, the intensity with which I'd tackled wedding planning had surprised me too, but it wasn't like I was insisting we absorb every wedding tradition into our ceremony. Just a few I felt were important. Like the "Something old, something new, something borrowed, something blue" that had been adhered to by generations of family on my mom's side.

I poked Morgan's thigh. "Speaking of traditions. Is this hazing part of some British wedding thing? Wind up your soon-to-be wife as much as possible?"

Morgan looked aghast. "Of course not. I was simply pointing out how we'd adapted these traditions you're so keen on to suit ourselves. For example, both of us having two Maids of Honor, not to mention this bachelorette party, which technically isn't a bachelorette party. Simply a relaxing gathering of friends."

"Nice recovery," I mumbled, sipping my champagne.

She bit her lower lip, but the twitching at the edges of her mouth gave away her smug amusement. "I thought so."

This shared not-really-a-bachelorette-party night had actually been Morgan's idea, something she'd discovered while embarking upon her usual routine of Googling anything she didn't know. Given all the new things I'd introduced my almost seven-hundred-year-old, Head-of-Death's-Minions fiancée to in the year we'd been together, she Googled quite a lot.

I'd been surprised that she'd suggested we have a gathering, albeit a very small one, and even more surprised when she'd said she was going to join me, which was apparently a modern thing to do for same-sex couples. Given her slightly workaholic nature, the fact that she was head of Death's Minions and oversaw the other Minions worldwide, and the fact that people kept dying and needed us to complete their afterlife contracts with them, Morgan taking a night off to relax was monumental.

She fidgeted. I knew what that fidget meant. I leaned over and grabbed the platter of food and a small plate. She murmured her thanks, took the plate and began loading food onto it.

Georgina glanced down the hall at a closed door, Mom's bedroom. "Are you sure we're not being too loud? Does your mom want to come out and join in?"

I laughed. "We're fine. She's got her headphones on. And no, but you're sweet. She was emphatic that this was for the wedding party only." Kind of. We were missing two people.

As if reading my thoughts, Emma gushed, "We're really sorry Serena and Imogen couldn't stay after the rehearsal and join us for drinks, Morgan." She lowered the level of champagne in her glass by a quarter of an inch.

Morgan raised her champagne flute in response. "Ah yes. And I know they're devastated at not joining in the festivities, but as you know, they work night shift." Her voice was utterly steady and sincere.

I knew my friends would accept what she'd said at face value. Explaining exactly why her two Maids weren't here—

because they'd had to go back to work in other countries around the world—would lead us down a rabbit hole. Imogen and Serena would arrive first thing in the morning, having blinked themselves to San Francisco in, well...the blink of an eye.

None of my friends knew exactly who or what Morgan, and me for that matter, was. And that was for the best. Scratch that. Emma *thought* she knew because Morgan had administered her afterlife contract years before, but as I'd learned when I'd been turned into one of Death's Minions, what you got told in school about the minions left out most of the important and interesting stuff. At some point in the future, we might have to explain why neither of us seemed to get any older. That was a problem for later and one Morgan, as the oldest of Death's Minions, had centuries of experience with.

Emma shot a glance at me. "I'm surprised Jane didn't throw a hissy fit about missing some members of the wedding party tonight."

Morgan looked from me to Emma, confusion written in the scrunched-up lines of her face. "What do you mean?"

Tension I really didn't want to be experiencing right before my wedding slid under my skin. "Jane's traditions" had been the source of much teasing during the wedding planning, and while I knew my friends meant it in good fun—and for the most part I'd taken it as such—the night before I was due to get married was perhaps not the right time to dig in. Before Emma could respond, I reached out and nudged her with my toe. "Do you mind? I feel like I missed the part where it said this was going to be a 'pick on Jane for wanting her wedding day to be special' event."

Morgan tried to interject with something that sounded like, "Jane's just..." Then she floundered. A helpless look was thrown in my direction.

"There's no need to be polite, Morgan," Emma said. "Let's be honest here." She turned to me. "Jane, I adore you but you really are traditional and boring, as much as you keep trying to pretend you're not."

"I am not!" I spluttered. "Traditional that is. Boring, yeah I'll wear that one."

"What about Old-New-Borrowed-Blue?" Georgina mused around a mouthful of cheese. My friends knew all about my unwavering insistence on following my mom's family idea of that old bride's tradition, which, now that I thought about it, had probably set me on the path to wanting other traditions. For months, everyone around me had quietly listened while I fretted about what I would do for each item on the "Something List."

"What about it?" I muttered petulantly. "Plenty of people do that one."

Emma slowly nodded. "Riiight. But do they do it with the same manic intensity as you have?"

"I have not been manic. Just…dedicated." I held up my aunt's sapphire ring on my right ring finger. "Borrowed and blue. And the new is…" My cheeks heated and I mumbled, "Never mind. I have something new to wear." Something I hoped Morgan would enjoy when she removed my dress tomorrow night. Tomorrow night, when we'd be legally married. I'd thought about that fact, obviously, *being married* to Morgan nearly every day. But really thinking about it, about everything it meant for us, was a whole other wonderful thing all together.

Morgan shifted slightly, uncrossed then recrossed her legs. I knew my empathetic and intuitive fiancée had picked up on my mood swing from happy to happy and a little horny. Under her breath she begged, "Stop it."

"And the old?" Georgina prompted.

I pushed aside thoughts of tomorrow night and the associated stomach-fluttering excitement. "A gift from a good friend. I'm expecting her to deliver it any moment." Had been expecting it since she'd said last month that she would take care of Something Old.

Any moment was apparently right now. Cici La Morte, more commonly known as Death, apparently had better intuition than I gave her credit for. That, or she just had excellent timing. The bond I shared with Cici meant I always knew when she had come earthside from her home in Aether, which existed in one of the many spacial planes around the universe. I sensed her in my space as a feeling of warmth and connection.

Mercifully, Cici used the doorbell instead of just appearing in the house as she usually did. Having Death suddenly arriving in our living room would cause far more questions than I felt like answering at this moment. Morgan was halfway to the door before I could even think of what to say. "I'll get it," she called over her shoulder.

I stood as Death swept into the room with her usual aura of presence and power. None of my friends had met Cici and both Emma and Georgina looked stunned, transfixed, and in Emma's case—more than a little interested. I didn't blame them. Part of Cici's charm and appeal was in her appearance, and I'd yet to meet someone who didn't find her attractive. Though the deep brown of her hair, porcelain complexion, full sensuous mouth and green eyes which changed color along with her mood remained the same, it was almost as if she projected what people most wanted to see.

Cici smiled at my friends, cupped Morgan's cheek in passing, then came for me. She clutched both of my hands. "Jane, my darling, may I speak with you a moment?" She flashed a smile that immediately flooded me with warmth.

Alongside the warmth that always came with being near her, was a rush of excitement and relief. She had brought my Something Old for me. "Sure."

Morgan moved to my side, sliding an arm around my waist. "You're not staying, Cici? We're having a…bachelorette gathering." She glanced sideways at me. "I think it's going rather well."

Cici didn't hesitate. "Hmm, yes. Sounds delightful. I can stay for a short while, once I've finished speaking with Jane, that is." Her eyes slid to the other two people in the room and with a cheeky little wave, she added, "I would so like to meet your friends, Jane. Now, come outside with me."

When we were outside on the porch, she took my face in both hands and kissed each of my cheeks, the touch of her lips lingering until her power suffused me. "You and Morgana are both looking simply radiant, darling. Are you ready for tomorrow?"

"I am. We are." I leaned against the railing, remaining close enough that Cici and I were still touching lightly. The proximity of her was soothing, revitalizing.

She studied me in a way that made me feel she somehow knew exactly what I was thinking, even though I knew she couldn't. Though possessing many extraordinary gifts, Death was not a mind reader, just incredibly perceptive. Almost as perceptive as Morgan. Cici's eyes—the mossy green they were when she was relaxed—softened as she smiled. "Ah yes, I promised you something, didn't I?"

"Yes, you did, Mistress." There was no need to say anything further. Cici didn't forget and she never broke a promise.

Now Cici flashed her Mona Lisa smile, when she knew something and had chosen not to divulge it to me. "I will deliver your Something Old to you tomorrow before you say your vows. I wish to ensure it is in perfect condition before I give it to you."

I worried my lower lip with my teeth and nodded my understanding. There was nothing I could do or say. You didn't argue with Death.

Cici brushed her thumb over my lip. "Now, now. No fretting. Tomorrow will be everything you and Morgana have hoped for and then more. Trust me," she purred.

"I do." Damn it. I hadn't meant to let that one slip.

"Excellent." She took my face in her hands and pulled me to her, bending to kiss my forehead. "Your mother has told me about the importance of the Smith women incorporating this particular wedding tradition into their ceremonies." Cici grinned and added, "And of course, she was quick to remind me that given her unmarried status, your strict adherence will make up for her breaking the custom."

One of life's greatest mysteries was how my mom and Death had become best friends from almost their first meeting. Morgan and I would often come home from work to find Cici and Mom in the living room together—Mom doing puzzles or brain games on her iPad while Cici sat on the couch, knitting. Sometimes there would be conversation. Other times just the quiet companionship of friends who simply enjoyed being near one another.

"Yeah." I tucked my hands into my pockets, hunching my shoulders. "I know it's kind of silly, Cici, but it's my family thing."

"Yes, my darling. And I, best of anyone, know how important family is. You are part of mine and I will never fail you." She gently tugged my arm until my hand came out of my pocket and then took my elbow. "Now let's get back inside. I would like to get to know your friends a little better."

Oh shit. Apparently we were also going to fulfill the tradition of a member of the wedding party hooking up with one of our friends.

Cici behaved as she always did around humans who were enamored with her—graceful, charming and flirtatious, the kind that made people feel wanted but at the same time made it clear they didn't have much chance. Emma and Georgina had been given vague explanations about who Cici was—the woman who owned the company Morgan and I worked for, which wasn't really a lie—and both of them seemed immediately enraptured by her, Emma especially.

The looks Morgan kept shooting my way made it very clear she was trying to hold on to her mirth at Emma's googly eyes. So far, she was succeeding.

"Where are you from, Cici?" Emma asked. "I can't place that accent. European?" She probably thought nobody would hear her but I did, and I knew Cici and Morgan would too when she murmured, "So fucking sexy."

Morgan snorted then quickly covered the sound by coughing into the crook of her elbow.

"Many places," Cici offered smoothly. "But yes, I have spent a great deal of time in Europe."

Emma couldn't have looked more interested if she'd leaned forward, rested her elbows on her knees and propped her chin on her fists.

Morgan and I were superfluous to this conversation, and apparently satisfied that the other three were occupied with their conversation, and satisfied with food and beverages, Morgan turned slightly away from them. "We should probably go to bed soon," she said quietly. "Having bags under my eyes in our wedding day photographs doesn't rate highly on my wedding list."

Emma managed to tear herself away from being smitten with Cici long enough to ask, "Aren't you guys spending tonight apart?"

"Yes," I answered.

At the same time, Morgan blurted, "No!"

Emma laughed. "Boy, you two really need to communicate more."

Morgan remained silent, childishly stewing and leaving me to answer, "We have communicated, we *do* communicate. We just have different ideas on this particular thing, that's all."

Cici slowly swirled the wine in her glass. "Differing ideals is part of what makes a strong couple. The challenges your lover gives you every day forces you to be better." The look she gave each of us was soft, like a mom with her favorite children. She rose gracefully. "But your fiancée is correct, Jane. You should both rest before your special day tomorrow."

After Cici had assured Emma and Georgina that she would indeed see them both the following day at the wedding, Morgan and I bundled them into a car back to Emma's place, while Cici helped my mom with her bedtime routine. Usually it was me or Morgan, or one of Mom's regular caretakers, but on more than a few occasions Cici had helped out if Mom was getting tired.

I'd barely locked the front door again when Cici swept down the hallway toward us. "Pamela is resting comfortably. Come now, Morgana. It is time to let your bride to be rest as well."

Morgan shot daggers at Cici. "I would like to state for the hundredth time that this particular tradition is one I am most certainly *not* on board with."

Cici ignored Morgan's petulance and bent to kiss my cheek. "Sleep well, darling Jane, and I shall see you in the morning." She disappeared without another word.

I followed Morgan as she stomped upstairs while muttering about the unfairness of being forced to stay the night in Aether, and what about one last session of sex before we were married, and stupid modern traditions, and how this whole thing was most unfair and incredibly stupid. I let her be because listening to Morgan's petulance was adorable and it was all I could do to stop myself from laughing.

Morgan packed a small duffel with quick, jerky movements, still mumbling and muttering. Finally she stopped talking to herself and spoke to me. "I hope you're happy with yourself."

In my pleasant little champagne bubble of not drunk but definitely not sober, I nodded and confirmed, "I am. It'll be worth it tomorrow. Trust me."

She kissed me quickly, but not gently, then moved to the corner of our room beside our walk-in and with a sigh of exasperation and a kiss blown in my direction, left the earth realm.

The moment Morgan had left to spend the evening in one of the many spare bedrooms in Cici's mansion, I showered, washed my hair as I'd been instructed by the hair person, and crawled naked into bed. As soon as my body touched the cool sheets, I regretted my insistence on this stupid wedding tradition. Damn it. Nerves and excitement mingled with a touch of worry about everything that would happen tomorrow.

I knew that in the scheme of things, the actual ceremony wasn't all that important. These little things I'd tried so hard to make exactly perfect wasn't what was important. What *was* important was that tomorrow I would legally tie myself to Morgan. Though thinking about it, considering the depth of our feelings and the fact we could easily exist until the end of humanity, a ritual that was nothing more than a legality seemed kind of silly. Maybe I had been stupid, insisting on us being apart for the night when we could have slept together and had sex one last time as not-wives.

We'd made love that morning in the shower, quick and dirty, while we got clean. Morgan had held me against the cool tiles and thrust her fingers deep inside me until I climaxed in a helpless trembling mess. Then she'd turned into a trembling mess when I knelt between her spread thighs and buried myself in her heat as water cascaded over us.

The sensation I always had when thinking about her started in my belly as an excited fluttering which spread downward. Oh, double damn it. I let my hand wander, brushing my nipples before sliding my fingertips down my stomach. I lingered, lightly touching the skin just below my belly button. I'd just moved my hand lower when the air in the room shifted.

Self-pleasure took a backseat. I sat up and stared at the place Morgan had left. As always, I sensed her a millisecond before she arrived and felt the rightness that always came with her being near me. A quick glance at the bedside clock told me Morgan hadn't even lasted forty-five minutes away.

"This is dumb," Morgan declared the moment she'd appeared beside our walk-in. "I am vetoing this particular wedding tradition." She gesticulated wildly, as if she thought I was going to disagree with her being here. No chance of that. "The whole point of being apart on the night before one's wedding is so you'll be extra excited seeing your soon-to-be spouse at the altar. Jane, love of my life, being apart from you for any time pains me greatly. Seeing you after any length of separation, be it an hour or minutes, makes me feel as though I can breathe again. Therefore, I deem us being apart for the few hours of getting ready time prior to the ceremony enough to fulfill the reason behind this custom."

"Okay."

Her left eyebrow slowly rose. "Okay? That's it? You're not going to argue?" She crossed her arms. "My love, you have been, dare I say it, anally-retentive about almost everything relative to our ceremony, and now you're just going to let this go?"

"Yes. And I know. But with you here I realize how stupid it was of me to think I could spend a night apart from you. Now come here."

But she didn't move. Instead, her gaze raked up and down my sheet-covered body. "Are you naked?"

"Yes." I usually slept naked, even if we hadn't made love, so I wasn't sure why this was such a revelation.

"Jane." Morgan's full, sensuous mouth turned upward in a smile so sexy I wanted to kiss it. "Were you going to masturbate because I wasn't here?"

"I thought about it." After a pause I admitted, "More than thought about it. You interrupted me just getting started."

"Then I'm very glad I returned." She crossed the room and bent at the waist to kiss me. "That is something I do not want to miss." Morgan sat on the end of the bed and with a small flick of her wrist told me to, "Carry on."

I slipped my hand underneath the sheet, pausing just below my belly button. Morgan's expectant gaze lingered on what remained hidden, and after long moments she tore her eyes away from where I was lazily stroking my belly under the fabric, and asked, "Do you require some encouragement?"

A deliciously naughty idea popped into my head. "Now that you mention it, yes."

She picked up on my meaning immediately. "Well," she mused, "about these strippers…"

"Alleged strippers," I corrected.

"Right." Morgan crawled backward off the bed and once upright, she unbuttoned her shirt and drew the side off her shoulder. Her fingertips lingered teasingly on her collarbone. "Having researched the things one might encounter at a bachelorette's party, I know that Emma and Georgina's joking about strippers wasn't actually much of a joke. Considering they didn't deliver, and despite your protestations that you did not want an exotic dancer, I think you deserve a show. A *private* show."

My stomach did a slow, excited roll at the suggestion. "Should I put on some music?"

The other side of Morgan's shirt fell too. "I don't know. Should you?"

I raised my voice so the home organization system could hear me. "Alexa. Play stripper music."

Alexa took a few seconds before she responded, "Playing Amazon Music's Pole Perfection."

Rihanna's "Work" pumped out through the hidden speaker in our room. Morgan's eyes were as big as the moon and I could imagine her panicked thought processes.

I butted in. "Alexa, stop. Play *stripping* music."

Alexa thought for a moment, then tried again. "Playing Amazon Music's Pole Perfection."

I cut her off before she could play the same song—the beat of which was far beyond Morgan's dance capabilities—or something equally as funky, with a sharp, "Alexa, off." Apparently she only had one playlist for strip-tease music.

Throughout my exchange with the AI, Morgan had been teasing the zipper of her pants down until the fabric of her panties was just visible. "Perhaps you should specify you want Pandora to play you a sexy song for your almost-wife to strip to?" she mused, fingers playing over her open zipper.

"True. Or I could do it the old-fashioned way."

Morgan adopted her thinking face. "You're going to find a minstrel to play lute for us? Best send out the carrier pigeons now if you want him here in time."

I slow-clapped her. "Ha-ha. Not quite that old fashioned. I was thinking more like…" I fumbled for my phone, scrolled, and started up Bad Company's classic, "Feel Like Makin' Love."

Morgan heaved a sigh of relief. "Thank you. That previous song was well beyond my dancing abilities."

I extracted my teasing hand from under the sheet and gestured for her to start her show. "Then show me what your dancing abilities are," I murmured.

Morgan Ashworth was many things, not least among them lithe and graceful with movement that always looked effortless. But despite that grace, she couldn't dance *at all*. Her version of a striptease was to shimmy and gyrate, as she shuffled around to the beat. Kind of. Mostly she jiggled and swayed—which did wonderful things for her breasts—as she slowly removed articles of clothing and flung them about the room.

After a few minutes, by which time she was down to nothing but underwear, I decided I'd had enough. Not of the dancing, which was hilariously adorable. Of her being clothed. "Mercy," I begged. "No more dancing. Just strip."

Morgan's hands slid over her bare breasts and down her stomach. She paused just above the waistband of the lace-edged thong she wore. "On…or off?"

"Are you *really* asking me that?"

She turned around, bent forward slightly and slid her panties off. She remained in that position for an excruciatingly long time before she faced me again. My fiancée's hands came up to cup her breasts and she teased her nipples between thumb and forefinger. The entire time she fondled her breasts, she kept intense eye contact with me, as if daring me to say something. I kept silent until one hand slid down her stomach to linger in her pubic hair.

I swallowed and worked my tongue around the inside of my mouth, trying to find saliva to talk. "Oh, that's not fair. At all."

Morgan's fingers moved lower and disappeared inside her folds. She exhaled, and when she answered me, the words came out slightly clipped. "I think it's very fair, considering you were in the midst of pleasuring yourself when I arrived."

"Midst?" I squeaked. "I hadn't even touched myself. Not properly." I indulged myself, watching her watching me as she slid her fingers over her clit.

"Well that's a pity," she drawled. "Now you have to wait."

"Is this why you came back tonight? To make me watch you while you make yourself come?"

"Not at all. I'm simply taking advantage of a situation."

She had an expression of deviousness I recognized, and based on her mood, I took a chance. "Then you're being cruel. *And* you've been a very bad girl coming back here, you know that, right?"

"Mhmm."

I threw the sheet off myself and got out of bed. "And bad girls get punished, don't they?"

Her breathing hitched. Bingo. Morgan's response was a whispered, "Yes."

"Come here."

She let her hand fall away from between her thighs. After a pause she approached the bed. "Now what?" The question was facetious, deliberately so, designed to taunt me.

It did that. But it also made my stomach flutter. "Face down on the bed. Eyes closed."

She complied without a word or hesitation.

"Can I trust you to stay still and keep your eyes closed or do you need some help?"

The scarves of silk and satin and wool that Morgan so often wore were wonderful tools for light bondage or covering her eyes. After centuries of being alive and all the weirdness associated with that and her position as the most senior of Death's Minions, I knew Morgan often had an uncomfortable sensation of not quite knowing who she was. I'd learned in our early stages of "Are we dating or what?" that one of the best ways to bring her back to herself was to force her to focus on every sensation except sight. And she loved nothing more than me taking charge and giving her the respite of not having to be in control.

"I can keep them closed," she breathed. "I'll be still."

"Good." I climbed back onto the bed and settled myself on top of her, sliding my hands up her arms to pin her hands to the bed. "Keep your hands here."

Morgan nodded. She was a little taller than me, and I let myself slide down her back slowly as I kissed, licked and sucked the skin of her neck, shoulders and back. The sensation of her warm skin against my nipples made them harden, and when Morgan deliberately lifted her hips so her ass pressed into exactly the right spot to put pressure on my clit, my breathing caught.

"Spread your legs," I demanded. Or it would have been a demand if I hadn't been so undone by the grinding of her ass against me which was making my breathing catch in my throat.

Underneath me, Morgan took her time to part her legs and the moment she'd spread apart I raised myself up so I could access what I most wanted. My hands roamed over the smooth, warm skin of her ass and backs of her thighs. Morgan bucked when I brushed my fingertips over her inner thighs and drew them upward. I lingered against her wetness for a second, delighting in her response to my touch. "Is this what you want?" I murmured as I drew slow circles around her clit and teased her entrance.

Morgan turned her head slightly to the side and choked out a single word. "Please."

She was so wet and ready that my fingers slid easily into her heat. Morgan and I both let out a quiet groan as I thrust into her. She raised herself slightly. "Can I touch myself?"

"No." I exhaled a trembling breath. "I told you before where you have to keep your hands."

Her fists curled in the sheets and the moment she'd gripped the sheets I withdrew my fingers and slid them forward to her clit. Morgan's, "Oh, God," was muffled in the sheets as I kept up the rhythm I knew would bring her quickly to climax. This first time I wanted us to be fast. We could have slow later.

I straddled the back of her thigh, sliding myself up and down her sweat-slick skin, rolling my hips against her. The effect of pressing against her was an immediate flood of arousal—the deep, leg trembling kind. I kept sliding, rocking myself against her as I played with her clit, and it only took Morgan a few moments to catch on. "Are you fucking yourself on my leg while you're fucking me?" she gasped.

"Yes."

She bit the skin on the inside of her bicep but it didn't stifle her moan. It was a deep moan of pleasure and frustration all rolled into a sound that sent a roll of desire through me. Morgan inhaled a shaky breath. "That is vastly unfair."

I showed her just how fair it actually was by driving her closer to climax as I brought myself to the brink. The sensation of my clit against her sweat-wet skin, which had been made even wetter by my arousal, had me so close that I had to consciously slow down and focus my attention on Morgan's pleasure.

Slow down, not stop.

As my fingers worked through her folds, teased her entrance, slid inside and back out of her wetness, and then played around her clitoris, I kept my own slow and steady rhythm against her thigh. Morgan began to writhe beneath me and her breathing rose to meet my own panting, gasping pitch. She exhaled a desperate, "Jane, *please*."

I drew my finger back and forth over the underside of her slippery clit, and she choked out a moan as she came. The sound of her climax, the way she bucked under me and inadvertently pressed her thigh more firmly against me sent me spiraling into release. I tried desperately to keep going and draw out her pleasure, but my limbs gave out and I collapsed forward onto her back.

Pressing kisses to Morgan's skin I carefully disengaged our limbs and climbed off her. As I reached for the sheet to cover us, Morgan rolled onto her back. She flashed me a cheeky grin. "Now I'm very glad I came back tonight."

"Me too." I settled against her side.

We lay quietly together, stroking skin, twining fingers, enjoying the mutual satisfaction of our lovemaking. Despite the relaxation suffusing me, there was clearly some emotion of mine that Morgan was picking up on. She stroked the edge of my jaw with her fingertips. "What's wrong, love?"

My eyes widened. "Nothing. Really." After a pause I added, "It's not anything *wrong*."

"Mmm," she mused. "Okay then. Not wrong, but you're still worried." Morgan's thumb brushed lightly over my lower lip. "I'd wager I know why."

"Probably," I whispered. There was little about me that she didn't know.

"Sweetheart, are you really worried about a wedding superstition?"

"Well, yes. No. I mean, I don't know. It's just part of the Smith wedding tradition and I feel like I should be part of that for me and also for Mom who didn't. And I have everything but the old. And I *know* Cici promised she'll give it to me before we walk down the aisle, but I just want to be totally prepared. I know, I know," I added when she didn't say anything. "I'm being a stupid bride."

She kissed me. "First, you're not stupid. And second, I love your obsession with this one thing."

"I know I'm being ridiculous about it." I sat up and the sheet pooled around my waist. Picking at the fabric, I mumbled, "I guess I'm just worried about what it is, that's all. Like will it match the dress? Will it be out of place? I would have liked a little more time to be sure, that's all."

"Do you really think that Cici La Morte would ever let you appear in public with something she's given you that doesn't perfectly suit your outfit, your mood *and* the surroundings?" Morgan lightly stroked my cheek with her fingertips. "Jane, she practically invented fashion and accessorizing."

"True," I conceded. "Have you seen the thing she's giving me?"

"I have."

"And?" I prompted when she said nothing more.

"And what?"

"Is it nice?"

"I think so." Morgan's expression turned serene. "Very suitable. A beautiful piece. I think you'll be rather pleased with it."

"What is it? Because my dress and shoes and jewelry and all that are already set and can't be changed or swapped out. So it's got to be something that complements my outfit somehow, but I can't figure it out."

"If I tell you it'll ruin the surprise, like seeing my dress before it's time. But trust me, your Something Old *definitely* complements your outfit."

I fell back onto the bed and covered my face with my pillow. "Ugh! You're being so frustrating."

Morgan pulled the pillow away and then covered my face with soft kisses. "I know. But I'm sure you'll cope until tomorrow."

"Doubtful." I propped myself up on my elbow. "What about wedding traditions for you?"

Both eyebrows rose in surprise. "What about them?"

"You've been so quiet about it all, just letting me obsess over everything and going along with pretty much everything I've suggested. Should you have like sheep intestines draped about you or something for your traditional wedding thing?"

Her laugh was a sudden loud burst of mirth. "No, sweetheart. I think you're confusing my fourteenth century birthdate with another period entirely. Something else I'm not entirely sure of to be honest." Morgan pulled my arm until I was lying down again. "I had considered wearing a cotehardie, full damask with stripes and billowy sleeves, but it felt a little weird and totally wouldn't suit our theme and color scheme."

"True. But I wouldn't have minded if it made you happy and made you feel like you were sticking to your birthplace traditions."

Morgan smiled, her eyes creasing at the edges. "Jane, I have lived for so long and moved around so many places that I honestly don't feel a great tie to, or need to adhere to, the customs of England in the thirteen hundreds."

"Oh. True."

She sketched a dismissive wave. "I mean, if we're going by the traditions of my birthplace and time, we're actually already married."

"Really? How so?"

"Well..." She lowered her voice. "We've had sex which counted as consent to marry, and back in my day it would've created a legally binding marriage." She leered. "A whole lot of consent in our case. And we've exchanged engagement rings and many other things that would technically count as the gift my people would give as consent to marriage."

"Gifts like what?"

"Usually a ring, but I recall all manner of things being offered—a vase, a bowl, and even a set of sewing needles. So we've had all manner of consent, which is all that was required back then to be married."

"Why didn't you tell me this earlier? We could have saved ourselves all this hassle, skipped the ceremony and just gone for our honeymoon."

"True, but I think there would have been people lining up to express their disapproval, all the way from your mother to Cici and beyond to Hera, Hades, Lucifer and all those other Afterlife Committee members who are strangely invested in our union."

"They care about you, babe. They've known you for centuries."

"Mmm," she agreed. "But if Lucifer wears one of his stupid English Premier League jerseys to the wedding, I might flay him. That is the very opposite of *dressy casual or semiformal*."

"It's a bracelet, isn't it," I blurted. "Cici's thing for me is a bracelet." It had to be because that was the only thing that would work with my already set outfit.

Both of Morgan's hands came up in exasperation. "No more. We're not talking anything wedding until we're standing at the altar tomorrow."

"Fine." Instead of being a forceful-yet-unhappy-with-the-situation agreement word, it came out more like a child's whine.

Despite my tone, Morgan carried on as if I'd agreed with her rather than sulked about the situation. "Perhaps I shall find some other way to take your mind off this particular issue."

"What exactly did you have in mind?" I asked, knowing even as I posed the question what her answer would be.

"I want to make love again." She covered my body with hers and lowered her lips to within a breath of mine. Her voice was pure seduction. "But this time, it's going to be more than just my thigh giving you an orgasm."

Morgan left just after eight a.m. for the hotel where she'd be getting ready, and my Maids of Honor arrived midmorning with bottles and brunch which occupied me until the beauty people arrived. Hair and makeup were a blur while Emma and Georgina flitted around and kept me occupied with small glasses of champagne, large glasses of water, and snacks, in that order, repeated throughout the day.

And there was still no Cici.

The roving photographer was unobtrusive and sweet, and once my hair and makeup had been done and I was about to get dressed, she quietly asked if I was nervous. I forced a smile. "Not at all. Just waiting for something. Someone who'll give me something."

She nodded and snapped another photo. I excused myself, and in nothing but the brand-new lingerie and garter belt I'd picked for Morgan's wedding night surprise, with a silk robe over the top, I wandered downstairs to my mom's bedroom. When I knocked on the closed door and called her name, I was greeted by a muffled, "Yes, Jane?"

"Are you ready for my help?" My quadriplegic mother could dress herself in her usual daily clothing of loose pants and free-flowing tops, but her outfit for today would require some assistance.

"I've got it, thank you," she called back. "Veronica is taking good care of me." Veronica, Mom's main caretaker and almost a member of the family now, was a certified angel. I hadn't even realized she was coming to help Mom before attending the wedding as a guest herself. After a beat, Mom added, "You girls concentrate on yourselves."

I let my hand linger on the closed door as I tried to tamp down the sense of unease. It felt like something huge was about to shift, though rationally I knew nothing would really change after today except for legality. Morgan and I would still be together, living in this house with my mom, working and doing everything we always did.

Because I was an expert at analyzing myself, I knew my strange sense of disquiet came entirely from the fact that I was missing the thing Cici had promised to bring me. There was still time before we had to leave for the venue, time for Cici to arrive with the final piece. But I couldn't shake the feeling that she should have been here by now. That I should have it ready to add to my carefully planned dress-jewelry-heels-hair-makeup combination.

Cici never let down those she loved, so why did it suddenly feel like I might be the first?

Back upstairs, standing in front of the full-length mirror beside our walk-in, inches from where Morgan had left and arrived last night, I stared at my reflection. I'd never imagined myself in a wedding dress—mostly because I'd never pictured myself finding my soulmate. The image of me ready to legally bind myself to the person who made me feel so alive, so loved, so *enough* almost made me cry.

Georgina's quiet, "Jane? You ready?" broke me from my contemplation.

"Mhmm." I turned around and carefully gathered my dress so I could walk downstairs.

The moment I came into view, Mom covered her mouth with a hand, and probably would have exhaled some sort of sound of excitement and love if Veronica hadn't loudly beaten her to it. The photographer, bless her, broke the building emotion by holding up her camera and apologizing that it was time for a final round of photos before we left.

We posed for photos by Mom's roses, and by the time the Aston Martin that would carry me to my wedding rolled into the driveway, Cici still hadn't arrived with her promised item. Goddamn it. Closing my eyes, I tried to sense if she was earthside. Nope.

I could duck to Aether to see her…

As quickly as the idea came to me, I discarded it. Not only was I supposed to be getting in a car *right now*, if Emma's exasperation was anything to go by, but traveling to Aether to demand something of Cici wasn't really the done thing. Especially not while wearing a wedding dress. She was probably going to give it to me moments before I walked up the aisle. That had to be it.

We arrived at the sprawling ranch-style venue in the Castro Valley right on time, and as we drove slowly toward my drop-off point, I spotted the vintage Rolls-Royce that Morgan had chosen for her transportation. She'd beaten me to the venue, and the car was parked just to the side of the path that we'd walk together. The van transporting Mom was also there. She'd already been lowered by the mechanical wheelchair platform out of the back and was maneuvering herself toward Morgan, ready to gush.

Apparently my driver had taken a scenic route.

Morgan slipped from the back of the Rolls-Royce, followed by Cici, Imogen and Serena who each held on to a portion of the train of Morgan's dress. I saw Morgan just before she spotted me, and the wave of emotion hit like a tidal wave as a rush of joy and love and awe and a million things in-between. She looked so beautiful that all I could do was raise my hand in a feeble, "Hey, hi, nice to see you," wave while my insides were leaping about with excitement.

Morgan's dress was modern and not modern, and I loved how she'd managed to mix the two styles to blend her life before and her life now. The dress clung to her body with intricate lace and beading glittering in the bodice that fell away in elegant lines of fabric. Her blond hair was down around her shoulders, curled loosely. As I approached her I could see she was blinking to hold back tears.

She spoke first, hoarse and husky as she looked me up and down. "Jane…" A nervous swallow. More blinking. "You look…I can't even think…I—" After a short laugh, she managed, "Wow."

"I think that about sums up my reaction. You look so beautiful, and I just…" After a shaky breath I managed, "I love you."

"I love you too."

Cici placed Morgan's hand in mine then closed my other hand over the top. "And I love both of you, very much." She studied us, and apparently satisfied, nodded and stepped away.

I felt like melting, and of course I couldn't ask her for my Something Old now in front of everyone when Morgan and I were about to walk down the aisle. Cici studied Morgan, a knowing smile tugging the edge of her mouth before she turned to me. She said nothing, just laughed, low and melodic. After a quiet, "Oh, Jane," Cici winked at me then walked away to stand by my mom without giving me the trinket or piece of jewelry or whatever it was to complete my Old, New, Borrowed, Blue. And though I knew it was stupid, and in the scheme of things was a complete nonissue, the idea of being the first one in my mom's family not to continue this tradition felt weird and wrong and surprisingly upsetting.

Morgan turned our hands until she held both of mine. This touch, her grip was immediately grounding. She pulled me slightly away from the group and when we had some privacy, quietly asked, "What is it?" The way she asked the question made me feel as if she knew the answer but wanted me to tell her.

But I didn't know how to tell her, how to express something that was so upsetting but at the same time, really didn't mean anything. It wasn't stopping Morgan and I from binding ourselves to one another. It would have no bearing on our eternity of happiness. But it *was* one thing tying me to my family, my human family, who I would outlive by thousands upon thousands of years.

So I shrugged and mumbled some indistinct syllables.

Morgan—intuitive, loving, self-sacrificing Morgan—laughed. "Something Old, yes?"

I nodded, trying to articulate around the tears threatening. Tears of joy because I was minutes away from marrying the love of my life, and tears over this custom, which now that I thought about it was really pretty ridiculous. "I'm sorry," I managed. "I know it's dumb, it's just…"

"I know. And it's not dumb at all." Her expression softened and I could see the glint of tears in her eyes. "But, sweetheart. It's been right in front of you this whole time. The answer to your dilemma is staring you in the face. Literally." Despite us not being anywhere near the kissing part, she kissed me. Framing my face with both hands, she kissed me again, lingering until my upset melted. "It's me. I'm your Something Old."

I was the biggest dumbass on the planet. In the universe. I could say that for a fact, having been around the universe. It'd been so obvious and right in front of my face this entire time. My Something Old was my almost seven-hundred-year-old fiancée. She certainly qualified.

I exhaled, "Oh. Ohhhh."

Morgan took my hand again. "You can't wear me, obviously, but I am right here by your side." She kissed my knuckles. "Are you ready to do this?"

I nodded. "I've been ready to do this since I first met you." I wrapped my arm around her waist and immediately felt something out of place. I patted her waist, then her hip, trying to work out what felt wrong. "What's that?"

Morgan's voice was low enough that only I would hear her, and completely deadpan. "I'm wearing sheep intestines under my dress."

See how Jane and Morgan's story started in Reaping the Benefits *available from Bella Books or your favorite retailer.*

About the Authors

Kay Acker grew up in northern Alabama and lives in southern Vermont. She and her wife play tabletop games with friends and enjoy the daily antics of two cats. The first queer romance novel Kay read was found in a public library and hidden in her room until well after the due date. She now borrows, reads, and writes them openly.

❧

Celeste Castro (she/her) is an American Mexican from small-town, rural Idaho, where most of her stories take place. She grew up with learning disabilities, though she always kept a journal. In addition to fiction, she is a staff writer with Hispanecdotes, an online magazine for Latinx writers, where she publishes essays and poetry.

❧

Jessie Chandler is the award-winning author of the *Shay O'Hanlon Caper series* and the *National Protection and Investigation Unit Operation* series. Two too-adorable-for-their-own-good pooches allow Jessie and her wife of twenty years to hang with them in Minneapolis, Minnesota. When Jessie isn't writing, you can find her selling T-shirts, books, and other assorted fun stuff at festivals, craft shows, and a multitude of other strange locations.

❧

Jaime Clevenger lives with family—a wife, two kids, two cats and a dog—in Colorado. Most days are spent working as a veterinarian, writing (primarily romance but also erotica and fantasy), swimming and eating cookies. Jaime prefers not being tied to a pronoun and will happily respond to any.

Kate Gavin (she/her) is a native Midwesterner, currently living in Ohio. When not staring at a computer screen for her day job or this writing gig, she spends her time retrieving items from her thieving dog, playing video games, and bingeing TV shows with her wife.

❦

M.B. Guel (they/them) lives in LA and has recently released their debut novel, *Queerleaders*, with Bella Books. They love using their experiences as a non-binary Latinx to queer up all the tropes.

❦

Louise McBain lives with her family and pets in Washington DC.

❦

E. J. Noyes (she/her) lives in Australia with her wife, a needy cat, aloof chickens and too many horses. When not indulging in her love of reading and writing, E. J. argues with her hair and pretends to be good at things.

❦

Tagan Shepard (she/her) Tagan Shepard is the author of five sapphic fiction novels, including the 2019 Goldie winner *Bird on a Wire*. When not writing about extraordinary women loving other extraordinary women she can be found playing video games, reading, or sitting in DC Metro traffic. She lives in Virginia with her wife and two cats.

Cade Haddock Strong (she/her) Cade spent many years working in the airline industry, and she and her wife have traveled all over the world. When not writing, she loves to be outside, especially skiing, hiking, biking, and playing golf. She grew up in Upstate New York but has lived all over the US and abroad, from the mountains of Vermont and Colorado to the bustling cities of DC, Chicago, and Amsterdam.

❦

Dillon Watson resides in the southeastern United States. She has won Goldies (Golden Crown Literary Society) for Best Debut Author and Best Contemporary Romance. She has also been short-listed for a Goldie in the categories of Best Paranormal/Horror and Mystery/Thriller, and a Lammy (Lambda Literary Foundation) in the Romance category. Her novels include: *Keile's Chance*, *Back to Blue*, *Full Circle* and *The Secret Unknown*.

Bella Books, Inc.

Women. Books. Even Better Together.

P.O. Box 10543
Tallahassee, FL 32302

Phone: 800-729-4992
www.bellabooks.com